ARLENE McFARLANE

Murder, Curlers & Cruises

A Valentine Beaumont Mystery

MURDER, CURLERS, AND CRUISES
Copyright © 2018 by Arlene McFarlane

MURDER, CURLERS, AND CRUISES is a work of fiction. Names, characters, places and incidents either are the product of the author's imagination or are used fictitiously. Any resemblance to actual persons, living or dead, events, or locales, is entirely coincidental.

ISBN-13: 978-0-9953076-5-0

Published by ParadiseDeer Publishing
Canada

Cover Art by Janet Holmes
Formatting by Author E.M.S.

Acknowledgments

To start, I thank you, my devoted reader. If you're holding this book, you've hopefully enjoyed books one and two. What a pleasure it is to write more Valentine adventures for you!

My humblest appreciation to Chief Scott Silverii, Ph.D. and Detective Constable Sandra Courtney for graciously answering all my questions on police matters. Any mistakes I've made in these pages are my own.

Enormous thanks to Major Anna Richland. You gave me utterly amazing insight into what it's like to be in the U.S. military and how to breathe life into characters who serve. If you ever have a hair or beauty dilemma, I'd be happy to return the favor. (*wink*)

Oodles of shiny gold stars for my team: My editor ~ Karen Dale Harris, formatter ~ Amy Atwell, cover artist ~ Janet Holmes, and proofreader ~ Noël Kristan Higgins. You've been kind, patient, and humorous, and those qualities have made this journey a marvelous one.

Big hugs and deepest gratitude to *New York Times* and *USA Today* Bestselling Authors Liliana Hart, Darynda Jones, and Wendy Byrne for your dazzling endorsements. Your delightful words have warmed my heart and put a bounce in my step!

Cuddly squeezes to my family for your endless love and support. I'd attempt to write down the million ways you fill me with joy, but there wouldn't be enough ink in the world to complete the task. My endless sloppy kisses will have to do.

Lastly, and as always, thanks to God for Your rich blessings. You are my rock and foundation.

To Eden & Hart:

You are my greatest joy. I love you always. xo

Chapter 1

Grandma Maruska once said, "Nobody's past is very interesting. It's the future that counts." While that last part may be true, one's past *could* be indelible. How many beauticians, for example, use their salon tools for catching criminals? And how many continually find themselves caught up in murder investigations? That's where the interesting part comes in with me.

My name is Valentine Beaumont, and I own a full-service salon in Rueland, Massachusetts. Beaumont's is an open-concept shop with soft lighting and rustic Mediterranean decor. It's not grand by beauty standards, but it does have a small amount of class. I have three employees ranging from extremely talented to she's-got-scissors-in-her-hand—run-for-your-life!

While I do my best to manage the shop, I also do my utmost to stay clear of homicide investigations. Unfortunately, I'd failed miserably in both areas. And falling hard for Roman warrior-like Detective Michael Romero when he'd been assigned the strangling in my salon four months ago was only complicating my life since now there was also Jock de Marco.

Jock was one of the extremely talented at Beaumont's. He was six three—or four—and was Hercules in the flesh, with muscles in places I didn't know had muscles. He had

Argentinean blood, was raised in a salon, and could turn a Plain Jane into a knockout with the mere touch of his comb. In another life, he'd also served a stint in the navy and had later fallen into stunt work. These were the few things I knew about Jock. The rest remained a mystery.

Presently, I was standing inside the Miami airport, watching Jock maintain a safe distance from Max and Phyllis, my two other employees. We'd flown in from Boston and had collected most of our bags, so we could board the bus that would take us to our ship for the six-night Caribbean "Beauty Cruise" for four I'd won for the salon.

I tapped my toes inside my rhinestone-heeled straw sandals, uncertain if winning the trip for us all was a blessing or a curse. Not only was I anxious about being on the high seas with someone whose touch evoked longing and sparked bodily desires I struggled to ignore, but my meddling parents and my father's sweet but oblivious aunt were also coming along since the cruise was open to the public. I took a deep breath, put all that to the back of my mind, and ambled over to Max and Phyllis. I had news to share.

"Is this going to take long?" Phyllis pulled apart a Cuban roll from the Portly Pig's kiosk. "Because I'm on a new diet, and I'm not supposed to starve myself."

Phyllis was less of an employee and more of a liability. She performed pin curls and finger waves on the near-sighted and hard-of-hearing, so her lack of talent usually went unnoticed. Most smart business owners would've shown her the door long ago—and I'd unsuccessfully tried that once—which said something about my managerial skills. But mostly, I kept her on because she was blood on my mother's side. And while it wasn't easy facing disgruntled clients, compared to familial guilt, it was the lesser of two evils.

"Yes, that'd be a real shame," Max said. "*You*, going without food. You might almost fade to a ton."

Max, on the other hand, had been with me since I'd

opened Beaumont's almost ten years ago. Apart from his love of riling Phyllis, he was the yin to my yang, the up to my down, the pesky brother I never had. And his innate sense at beautifying others was a genuine gift.

"For your info"—Phyllis shook her roll in Max's face—"I heard Dr. Oz had a guest on his show the other day who said you could lose weight by eating spareribs and cornbread."

Max's eyebrows shot up. "Was he wearing a polka-dot costume and red rubber nose?"

"As a matter of fact, he was a physician with a best-selling book."

"Dr. Seuss? Oh, wait. He's dead." Max shook his head. "Like this dimwit idea of yours."

Phyllis puckered her lips at Max and scrunched her eyes like she was ready for a fight. Thing was, we'd heard it all before. Phyllis would go on a diet. We'd walk around on pins and needles while she starved herself and ranted at everyone. And in the end, she'd gain back her weight, plus ten pounds. This diet actually sounded promising. At best, it wouldn't require much willpower.

Speaking of which…my gaze slid to Jock, and suddenly my ears got hot. He stood relaxed yet alert. Arms crossed, legs wide. Atlas determining how to hold the world on his back. He wore a lime-green T-shirt that begged you to count the hard ripples down his abs. His long, darkly streaked hair had grown back to a natural chestnut brown, complementing his mocha skin, his face a replica of a young Dwayne Johnson's—at least I'd been told.

If I was totally honest, I'd admit my ears weren't the only thing that heated up when I thought about Jock de Marco. At the moment, I felt my underwear almost sizzle off from his caramel-eyed hot stare. But he was an employee, and I refused to get romantically involved. In addition, I was still working out feelings for Romero. The fact that the two men had met when I was unsure where I stood with Romero only created unspeakable tension. They each had their individual skills and tended to their own business. But overall, I was fighting a losing battle swearing off men.

At 5'4" and 118 pounds, I led the parade over to Jock, feeling slightly bigger than my size 7/8 britches. I parked my luggage by my side, put up my chin, and cleared my throat. I didn't make eye contact with Jock, but the heated tension was there. He uncrossed his arms and rested them at his sides, waiting for me to speak.

I ignored the thumping in my chest from his closeness, remembering who was in charge here. "I was saving this until we landed," I said, feeling a tad guilty for not sharing my news with everyone earlier. "As this is a beauty cruise, there's going to be a competition on board tomorrow to kick off events. You'll choose a model from the passengers and fix her hair and makeup. Tools and supplies will be sponsored by Adore It Products. Prize is five thousand dollars."

I exhaled and gave myself some slack. Truth was, even my own stylists would be my opponents, and if I wanted to win and donate my prize money to the new children's wing at Rueland Memorial, the less competition the better. Plus, this was supposed to be a fun vacation for everyone, right? Competing would be like working. Who'd be interested?

Max and Phyllis started eyeing the possibilities for models and bickering about who'd win the contest. I'd already decided to ask Tantig, my father's aunt, to be my model, and I intended on presenting the idea to her once we set sail.

Jock watched Max and Phyllis for a moment, then took a step closer, wrapping his arm around me in my cute tie-dyed summer dress.

He smelled like leather and citrus after a rain, and it never ceased to test my self-control. "May I speak with you privately?" His voice was low.

"About the contest?" I stepped back from his grasp and caught myself before falling over my luggage. I straightened my shoulders and looked him in the eye. "I'm sure whatever you want to discuss can be said right here."

He tilted his head in an if-you're-sure gesture, then swept a stray lock of my hair behind my bare shoulder. His fingers lingered, causing tingles across my skin. "It's about the sleeping arrangements."

Max and Phyllis choked back their quarreling, staring at us bug-eyed. And my mother, who was sitting ten feet away in her oversized straw hat, poked up her head with interest.

I swallowed down a lump in my throat. I recalled the kiss Jock had given me little more than a month ago in the salon. He was right when he said I wanted him bad, but he'd have to strip me naked before I admitted that. I drew in a deep breath, remembering his full lips, supple and demanding. Heat rose from my stomach to my face, followed by a nervous fluttering inside.

I put the memory aside and yanked him behind a pillar, out of earshot and hopefully out of my mother's line of sight. "We discussed sleeping arrangements before," I whispered. "You're bunking with Max, and I'm sharing a cabin with Phyllis."

"I have a better idea."

"You think you and Phyllis should share a room?" I could be so clever.

He pinned me to the pillar, his hard thighs pressing into mine, his hands flat on the column on either side of my head. "Actually, I had something else in mind." His hot whisper tickled my neck. "And I think you know what that something is."

Yes, oh yes. I could feel that something, pushing into my pelvis. "Oh, well," I sang lightly before I melted in a puddle on the floor. "I guess you're out of luck."

He shoved off and flicked my chin. "We'll see."

I slid past him, took a shaky breath, and was halfway back to the group when Tantig shuffled over in her sweater and polyester dress. "I need my Xalatan," she said dryly.

Tantig was the grandma I never had. She was also a short, white-haired prophet of bad tidings. She never raised her voice or became anxious in a family where one had to be loud to be heard. Instead, her Armenian accent would come out in a bland monotone. "She's going to have a strrroke," she'd say when I was a child running around at play, or "You'd bett-air call an ambulance. She's going to brrreak her neck."

My parents didn't go far without taking Tantig with them, whether it was to Zettle's to pick up her dry cleaning or to Kuruc's European Deli to buy ingredients to make paklava.

I walked Tantig over to my mother, reminding myself this was going to be a wonderful vacation.

"I've got her eyedrops here somewhere." My mother rummaged through her bag, clutching passports, boarding passes, her wallet, and about three other things she wouldn't dare set down. The thing about traveling was my mother trusted no one, and she trusted my father even less when it came to ensure nothing got stolen or lost.

Tantig waited patiently on my mother, then glanced up at Jock. "Who-hk are you?" Some of Tantig's words were embellished at the end with a throat-clearing sound.

Jock bent his head down, a mixture of humor and respect in his eyes. "I'm Jock."

"What's a Jock?" Tantig asked.

It was a good question, one in which I was still trying to find the answer.

After my father had collected their bags, we moseyed over to a woman in a blue uniform who was holding up a sign with the cruise line logo across the top and *BEAUTY CRUISE* in small letters underneath. She smiled pleasantly despite the swarm of people knocking down luggage, waving passports in her face, and firing questions. Everyone wanted to know why we weren't boarding the bus. Remarkably, the woman remained chipper. Wait till she met our bunch.

"What's the hold-up?" demanded a shrill, girlish voice above the others.

Everyone fell silent and looked around for the owner of the voice. Finally, the cruise lady lowered the sign and peered down. The crowd thinned, and I saw where everyone was gawking.

Standing at about three feet high was a little person, hands on hips, blond hair in a ponytail. "What gives anyway?" she said. "We hitching a ride on one of those shuttle buses or what?"

The cruise lady smiled as one would when dealing with a child. "We're waiting for two more passengers. Then we can board the shuttle."

"Hey, if the morons can't get here on time, I say we push off without them. And stop staring at me like I'm from *Toy Story*. I'm Lucy Jacobs. Everyone got that? And yes, I'm a little person. I recognized it before any of you saps did. So stop feeling sorry for me. I'm plenty big where it counts."

"Yeah," Max whispered. "In her vocal cords."

Lucy whipped around. "Who said that?"

Max mutely pointed at Phyllis from behind her head.

Lucy aimed a stubby finger at Phyllis. "I'll be watching you."

Phyllis glanced up from tearing a meaty piece of pork from her sandwich. "Huh? What's she talking about?"

"Nothing, dear," Max said. "Enjoy your snack."

We all watched Lucy Jacobs strut over to a chair, hike onto the seat, and swing her legs furiously under her.

Just then, a thin East Indian man, medium height, in a white suit raced toward the crowd, hands flailing in the air, knapsack swinging on his back. "Do not let the bus leave without me!"

The cruise lady scanned the opposite side of her sign and gave a puzzled but professional smile. "You must be Kashi. Kashi...Farooq?"

The man caught his breath and pushed up his steel-rimmed glasses. "Yes. Do not be fooled by the Arabic name.

I am Indian through and through. And devilishly handsome, if I do say so myself." He gave an apologetic smile to the group. "I am here for the beauty cruise, but it seems my luggage is on its way to Malaysia, and for this I am most upset."

Lucy hopped off her chair, hands on hips. "If it isn't our four-eyed jungle boy, Cashew."

"*You!*" A murderous look filled Kashi's face. "You are the reason my luggage is flying across the ocean." He made tight fists. "I knew you were up to something when you slipped through the opening where the luggage slides out. You stopped mine from ever coming through. You terrible human being!"

"Relax." Lucy waved him off. "So, you're missing a robe or two. I'm sure we can swipe a tablecloth from the captain's table and wrap it around you."

"You *nasty person!*" Kashi lunged for Lucy. "My cat has more class than you!"

"Aaaaah!" Lucy ran around in circles, making a path over chairs and around luggage.

"Stop her!" he cried, arms flapping. "Kashi is well-respected in New York. I am not a jungle boy or…or some garden variety peanut."

Nobody knew who to grab. Except Jock. He swooped Lucy up by the collar and carried her, like a kitten by the scruff of the neck, back to her seat.

The crowd sucked in air at Jock's strength, and the cruise lady promised Kashi his suitcase would be retrieved and delivered to the ship as soon as possible.

Everyone had just settled down when the second passenger we'd been waiting for reared her ugly head. None other than Candace Needlemeyer, my archenemy who owned Supremo Stylists three blocks from Beaumont's.

I'd gone to beauty school with Candace, and she'd been a sneaky, lying cheat who'd taken pleasure in making my life miserable. If she wasn't secretly yanking out clumps of hair from my mannequin's head, then she was soaking all my tools in oil, making it impossible for me to grip anything. I'd bid her farewell when we'd graduated, thinking I was rid of her. Then she opened a shop in the same neighborhood and did her best to one-up me and steal clients.

There was a sharp pain in the back of my eye as I relived Candace's efforts at enticing Max to work for her, not to mention her more recent attempt at luring away Jock.

She pushed past people and came to an abrupt stop three feet from me. "What are *you* doing here?" She fluffed her blond mane like it was free and flowing instead of stiff and coated in hairspray.

I narrowed my eyes at her. "I won this trip, not that it's any of your business." Truth was, this trip happened so suddenly I barely had enough time to close the shop and promise my clients a ten percent discount next time they came in. Here I'd been afraid Candace would swoop in and steal my customers while I was gone.

My fingernails dug into my palm so ferociously I almost drew blood. "How did *you* get here? I didn't see your broom parked outside. And you sure as heck weren't on the plane." I didn't like talking so mean, but Candace brought out the worst in me.

She tapped her glossy red luggage handle that matched her glossy red lips and nails. "I was in Jacksonville for a few days, visiting a friend, if you must know." She looked over at Jock and winked. "I flew into Miami this morning for the beauty cruise."

Ugh.

"Fortunately," she continued, "my staff stayed back to work."

More likely, they chose working over going on a trip with Candace. This ship wasn't going to be big enough for the two of us. I looked up in a silent prayer and told myself to let it go. Candace wasn't going to interfere with my vacation.

Ten minutes later, we all piled onto the shuttles. Thank God Candace boarded one of the other buses. She was out of my hair and at the same time could make enemies with a whole new group of people.

Tantig sat beside Kashi who, at present, was pressing his straight brown nose against the window. Max and I settled in behind them. The bus driver welcomed us, said a few pre-cruise words, and took off with a lurch.

Tantig stared over Kashi's shoulder. He turned from the window, smiled at her, and leaned back so she could have a better view of the passing palm trees.

She put her lips together and blinked. "I wear a pacemake-air," she said flatly, likely not noticing the view.

Kashi glanced over his shoulder at us as if maybe he'd missed something. Getting no response from us, he nodded at Tantig. "That is indeed noteworthy."

She did her usual pursed-lipped half smile, and Kashi took this as an invite for more conversation. "May I learn what is your age?"

She raised her chin along with a *tsk* of her tongue. The silent *no*.

Kashi smiled, undeterred. "You must be seventy-five, yes? Or eighty?"

Tantig shifted her eyes at Kashi. "I'll give you a Tic Tac if you stop asking how old I am."

Kashi laughed. "You dear little pasty-skinned woman. You remind me of my grandmother." His face brightened like an idea occurred to him. "I have a gift for you, made with Kashi's own hands." He buried his head in his knapsack and came up a second later, clutching something that resembled a cockroach with glittering gemstones and blond hair swirled on the sides. "I call it Kashi's 'Get Out of Town' brooch. My own creation made from human hair. This one is for you. Kashi's 'Get Out of Town Marilyn.' Named after the legendary Marilyn Monroe." He placed his brooch on Tantig's sweater lapel, and she gave another tongue click.

"Tank you." Her words were sincere, but I knew she was thinking she could do without the brooch.

I relaxed in my seat and breathed in the blue skies of

Miami and warm air blowing through the windows. I couldn't believe we were here in the Sunshine State, getting ready to board a cruise ship. Apart from work, I'd managed to pay my landlord my house rent and ask my neighbor Mr. Brooks to take care of my cat, Yitts. There was nothing left to do but enjoy myself.

My gaze roamed back to Kashi's shiny black head of neatly cut hair, and my brows creased. What was that confrontation in the airport with Lucy Jacobs all about? Kashi had said he was here for the beauty cruise. Was Lucy here for the same reason? Kashi had also mentioned New York. Was Lucy from New York, too? Had they been involved with each other? Was that skirmish work-related? I did a half shrug. It was none of my business. I was here for the contest. I didn't need something else to worry about.

Max was up and down in his seat like a jack-in-the-box, sweat on his lip, white-knuckled grip on his carry-on bag.

"What's the matter?" I asked.

His eyes were wide as we careened around a corner. "I didn't want to say anything, but—"

"But what?" I slid back to my side of the seat.

"But I have a problem with water."

"As in, you're worried about how clean the beaches will be? Or worried about drinking it?"

"More like worried about deep, deep water...and drowning."

I sighed, remembering Max's nausea and white face on our ferry ride to Martha's Vineyard a month ago. "You waited until we were minutes from boarding a cruise ship to tell me you're afraid of drowning?"

"*Shhh!*" he spit out. "It's not something I want the whole world to know."

Sort of how I felt about being related to Phyllis. "Why didn't you tell me this earlier? Like maybe when I told you we won the cruise?"

He rolled his eyes. "Because I didn't want to miss out."

"Terrific. Now what?"

"As long as I don't go anywhere near the ocean, I'll be fine."

"Going to be kind of hard on a cruise ship, don't you think?"

Bad enough I had my family vacationing with me, Candace on board, and Jock planting lustful thoughts in my head. Now I had Max's phobia to deal with, too. What else could happen?

My gaze wandered to where Jock leaned against the dashboard of the bus. He had one leg down on the step, at ease, like a tour guide. He talked comfortably with the bus driver and, as if sensing my eyes on him, turned his head and winked.

I jerked down in my seat, my skin suddenly hot. I squeezed my eyes tight, picturing the upcoming week. Hot lazy days. Long sweaty nights. Bikinis. Swim trunks. Tanned, oily skin. Drinks with tiny umbrellas. Dancing, romantic locations, being under the same roof, knowing Jock was only seconds away. *Whew.* I forced open my eyes, my heart beating wildly. This was not a good idea. Jock and I together on a cruise.

"Right." My throat thickened. "I can handle this." There was no way I'd be swept into the Jock de Marco lair. As long as I stayed away from the piña coladas, I'd be good.

Max cut me a look. "What can you handle? And why are you halfway to the floor?"

"What? Nothing." I straightened in my seat.

He nudged me, fanning himself with a brochure. "Speaking of handling things, looks like Jock's on the hunt, and you're the prey."

I grabbed the brochure out of Max's hand. "In another hour, Jock will be swatting off bikini beach babes. And a minute ago, you were fretting about deep water."

He ripped the pamphlet out of my hand. "Thanks for reminding me."

My mind shifted from beach babes to the new *police* babe Romero was flying off to California with on a case.

Belinda. Yuck. To add insult to injury, when he'd phoned to share the news, I could hear her silky voice in the background, asking for a file. He'd faded for a moment, presumably looking for the file, and then they'd mumbled something to each other. Last thing I caught was the sound of her flirty laugh.

Steam piped out my ears at the memory. I'd heard other women laugh like that around Romero, a laugh that implied they were his for the taking. Not something I liked to think about.

I wasn't sure what Romero and I had, but when he'd indicated he wanted a relationship, I presumed he meant more than a casual association. Yet what if I was wrong? What if he merely wanted another playmate to fit his hectic work schedule, like the playmates who'd decorated his past, no strings attached?

Maybe I was too much effort. So what if I wasn't playmate material. *Ooh.* Being with Romero made me too vulnerable, too emotional, too crazy. We couldn't even get through a conversation without wanting to kill each other. Then again, amid the hollering and doubting, there'd also been kind acts, caressing, and plenty of sexual tension. At times, I was so close to ripping off his clothes, it was like my nipples were on permanent standby.

I tapped my fingers on my lap, trying to think about something else. But the truth was, I wanted to know what Romero was up to. He said he'd call from California. Why hadn't he? Was he ticked because Jock was going on the cruise? The tension between them was palpable. Maybe Romero had never truly accepted the fact that Jock worked at Beaumont's. Or was he too busy with his new partner to call? Oh *hell.* I tugged out my cell phone and pulled up his name.

Max eyed the screen and shot me a look.

"What?" I asked.

"I'm not saying a word."

"You think I'm wrong to phone him."

"You mean to check up on him."

Just once I'd love for Max not to be so bloody perceptive. And why did I tell him about Romero in the first place? "That's not what I'm doing."

"What do you call it? And your nose is twitching."

Darn. I pinched my nose. "Maybe I'm phoning to apologize."

"Apologize!" He slapped my hand away from my face. "For what?"

I shoved my phone back in my bag. "Nothing, okay? I'm not calling. Period."

The bus squealed to a stop, and everyone but Tantig and Max swiveled their heads to the windows.

Max gripped the headrest in front, his face pale green. "Can you see water?"

Kashi's glasses steamed up. "Lots and lots of water! That is what I call a cruise ship!"

"Feeling Hot Hot Hot" blared from a distant speaker, and everybody hopped off the bus and formed a conga line. Max squeezed his eyes tight and put a death grip on my arm until we cleared any sign of water and were inside the cavernous cruise terminal.

After we went through security, showed our cruise documents, and had our pictures taken, we stepped sweaty but elated onto the ship.

The festive atmosphere gave me goose bumps, and I was all but salivating at the smells that were an intoxicating mix of the sea, coconut oil, and something extraordinary. Probably our dinner being prepared by a world-class chef.

We waited in line to shake hands with Captain Madera, and Max got all dreamy.

"Isn't he handsome?" He gazed at the captain, his color miraculously restored. "All that premature white hair and gorgeous tanned skin. So debonair."

We were inching along when Lucy shoved past us with a big blue suitcase. "Will you get out of the way!"

In Lucy's wake strode a tall redhead toting a white snakeskin suitcase, her beautiful hair flowing down her bare shoulders onto a white cotton dress. "Lucy," she said gently, "these people have been waiting ahead of us."

"And you're telling me this because?" Lucy cocked her head up at the redhead. "I've got to get a good spot by the pool and plan my attack on this contest." She put her little hands on her hips. "You know how hard I work, Sabrina. I'm here for a good time, not a long time." She nodded at her suitcase. "Which is why I said not to leave our bags with any dumbass porters to lose between the dock and our room. Now grab the heavy thing for me."

Sabrina planted her feet firmly. "You go ahead. I'll see you later."

Lucy gave her a mean glare. She clutched her suitcase, gave a salute to the captain, and bopped the bag down the steps behind her into the ship.

"Bravo!" Max said in a hushed tone.

Sabrina turned to Max and me as if she'd forgotten there were people around. "Lucy's not that bad." She grinned. "She's just straightforward, honest, and…"

"Bossy?" Max finished, then put on a bright smile for the captain.

We all shook hands with the captain, then veered over to a Beauty Cruise sign-in desk. We got our packages, and Sabrina fell into an easy conversation with us about the makeover contest. "Lucy's determined she's going home with that contest money." She sighed. "If nothing else, she's got self-confidence." She dug into her package. "Look, the rules."

Max opened his package and scanned the rules. "If I win, I could buy that hot tub I've had my eye on." He smiled. "Or maybe I'll take up golfing."

While Max was mentally spending his winnings, I thought about the talent I'd be competing against. Now that I was here, it was sinking in that this wasn't a simple local contest with a gift-card prize to Friar Tuck's Donuts. Five thousand dollars could buy a lot of things.

"If you win, lovey, what are you going to spend the money on?"

I gave a small smile. "The new children's wing at the hospital. They're close to reaching their goal, and I figure I can help out a bit." Actually, I'd pledged to help out a lot. So far, I'd only donated the equivalent to a new pair of shoes. Expensive shoes, but still. Sure, I could add a few updates in the salon, buy some new equipment, and get ahead on my mortgage. But then I thought about playing Mon Sac Est Ton Sac—my made-up hairdressing game— with the hospital kids. I'd empty my bag on one of the beds, and they'd adorn me with bows and false lashes and nail polish, and the beauty of it was, there were no rules or guarantees I wouldn't look like a clown. I warmed inside, recalling their squeals of laughter at my appearance after they'd finished beautifying me. Yes, their need for an improved environment easily topped my needs.

"Oh brother." Phyllis dropped her carry-on in a heap. "Who are you anyway? Mother Teresa? Why don't you spend it on something big?"

Max turned to Phyllis as though he'd cruelly been reminded she was on board. "Like a side of beef?"

Phyllis went starry-eyed. "Like a thousand lottery tickets."

"Oh, that's brilliant," Max said. "Win it, and then lose it."

The boat swayed slightly, and Phyllis gagged, bending forward. "Uhhhhh, I don't feel well."

So much for her new diet being off to a good start. I dropped my stuff at my feet, and before I could reach out to help, she threw up all over Max's shoes.

An hour later, after a routine safety drill and lecture on lifeboat stations, passengers went off to play shuffleboard, mini-golf, and search for the casino for when it opened later. My parents, Tantig, Max, and I settled on the lower deck around the pool, watching activities from the sidelines until our early dinner seating. Phyllis was in our cabin turning different shades of green.

There was nonstop action all around us. A group of sports jocks at the far end of the pool slugged back Coronas and laughed at football bloopers playing on a mega-screen on the upper deck. Candace was in the middle of the group, laughing it up with them. One tiny man with a willowy white beard sat, head resting on his arm, at the edge of the bar, getting a head start on becoming the happy-hour drunk. More power to him. The strongest drink I was going to swig was a Shirley Temple.

I ordered a tall glass and looked from a group of people splashing in the water to others basking in the sun. This looked like a good idea to me. I dragged a lounge chair out into the sun and dug into the contest rules.

Max had his chair back five feet in the shade next to Tantig, crossword-puzzle book from the beauty package under his nose, sangria in hand. "Tantig," he said, "what's a six-letter word for revenge?"

Tantig didn't turn an inch, but I did catch her eyes roll skyward. "Who-hk cares?"

"Listen to this," I said over my shoulder to Max. "Contestants will be given three hours to produce the finished look on their model. Any means of treatment may be used."

Max flopped his crossword down. "I can't wait! I'm going to give them one hundred percent Max in this competition!"

My father stared blankly at Max like nothing he said would ever surprise him. Given Max's flamboyancy, that was probably a good thing. He looked at his watch and grumbled that he might as well stroll the deck if supper wasn't for another hour. God forbid we make my father wait until eight o'clock to stuff Alaskan king crab down his throat. He clasped his hands behind his back and wandered away. Likely thinking how nice a Cuban cigar would taste right about now.

My mother jammed sneakers onto Tantig's feet, then plunked a hat onto her head and tied the ribbons into a huge bow under her chin. Tantig looked like Scarlett O'Hara with wrinkles.

"What are you do-ink?" she asked my mother.

"Getting you ready for a walk as Dr. Stucker recommended."

"I'm going to fire Stuck-air," Tantig said. "I wear a pacemake-air. I can't exercise."

"Dr. Stucker knows best," my mother said. "You can't sit and watch soaps on the satellite channel all week. You can walk every morning while we're here."

Tantig clicked her tongue and allowed my mother to drag her away.

I sipped on my Shirley Temple, lowered my sunglasses onto my nose, and lay back in my lounge chair, relaxing to the sounds of splashing and laughter.

"I'm going for a dip," Max said. "It's hot as Hades out here, and it looks like they're getting water volleyball going." He stopped at my chair and looked down pointedly. "Coming? Or are you still thinking about that six-letter word for revenge?"

Wiseass, needling me about Romero. If sarcasm were a country, Max would be queen. "I thought you needed to stay away from water."

"Pools are different," he said. "*Those*, I can see the bottom."

"Then go ahead. I'll be in later."

"Suit yourself." He stood at the water's edge, towel around his waist.

Lucy darted by out of nowhere and ripped Max's towel away from him.

"Hey!" Max shouted. "Did you see that? She stole my towel! That mini Jezebel."

"Jezebel was a seductress," I corrected, "not a thief."

"I don't care if she was a high priestess. She stole my towel." He took off flat-footed after her. "Jezebel!" he screamed until he was out of earshot.

Grinning, I closed my eyes and slid the contest rules under my leg.

The sun's rays were warming my skin when a hush fell over the deck. For a moment, the splashing calmed, and music stopped. Then I heard intense gasping as if a UFO had been spotted in the sky. Suddenly, something blocked the sun.

I squinted my eyes open at Jock, standing at the foot of my lounge chair, shades on his nose, towel slung over his shoulders, swim trunks low on his hips. Thor of the twenty-first century. A UFO wouldn't get half the attention.

I glanced at the women on either side of me, holding their breath. In a blink, they guzzled their margaritas and averted their gazes to the pool.

Jock sat, straddling the edge of my lounge chair. He pushed back my feet with his hands, the crescent-shaped scar on his ribs from his navy days hidden under his towel. "You're getting red."

With knees bent, I looked down at myself. I wasn't surgically enhanced curvy or waif-thin, and I didn't spend inordinate amounts of time at the gym, but thanks to good genes, Zumba class, and biking, I managed to keep in shape. How red I was getting? That was a matter of opinion.

He leaned in until I could smell his exotic scent, his eyes unreadable behind his shades. Grazing my thigh with his hand, he picked up the suntan lotion lying beside me.

He raised his shades onto his head. Then, eyes on me, he squirted white cream onto his palm. I stirred hotly inside at the way his penetrating gaze raked across my bare skin and prayed he was going to lotion his own body. He rubbed the cream in his large, strong hands, then stroked it on my right calf, lifting my leg to get underneath. I muscled my leg back down, my heart thumping madly, but Jock widened the gap as if he was spreading a wishbone.

He rested my leg across his thigh, and I swallowed hard, trying not to look at his trim waist or, dear Lord, anything lower. I focused on his anchor-and-rope tattoo on his left bicep, *anywhere* but on what his hands were doing to me, inside and out. Okay, I was having indecent thoughts about Jock. I was only human.

He massaged my inner thigh with his thumbs, eyes appreciatively on my stomach. "I like the white bikini. It's"—his full lips curled up a fraction of an inch—"virginal."

Gulp. My nipples perked up, and I self-consciously grabbed a towel on the guise of wiping sweat off my collarbone.

He slanted forward to squirt more cream on my bikini line, but I seized his wrist. "No!" I panted. "Thank you. I can do the rest."

"You sure?" His tone was low. "If you get too much color, I'll have to rub you down with therapeutic oil."

I heard the clatter of plastic on wood and noticed the woman beside me had dropped her margarita.

Ignoring the distraction, Jock lifted my shades over my head and looked deep into my eyes. "Of course, I might do that anyway."

I made a squeak somewhere in the back of my throat, my face hot. "Look…" I somehow scraped together a confident voice. "I'm here for one thing—to win that contest."

"I'm here to win, too."

I wasn't sure if that was a threat or a promise, but something told me we weren't talking about the same thing. I whipped off my sunglasses and leaped off the chair, thinking I'd cool down in the pool.

In one fluid move, Jock got up and slid his arm around my waist, lifting me off the ground. His lips brushed my ear. "You can't go this entire cruise avoiding me."

I broke free and crashed ass-backward into the water. *No*, I thought as I sank to the bottom, *but I'll probably die trying.*

Chapter 2

"You're going where?" Phyllis was on the bottom bunk, leaning on one elbow, steadying the garbage can under her chin while watching me dab foundation on my burned nose.

"Dinner." I snapped shut the compact and slipped on a pink halter dress. Then I moved a tiny bouquet of fresh-cut tropical flowers by her bed, hoping they'd make her feel better.

"Uhhhhh," she moaned. "Don't mention food. And get that vase away from me. Lilies alone are enough to make me puke." She hauled herself off the bed and staggered past her strewn luggage on the floor into the bathroom.

I tripped over her shoes, moving the flowers to the other side of the room. Muttering under my breath at her lack of order, I watched her pull back her hair and hunch over the toilet. Her soft mahogany curls were plastered to the sides of her cheeks from sweat, and there was a small patch behind her ear.

My heart mellowed. "What's with the patch, Phyllis?"

She angled her head toward me. "Ship's doctor gave it to me. Said I didn't have food poisoning or a virus. Just seasickness. But now my mouth's dry and my eyes are blurry." She faced the toilet again. "I hope the good part kicks in soon because I can't stand it much longer in this closet they call a cabin." She slammed the bathroom door shut with her foot and retched into the toilet.

I stifled back a gag and took in the size of the room. I had to agree with Phyllis. Being deep in the bowels of the ship wasn't the luxury accommodations I was hoping for. There were no windows, the bunk beds were narrow, and the shower looked like it wouldn't even fit Lucy. And good luck bending over with another person in the room. I grinned. Jock and Max would have an interesting time in their nest.

I finished dressing and was winding the sparkly ties on my pink sandals up my calves when the phone in our cabin rang. It was my mother, apparently testing the ship's amenities, and announcing we weren't sitting at the same dinner table.

I coughed in relief. Who could I thank for that?

"Do you think they're grouping the beauty cruise passengers together?" she asked. "Because I can talk to the captain and see what he can do about this."

"I don't think that's the captain's department, Mom." I picked Phyllis's sunhat off the floor. "They're probably providing meeting opportunities for people, especially singles."

"Singles? Forget I said anything." She quickly hung up.

I put the phone back on its cradle, thinking the bathroom was awfully quiet. "Phyllis?" I tapped on the door. "Do you want me to bring you anything?"

"Yeah, a gun."

If my mother donned her matchmaking hat, I might need one myself before the night was over.

Phyllis heaved again, and I left her to it. I swung my beauty bag over my shoulder, clicked the cabin door behind me, and faced Max and Jock's door across the narrow hall. I thought about knocking, then decided against it. Might give the wrong impression. Anyway, I'd see them at dinner.

Unaccustomed to the subtle rocking of the boat, I wobbled down the hallway, following the spicy aroma to the elevator. Boy, I was hungry. Poor Phyllis. She was missing out big time.

I rode a gazillion floors up and found the dining room decorated like something under the sea. Two elaborate dolphin ice sculptures formed a centerpiece in the middle of the room with an array of exotic flowers floating in a circle around the base. People sat at beautifully set tables of various sizes, already eating appetizers.

I spotted my family against the far wall, sitting with Kashi and three others. The banter seemed lively, and everyone wore a Kashi "Get Out of Town" brooch, except for my father. He wore his wedding ring and a dependable watch but drew the line at silly jewelry.

I turned to find my table and nearly knocked a fruity mai tai out of the hand of a short, gray-haired man in a straw fedora, Bermuda shorts, and a Hawaiian shirt.

"Watch where you're going in those damn heels," the man said, his knees and elbows so knobby a stiff breeze could snap them in two.

"Sorry." I stepped back and looked down under the man's hat into his face. "Mr. Jaworski?" I blinked wide-eyed at my landlord. "What are you doing here?"

"Valentine Beaumont!" he crowed, waving his mai tai in the air. "I'm on vacation. When you paid your rent the other day and told me you were going on a cruise with your family and a bunch of hairstylists, I decided to treat myself, too. An all-inclusive trip is just what Samuel H. Jaworski needs. Wouldn't you agree?"

Of course. Why the *H* wouldn't I agree? Just because tremors of anxiety were working their way up my spine? I peered from his sandals and nylon socks up to his beady eyes. First, my family. Now, my cheapskate landlord? I *eek*-ed out a polite laugh.

"I wouldn't be on this all-inclusive trip if it weren't for my lovely niece, my brother's daughter. She's also a hairdresser."

I let out a cough. There were two Mr. Jaworskis in the world? "You never mentioned you had a niece who did hair."

"Yeah, well, I do. When I told them about the beauty cruise, my brother said she knew about it and was already planning the trip, eager to win some contest. Seemed fitting I'd be here, too. I came down a day early, did some sight-seeing, and met up with her after we boarded the ship." He gave a hearty head shake. "Wait till you meet her. She's a real joker, that one."

"Nice." I tried to sound enthused, but it was futile.

He patted his shorts pocket. "It's about time I started spending my money. What good is it if you don't spend it, right?" He swirled his swizzle stick with a maraschino cherry and pineapple slice on the end. "I've got a real nice cabin, too. They even promised to leave those mint chocolates on my pillow every night. Real nice of them. No extra charge for the mint chocolates either. Where do you get mint chocolates for free anymore?"

"Probably nowhere." I moved back to dodge his rum-soaked breath and glanced over his shoulder. "Where is your niece?"

"She's around somewhere. Probably schmoozing with other hairstylists." He hoisted his glass in the air. "These mai tais are tasty. But you gotta tell them about the maraschino cherries. I got cheated last time, and I had to pay good money for that drink. When I buy a mai tai, I want my maraschino cherry."

If I had a jar of maraschino cherries, I'd dump them on his head just to shut him up. In fact, I'd probably never look at another maraschino cherry without thinking of Samuel H. Jaworski.

He gave me a creepy wink, then waltzed over to my parents' table.

Ugh. Me and my big mouth. Why did I tell him I was going on a cruise?

I shook off the prickly feeling of having my landlord on the same boat, then wandered in the opposite direction and found my designated table. I sat down, slipped my bag between my feet, and saw Max heading my way, a breath of fresh air in a crisp long-sleeved shirt and Italian-cut pants.

He sat beside me, placed his napkin on his lap, then gave me a once-over. "What happened to your nose?"

I put my finger to my burned nose. "One spot I forgot to lotion."

He gave me a sharp glare. "You mean Jock forgot to lotion."

Rat. He smugly took a sip of water, and I was having second thoughts about him being such a blessing.

We were trying to guess who'd be joining us when we heard a commotion at the entrance.

Lucy plowed into the dining room, shouting obscenities to an elderly couple who were obviously slowing her down. Passengers gasped in shock at her language, while Lucy zipped across the carpet like the Energizer Bunny.

Sabrina, in a purple floral dress, strode into the room a safe distance behind.

Smart. Keep the gap. But what was her relationship to Lucy? She never actually said. Were they friends? Co-workers? Relatives? Whatever it was, Sabrina didn't bow to Lucy's whims.

"Pretend you don't see them." Max studied the cutlery. "Maybe that little Jezebel's sitting at a table for one."

I stared at the empty chair beside Max, other things on my mind. "Where's Jock?"

Max raised his palms. "Said he had things to do."

"Like?" I tried to keep the anxiousness out of my voice.

He dropped his chin to his chest. "Do I look like his keeper? And why are you so interested? Earlier, you were convincing yourself you didn't care if he was marking his territory."

As we were locking horns, two blond, fluffy-haired beach babes clad in bikinis, sarongs, and flip-flops plopped themselves at our table, introducing themselves as hair-stylists. They were average in height with above-average hourglass shapes, and their tans looked like they'd been painted on with a roller brush.

"I'm Polly," the one with the bigger chest said. "And this is Molly."

I thought Max was going to have a coronary before he ordered his dinner. Since Jock had started working at Beaumont's, we were used to shapely women coming and going. But these two were showstoppers.

Max sputtered out a hello, extending his hand like royalty. "I'm Maximilian Martell. And this is"—his gaze lowered from Polly's tanned face to her bikini top, and suddenly the words got stuck in his throat—"Va-Va-Va—"

I gawked at Max while he practiced consonants. "Valentine Beaumont." I shook their hands, disregarding other eyes in the room zooming in on the blonds.

Polly giggled and pulled up her bikini bra strings. No easy feat, considering the weight being boosted. "We didn't know you were supposed to dress for dinner," she said. "But that nice maître d' at the door said not to worry. And we're just going back to the pool after anyway."

Max shrugged, finding his tongue. "Saves a step then, doesn't it?"

"Exactly!" Polly clapped her hands together, clicking her long, flower-painted fingernails.

A moment later, Sabrina and Lucy docked at the table. Lucy edged up between Molly and Polly's chairs, her chin barely reaching the table top. She looked right, and then left. "I didn't know they were serving watermelon as the main course."

"Where!" Molly exclaimed, breasts bouncing.

The maître d' wordlessly brought a booster seat for Lucy to sit on. She gave us all a defiant look, then hopped onto the seat and let the maître d' push her up to the table.

Max smiled, and I could see he was anxious to start the fun. "Polly and Molly—this is Lucy and—"

"Save the introductions, bub." Lucy nodded at the two empty chairs. "Where's that fat chick and the motorcycle hunk who were with you?"

Max stuffed a piece of bread in his mouth and squinted meanly at Lucy.

"Phyllis is seasick," I said. "And Jock"—I stared at the empty chair—"Jock's a mystery."

"I'll say," Sabrina said. "I saw him go into the captain's quarters when I was taking a tour."

"Ha!" Lucy barked. "You mean when you were snooping. Sabrina's a cruise junkie. She's already sniffed through every inch of the ship, including the bridge and the galley—or kitchen, to you morons. She's like a dog. Except I don't think she's peed on anything yet." She cracked up at this, slapping her hand on the table.

Everyone gaped at Lucy.

"What gives, anyway?" She narrowed an eye on me. "What's this Jock doing in the captain's quarters?"

It was a good question, but then nothing surprised me with Jock. He appeared when the mood hit him, and he left through trap doors. It was for sure *I* wasn't going to sit here, fantasizing over his whereabouts. Jock was an enigma. Period. If he wanted you to know what he was up to, he'd tell you.

"Wait a minute." Max eyed Lucy. "How did you know Jock rides a bike?"

She shrugged. "I can spot a biker a mile away. I have an eye for that sort of thing. And speaking of eyes"—she closed in on me—"I've seen yours somewhere before."

"Of course you've seen our Valentine before," Max said. "She's practically a celebrity after solving—"

I kicked him in the shin.

"Ow!" he howled.

Like I wanted the whole ship to know about my past association with homicides. And it wasn't such a long history. Only three. Plus, I didn't usually look for trouble. It found me.

"That's it!" Lucy said. "You stabbed a guy with a tail comb! Almost made a sprinkler out of him." She cranked out a laugh. "And they say we New Yorkers are crazy. Man, what are you doing here? You should be in the psych ward."

My jaw tightened. That first case was old news, and it'd happened years ago, *and* I'd acted in self-defense. Besides, it was the only way, in crisis mode, to stop a killer from getting away. Nonetheless, it continued to haunt me.

Lucy gasped openly. "And that was just the *one* crook! Any of you morons know she wrapped a perm rod around a guy's—"

I slammed my hand on the table with the speed of a bullet, and everyone jumped. "Look at that ice sculpture!" I exclaimed. "The dolphin's spraying water out its mouth!"

Everyone swiveled to look at the dolphin, the spray turning from pink to blue.

"Yeah, yeah," Lucy grumbled. "You've seen one ice sculpture, you've seen 'em all. I'm more interested in this contest tomorrow."

"Yeah!" Everyone piped, huddling closer to the table. I was just relieved we were moving on.

"Does anyone know who the judges will be?" Sabrina asked.

Nobody knew.

"I heard the models will be put in a separate room after the competition with their 'before' picture," Lucy said, "judged solely on how they look, not by who styled them or the technique used."

"I can't wait," Max said with glee. "Tantig will look like Zsa Zsa Gabor when I'm done."

"Tantig!" I swung my head toward him. "When did you ask her to be your model?"

"When you weren't around."

I drew my lips into a thin line.

"What!" Max lifted his shoulders. "I figured you'd want to fix up your mother. After all, she's Sophia Loren incarnate."

"Don't try and butter me up. Tantig was my first choice." I snapped a breadstick in two, mad at myself for not asking Tantig earlier when I had the chance.

"Quit your squabbling," Lucy said. "Doesn't matter *who*

you're doing. I'm going to win that contest if I have to jump the judges' bones to do it."

That thought put a sobering silence over the group.

The waiter came by and took our orders, leaving a complimentary bowl of jumbo shrimp on the table. We were all digging into the bowl when Mr. Jaworski strutted over. Splendid. If he mentioned maraschino cherries again, I was going to slit my throat with my knife.

"There she is!" he called out. "My little Lucy."

I almost swallowed a whole shrimp. *This* was Mr. Jaworski's lovely niece? His brother's daughter?

Lucy gave him a major eye roll. "Uncs, will you stop calling me *little*?"

I blinked in shock. Lucy was a Jacobs. Why the different last name? I spied her bare ring finger. Was she married but on the cruise alone? This didn't add up either. I smiled at Lucy. "Aren't you also a Jaworski?"

"Technically." She gave a flippant wave. "But you don't expect me to go by a loser name like Jaworski, do you? Lucille Jaworski. Sounds like a name you'd put on those ass wipes for babies. I changed it to Jacobs when I moved to New York."

Mr. Jaworski grinned from ear to saggy ear. "Didn't I tell you she was a real joker?"

"Don't cramp my style, Uncs." Lucy gave him a shove. "You're only on this cruise because..." She caught herself and swept a sheepish look around the table. "Uh, because..."

Everyone leaned in, waiting for the reason.

She patted her uncle's hand. "Because you're such a kind and, uh, generous uncle."

If there was one thing I knew about Mr. Jaworski, generosity wasn't it. Lucy clearly knew it, too. He slunk back to his table, muttering "brat" under his breath.

Nobody uttered a word after he left, and it was just as well. The sea air had made everyone ravenous, and when our meals came, we all got down to the business of eating, talking only about the contest.

After everyone devoured apple crumble for dessert, Lucy and Sabrina went off to secure their models. Molly and Polly went to re-soak their bathing suits. And Max and I wandered over to my parents' table. I asked my mother to be my model for the contest, and when she agreed, I gave Max a triumphant look.

"Come on, lovey," he said. "You can't hold a grudge forever."

"Watch me." I squinted at him.

He wove his arm through mine and led me out of the dining room. "Let's go for a stroll," he said. "You'll feel better."

I let him steer me down a row of boutiques, but all the contest talk at dinner had me more anxious about the competition. Max was right. My mother did resemble Sophia Loren, especially when she was dolled up. But what if I didn't win the contest? How would I earn enough money to donate to the children's wing?

We sauntered past a men's shop, and Max stuck his nose inside. Across the hall was a piano lounge, and the sound of a Ray Charles bluesy jazz song filtered out of the bar. I yawned, putting my concerns aside, then scanned the darkened lounge from the doorway. The only distinct thing I could see, apart from the pianist, was a wiry little fellow with a long white beard. His arm splayed across the bar, supporting his head to keep himself from falling off his chair. My gaze swept to the back of the lounge. Hold on a minute! What was this? Sitting under a soft floodlight in the corner of the bar was Jock de Marco, talking to the captain in what looked like a private conversation.

My mind replayed the discussion at the dinner table and Sabrina's revelation about spotting Jock in the captain's quarters. What had he been doing there? *Like I'd ask.* He'd be smug, concluding I was romantically interested. And I'd shave my head with a blunt razor before I'd admit that. I was merely inquisitive, like everyone else.

It wasn't as if the captain of a cruise ship spent his time hanging out with passengers. He wasn't on vacation. He had a job to do. Then again, Jock wasn't your typical passenger. Jock had a presence that was hard to ignore. Still, this was peculiar. Seeing him with the captain again now only confirmed there was something going on. I could feel it as sure as I could feel my heart leaping inside.

"Who are you looking for?" Max asked over my shoulder.

I yelped and clapped my chest. "Nothing! I mean, nobody!"

He did the Max stance, leaning to one side, finger pointed in my face. "You know your nose twitches when you lie?"

"Does not." I smacked his hand away. "I'm going to bed. It's been a long day." I glanced one last time into the lounge, then poked Max's chest with my finger. "And if you say his name one more time, I'm going to pluck out your eyelashes one by one!"

I stomped away, leaving Max with his mouth hanging. Okay, so neither of us mentioned Jock's name. Max could read me like a book. He could tell I was attracted to Jock. But there was also a part of me that was curious about him. Why I was being sucked in, yet again, to his enigmatic ways, I didn't know.

Chapter 3

When I got to the breakfast buffet the next morning, Max and my mother were sitting on either side of Tantig like bookends, looking at pictures. My father was at the end of the table, head down in his bowl of fresh fruit. He glanced up occasionally, eyeing the food stations as if breakfast might disappear if he didn't eat fast enough. Of course, this was hardly possible. The buffet looked vast enough to feed China. I filled my plate with eggs, pancakes, a strip of bacon, and fruit, and sat across from the Three Musketeers.

"Who-hk is that?" Tantig asked suspiciously, staring at a photo in my mother's hand.

"It's our wedding picture," my mother said. "The nicest shot I have of Bruce and me."

"Was I there?" Tantig squinted at the photo.

"Of course. That's you in the background."

I slathered syrup on my pancakes. "Why are you looking at your wedding picture?"

My mother lowered the photo. "Max said we need pictures of Tantig and me for the contest. Hard copies only, and this is all I could scrounge up. Bruce"—she poked my father's right arm—"give me your wallet."

My father leaned over his food protectively while he

dug into his pants pocket. Head still focused on his bowl, he handed my mother his wallet.

She rifled through the worn black leather, searching every compartment. "Where's that picture you kept of us from the Firemen's Christmas Dance?"

"I don't know," my father said. "It's so old it probably disintegrated."

My mother flipped his wallet shut and gave him a steely-eyed stare. The look was lost on my father. He didn't try to be insulting. He just didn't think before he spoke. He slurped the juice out of the bottom of his bowl, and I wondered if I should've taken my breakfast back to my room.

"Let's take a few shots right now." Max angled sideways, clicked pictures of my mother and Tantig with his cell phone, then looked back at me. "I'll upload them to the ship's computer and print them off before the contest. *Aaah!*" he screeched, dropping his phone on his bagel.

I looked around. "What's the matter?"

Max swallowed and pointed over my shoulder.

Phyllis barreled into the room, suddenly back to life in a flowing black-and-white checked dress, obviously one of her creations from the sewing course she'd taken a few months ago. She was hauling a little man with rumpled white hair and a long wispy beard. The man resembled a garden gnome without the red hat and suspenders and looked vaguely familiar. Phyllis spotted us and made a beeline for the table. The tiny man staggered to keep up.

"You were supposed to wake me this morning!" she said to me. She yanked out a chair for her friend. "Here." She pointed. "Sit."

The wiry man nearly missed the chair, a lifetime aura of alcohol surrounding him.

Everyone lifted their eyebrows, waiting for an introduction, when we heard Kashi in the background, making an entrance. "It is I, Kashi!" he said in his thick Indian accent.

My father rolled his eyes at yet another oddball in the

room and got up for the buffet table. I had a feeling he'd about had his limit of socializing.

The little man leaned his elbows on the table and gave a toothy smile, reeking of one hundred and ten percent proof. "Howth it goin'?"

All at once, it came to me. He was the drunk in the piano lounge last night and by the pool yesterday during happy hour. He had a four-inch-long gauze bandage on his left forearm that I hadn't noticed before, probably because both times I'd seen him he was using his arm to prop himself up. But he didn't look in pain. Of course, with the amount of booze in his system, a pile of garden gnomes could topple on him, and he likely wouldn't feel any pain.

"Who's your friend?" Max asked Phyllis, gaping at the black-and-white squares on her dress. "And why do I have a sudden urge to play checkers?"

Phyllis thwacked her matching purse on the table. "I can't make out his name." Her mouth went tight. "I call him Clive. Since I'd been sick in our cabin, I couldn't ask anyone to be my model. Now, all the good ones have been taken, so Clive's going to be mine." She snatched the bacon off my plate and wolfed it down. "Not the best choice for a makeover, but maybe the judges will be impressed with what I do with him."

Max bit off a sigh. "The judges would be more impressed if you gave up hairdressing."

I peeked over at my father at the buffet table. "Did you ask my dad? Maybe you can give him a new look." Doubtful, but I was trying to be encouraging.

"I don't think so. One time, your father came into the shop for a trim when you were out doing errands, and I told him I could cut his hair. He said, 'Not on your life.' *Waiter!*" Phyllis waved her arm in the air, her chequered sleeve fluttering like the final flag in a car race. "Coffee! And lots of it!"

"Phyllis," I said, "it's a buffet. You're supposed to get your own coffee."

She ignored me and continued waving to the waiter.

"You can't be in the contest," Max said in a hopeful tone. "You're seasick. Remember?"

"I'm over that." She lowered her arm. "The secret is echinacea and lots of water. My throat isn't dry anymore, and my vision's…almost perfect. Anyway, if I can stand without feeling nauseous, I'm good. Between my diet and all that hurling, I even lost ten pounds."

"They say the first ten pounds is water," Max declared, after the waiter brought coffee.

"I don't care what they say," Phyllis said. "I'm fit as a fiddle, and there's nothing that's going to stop me from winning that money." She exhaled down at Clive, who was sneaking rum from a tiny bottle into his coffee.

"Give me that!" Phyllis thundered at him.

He recoiled under her arm. "Yeow! Is she alwath like thith?"

"No," Max said. "She's being especially nice today."

"Good," Clive breathed out. "I left my wife at home so I could have peathe and quiet."

Max raised his eyes to me, and I knew what he was thinking. If Clive wanted peace and quiet, he'd have been better off at home.

The day at sea flew by with me pacing the deck, anxiously planning how I was going to fix my mother's hair and makeup so she'd wow the judges and make me a contest winner. I flopped down on a deck chair by the pool, recalling a new hair technique I'd learned a few weeks ago, when Max leaped out of the pool.

"It's three o'clock!" he cried. "Contest starts in an hour." Like suddenly he was worried how he was going to fix Tantig's hair. Served him right if he didn't have a plan. Stealing Tantig from under me.

He grabbed a towel, gave me a quick kiss on the cheek, and hurried down the deck. "Meet you there," he called over his shoulder.

I grinned inside, unable to stay mad at Max for long. I finished putting the required steps together in my mind for my mother's do, then abandoned my chair and made for my cabin. I passed Phyllis in the hallway heading in the opposite direction. "Where are you going?" I asked.

"To collect Clive," she said. "The little sneak got away on me."

I left her to her hunt and changed into my new white dress with a keyhole neckline. Professional yet fashionable! And since I wasn't coloring my mother's hair, it was the perfect choice.

Five minutes to four, two hundred stylists anchored themselves by their stations in the auditorium that now resembled a huge salon. Contestants were set up back to back in long rows, the aisle between their backs six feet wide. The room was equipped with enough beauty supplies to make over half of Hollywood.

The magnitude of the contest had me more nervous. How was I going to win that money for the children's wing, competing against so many? I decided not to focus on the numbers. I was as good as anyone else. I inspected the roomful of models. Obviously, some stylists had their work cut out for them. Like Lucy, working back to back with Max—who was stationed beside me. Lucy's model was a woman of about sixty, who looked like her heart had stopped beating at forty. If Lucy could turn her into a goddess, she deserved to win.

I smiled down at my mother, sitting in my chair, waiting to be dolled up. She wouldn't nearly be the challenge Lucy's model would be, but it was still going to be tough rising above and beyond the usual beautifying. I rubbed my hands together in anticipation. I'd just pretend I was in the salon, performing my magic.

Everyone was impatient to begin, puffing like a stampede of bulls at the starting gate. Speaking of bulls, where was my nemesis, Candace? I searched the floor again and spotted her in the reflection of my station's mirror. She was two rows behind our row of Phyllis, Max, and me—in line respectively. She caught me looking at her in the mirror and screwed up her nose in hostility. Fine by me. I wasn't going to be intimidated by Candace. I was here to win.

People were beginning to count down the seconds to four o'clock. Phyllis looked at Max, who glared across our row at Lucy, who stared up at Kashi, who was across from me.

Kashi's eyes glazed over to the next row at Molly and Polly, stationed between Candace's row and ours. The beach babes were working by Sabrina and other sane-looking people. Jock was nowhere in sight. Not that I cared. My mind was fixed on the children's hospital.

The whistle blew, Lucy climbed on top of her step stool, and everyone got down to the business of cutting, coloring, and making up their models, the clatter a decibel under earthquake proportions. Nobody knew who the judges were, but it didn't matter. Five thousand bucks was five thousand bucks. The pope could judge for all we cared. Everything was running smoothly, and then Phyllis's model began hiccupping. Loudly.

"Stop that!" Phyllis smacked Clive with her comb. "And stop drinking from my spray bottle." She wrenched the bottle from Clive and brought it to her nose. "Hey, what's in this?"

"Shhh," Clive said, blurry-eyed, leaning heavily over his chair. "Ith our little secret. *Hic.* Now, when am I going to turn into Antonio Banderas?"

Phyllis yanked him upright as if he had no bones. "You're four-eleven, chalky white, and built like a flamingo. Where do you see Antonio in your future?"

Max angled toward Clive while setting Tantig's hair. "Hey, cruise buddy, Phyllis said earlier she couldn't make out your name. Is it really Clive?"

"Not even clothe." Clive tipped to the side of his chair again.

"Will you shut up!" Lucy shouted over her shoulder. "Some of us have five grand to win."

Clive gave an ethereal smile, then slid off his chair and went face first to the floor.

"You promised to be good." Phyllis jerked him to his feet. "Now sit down."

Clive steadied himself, leering at Phyllis through bloodshot eyes. "I don't hafta listen to you. I can go home and hear thith every day." He staggered to leave, bumped into Phyllis's station, and tipped a jar of gel onto the floor. Gel splattered everywhere. Clive slipped in the goop, slid across the aisle into Lucy, and knocked her off her stool.

Lucy landed ass-backward onto Clive. "You idiot!" She rolled off him and clouted him with her hairbrush. Then she turned her wrath on Phyllis. "What kind of lamebrain are you, picking a drunk as your model?"

I didn't like Lucy calling Phyllis names. It was one thing for Max to call Phyllis names. They worked together every day and took pleasure in antagonizing each other. But I didn't like Lucy being mean to Phyllis. And I didn't approve of her abusing poor Clive.

She dropped her brush, and I bent to retrieve it. I noticed Molly in the next row, pointing at Lucy while whispering in Sabrina's ear. Sabrina looked at the clock and said something back.

I didn't think much about that, mostly because Clive snatched the brush from me and hurled it in the air, whacking Candace in the head two rows over. She yelped, looked past her mirror at me, nostrils flared, and pitched a full bottle of tint at me. I sidestepped to miss the bottle but wasn't quick enough. It hit me square on the chest, splashing red dye on my white dress. My *new* white dress. The dress I wasn't going to get dirty because I wasn't dyeing my mother's hair.

I pressed my lips together in fury. If anyone else had tossed the tint, I wouldn't have overreacted. But this was Candace we were talking about, someone who'd pushed my buttons since beauty school. Well, not today.

I reached behind me, grabbed my powder, and, despite my mother's protests at getting even, I whipped it at Candace. Maybe it was the first thing I seized, and maybe I was acting on impulse *again*, but Candace was not getting away with ruining my dress. Before she could retaliate, someone pummeled her with a bottle of shampoo. Suddenly, the room went wild. Rollers flew over mirrors, scissors sliced the air, tint bottles squirted like sprinklers, and there was massive screaming and hair-pulling.

"Valentine!" my mother shrieked. "*Do* something!"

I had the same thought, but first I forced her to duck to miss an airborne razor. Then I slipped on the gel and landed hard on a blow dryer.

"Someone's going to get killed," Tantig said in an even tone, head steady, eyes half-shut. The only one in the room unmoved by the chaos.

I crawled to my feet, rubbing my backside, struggling to stay calm.

"Nobody is going to get killed!" Kashi exclaimed. "Kashi is here to save the day!"

He tied a white towel to a broom handle and waved it in the air. "Please, may I have your attention, you crazy people."

Everyone quieted for a second, backing away from Kashi, most likely because he was getting ripe in his two-day-old outfit.

"Maybe all this beautifying is not doing it for you anymore. What you need is a hobby. Like me!" Kashi bowed. "As you can see, I make these spectacular 'Get Out of Town' brooches." He held one high. "Right now, you are thinking, Kashi, you are not only a handsome devil, but you are also very talented."

Within seconds, his white towel was on fire.

The whooping and hollering escalated.

Phyllis stood on a chair, waving her curling iron in the air. Someone else squirted water on Kashi's flag.

"Hold on!" Phyllis yelled. "Just *hold on* a minute!"

No one paid any attention. Everyone was having too

much fun trying to kill each other. Finally, Max did one of his ear-splitting whistles, and everyone froze mid-swing.

Phyllis nodded her thanks to Max, then glowered down at the crowd. "I spent all day yesterday puking in my cabin, and I finally got myself together to compete in this contest. I'm not about to get disqualified because of a bunch of loose-cannon hairdressers."

A guy with green hair poked his head above the throng. "Who died and made you king?" Silence followed, along with the smell of fear. "I mean, queen."

Phyllis narrowed her eyes. "And my vision's almost twenty-twenty, so I'd watch what you're saying. Now, I aim to fix up my model and win that money. Anyone else with the same agenda, shut up and get back to work."

"She's *baa-ack*," Max sang.

Everyone gloomily picked up combs and brushes off the floor.

Tantig blinked straight ahead. "Do I look young-air?"

"Almost, Tantig." Max worked fiendishly. "Almost."

After three long hours, I gave my mother a final appraisal. Not only could she have passed for a younger, gorgeous Sophia Loren, but there was a radiance to her complexion and timeless beauty to her face that even I had never noticed before.

I gazed over at Tantig. Max had worked wonders on her. Her white hair was swept up with soft curls kissing her face, and her makeup had been applied with such grace and precision, twenty years had easily been erased. It was up to the judges now.

We all filed out of the auditorium, snacking on hors d'oeuvres while the judges deliberated. There was a lot of guessing as to who would win, and after a tense hour, we were herded back in for the results.

Jock stood at the head of the room beside two senior crew members in white uniforms and a raven-haired supermodel who represented Adore It Products. Naturally. Couldn't send a middle-aged guy from management to represent the company. *Nooo.* Had to be a gorgeous knockout.

I rubbed my sore butt, hoping the blow dryer didn't bruise me when I fell on it. Then I looked down at myself, covered in powder, red dye that had now darkened, and other goop. *So what.* If I won that prize money, I'd be the one looking pretty.

Max flicked powder out of my hair. "What's Jock doing up there?" he whispered.

"He's Superman, remember? Leaps over tall buildings, has extraordinary hearing, X-ray vision." Boy, did I know about the X-ray vision. My loins warmed just thinking about his power to see through me.

Jock spotted me in the crowd and gave one of his penetrating looks, like he'd heard every word.

I almost swallowed my tongue, not that he'd care. He looked pretty cozy, standing beside the supermodel.

"He was a judge?" Max asked.

I shushed him. "We're talking about Jock, right? Anything's possible."

Max leaned in closer. "Isn't that what's-her-name, the Romanian supermodel?"

"Shhh," Phyllis hissed. "I'm trying to hear."

The supermodel put her lips to Jock's ear and whispered something that brought a devilish smile to his face.

He nodded and whispered something back, and I was having a hard time keeping calm. No wonder he wasn't participating in the contest. Probably contributing to the competition backstage. *Animal.*

Miss Romania brought her attention back to us minions and waved a check in the air. Then she spoke with a strong accent. "And the winner is…"

I held my breath, closed my eyes, and chanted, "For the kids, for the kids."

"Lucy Jacobs!"

"Woo-hoo!" Lucy dropped her bag by Sabrina. "Look out, you lowlifes. Let the winner through." She shoved people out of the way, and I choked back tears. I'd almost tasted that prize money. Now I'd let those poor kids down.

I glanced over at Lucy's model and fixed a sincere smile on my face. She did look incredible. More than incredible. Plastic surgery couldn't have breathed life into her like Lucy had in the past few hours.

There was grumbling among the crowd. Then Kashi slid a small item into Lucy's bag. Sabrina was two feet away, watching him. He moved closer and said something to her. She nodded and replied.

My eyes opened wide. What was that all about? Did Sabrina know Kashi? Were they playing a trick on Lucy? And what about Molly whispering in Sabrina's ear earlier? Was something going on? Or was my imagination running away with me?

"This is so unfair." Phyllis crossed her arms. "All I had to go through with Clive, and *she* wins. I'm going to the after-dinner buffet, then bed."

I knew how Phyllis felt. Disappointment flooded my veins. My pledge to the hospital wasn't enormous in the grand scheme of things, and it wasn't critical to the wing being built, but a promise was a promise. On top of which, Valentine Beaumont wasn't a quitter. I'd simply have to find another way to get the rest of the money.

"Don't forget," Max sang as she shoved off. "Only spareribs and cornbread. No fruit or veggies."

Lucy finally made it to the front and ripped the check away from the supermodel's hand. "I'll take that." She strutted down the aisle like a peacock, stopping short in front of Max and me. "Drinks are on me in my cabin." She gathered her things. "You losers coming?"

"Sure," Max said under his breath. "I love going where I'm appreciated."

Lucy's cabin was identical to Phyllis's and mine, same floor, different wing. Two bunks. Pee hole for a bathroom. She shared her cabin with Sabrina, who was presently pouring wine for everyone. There was a picture on the nightstand of Sabrina and Lucy that I thought odd but sweet.

I wasn't much in the mood for a celebration, but I congratulated Lucy on her win. While she was rehashing her big moment, I eyed the photograph. Looked like a third person had been cut out—all but one arm—so the photo would fit in the frame. I didn't want it to appear that I was snooping, which I was. But even from a distance, I could see there was something on the person's arm. A birthmark? A tattoo? A scrape in the photograph?

Sabrina held out a glass to me.

"No wine for me. Thanks."

"She can't handle herself after one sip." Max swooped the glass out of Sabrina's hand. "I'll have her share."

A few minutes later, there was a knock on the door. "Anybody home? It is I, Kashi."

Lucy flung open the door. "Cashew! Come on in. Hey, you're in a new suit."

"Yes." He overlooked the slight on his name. "My luggage arrived safely and soundly. I say we bury the steel hatchet." He pulled his hand from around his back. "To celebrate, I bring chocolate-dipped strawberries. Fit for a princess. You like?"

"Sure, I like. What do you want to drink?"

"Kashi is easy." He placed the carton of strawberries on the table. "A raspberry daiquiri in a martini glass with a slice of pineapple pierced with a green umbrella. Two straws."

Lucy cocked an eyebrow up at him. "We've got wine or beer."

"Beer is good."

The minutes flew by. I munched on a strawberry, trying to listen enthusiastically to the chatter though my mind was still on losing and letting down the sick kids. Max said something funny, and everyone laughed. Everyone but Kashi. He was busy emptying a vial of blue liquid into Lucy's red wine that was sitting behind her on the nightstand.

I almost choked on my strawberry. I gasped for air and grabbed Max's wine out of his hand.

"Hey!" He watched me toss back the last ounce of his drink. "What are you doing?"

"Time to go," I sputtered, heady from the wine rush. "Tomorrow's the first port of call."

"But Lucy was telling me about the time she played Dorothy in *The Wizard of Oz*."

He could've told me cannibals pee in their soup. Kashi spiking Lucy's drink alarmed me, and I had to do something before I screamed. I set the glass on the nightstand, deliberately knocking Lucy's glass over.

"Oops!" I feigned shock. "Clumsy me."

"No problem." Lucy reached for an unopened bottle of wine. "I can drink from the bottle."

"What was that all about?" Max wanted to know once we were stumbling down the hallway.

I pulled him aside to let another couple pass. "I saw Kashi slip something into Lucy's drink. What if it was poison?"

"I knew there was a reason I liked him."

I clouted him in the arm.

"Ouch! What'd you do that for?"

"This isn't a joke. What if Kashi had killed Lucy?"

He did a small shrug. "Then the judges will have wished they'd picked another winner."

Why me? "He also slid something in her bag when she went up to collect her winnings."

Max gave a dismissive wave. "Maybe he dropped a mint by mistake."

I blew air out my nose in frustration. "It wasn't a mint.

And it wasn't by mistake. Look, something's going on, and I'm getting freaked out. I've had enough experience to recognize bad karma, and I want to be far away from any disaster should there be one."

"Why didn't you say so? We're Thelma and Louise! You say *scoot*, I'm ready."

"You're never ready. You're always fussing, or moaning, or giving excuses."

"Yeah, but I'm ready when it counts."

Oh Lord. If Thelma and Louise had days like this, it's no wonder they drove off a cliff.

"Look," Max said, putting on his Mr. Rationale hat. "You're not thinking straight. All this sun and sea air is probably getting to you."

I tapped my toe. "We've been at sea for one day."

His eyebrows went up. "Okay. Maybe back in the cabin you didn't see what you thought you saw."

"I saw Kashi empty a vial of blue liquid into Lucy's red wine. What else could it have been?"

He looked up at the ceiling, pondering this. Then he brightened. "Maybe Kashi slipped Lucy something to help her sleep off the excitement of the day."

He evaluated my deadpan face. "Or maybe they're closer than we know, and he was giving her medicine."

I tried to keep from rolling my eyes, but they seemed to have a mind of their own.

"What!" Max countered. "We don't know what it's like to be a little person. Maybe Lucy needs certain supplements or medication to help her function."

He had a point. "Sabrina's her roommate. Why wouldn't *she* be the one to give Lucy meds?"

Max tilted his head back and forth. "Maybe Lucy and Kashi are more…intimate."

"Thanks for that thought."

Clearly, I'd be on guard from what I witnessed tonight. I'd especially keep my eyes and ears open where Kashi was concerned. But was I overreacting? Was Max right with his theories? I bit my lip. How would a detective view all this?

More especially, what would Romero think? Should I call him and find out? Reluctantly, I had to admit that getting his take on things would be a huge help.

We arrived at our hallway, and Max gave me a hug goodnight, then slid into his cabin. I tiptoed into our room, hoping Phyllis was asleep. I wasn't in the mood for more tirades on how unfair the contest was. I was in luck. She did a couple grizzly-bear snorts, then rolled toward the wall.

I slipped into the bathroom, dumped my bag in the fishbowl of a sink, and dug out my cell phone. I glared at the screen, apprehension suddenly filling me about calling Romero. Where was he? What was he doing? And why was I calling him about anything? He didn't even have the decency to let me know if he was alive or injured in some California alley.

I strummed my fingers on the countertop. It'd be too expensive to call anyway. Probably cheaper to wait until we pulled into port. But what about what I saw tonight? If nothing else, Romero would offer professional advice. Furthermore, hadn't my wealthy clients Birdie and Betty Cutler paid for a mega international calling plan as a going-away gift? Darn right they had.

I kicked off my heels and stood there, wiggling my feet on the cold tile, thinking of the night not long ago when Romero had shown concern about my foot. True, I was injured at the time and in the Berkshires investigating a murder. Not exactly a romantic getaway, but he'd been there and was worried about my well-being.

I stared at my phone, my heart giving a thump. I'd simply call his house on the off chance he'd wrapped up his case early and was now back in Rueland. That was acceptable, right? I absolutely drew the line at trying his cell number. If he was still working in California, he wouldn't appreciate me distracting him because of something I saw—something that was probably totally innocent. He'd only think I was checking up on him. I pressed my lips together, dialed his home number, and waited.

This was pointless. He wasn't home, and he likely never used his landline. If I hadn't found his home number on my own, I wouldn't even have it. I was about to hit END when someone picked up. My heart lurched, the anticipation of hearing his low, sexy voice almost too much to bear.

"Hello?" answered a voice. Not Romero. A woman.

What? Did I dial wrong? I gasped into the phone, then glanced at the readout. Right number. Wrong person. I forced back a dry swallow and hung up. *There. Happy?* Now this woman would tell him some heavy breather called and hung up. Like I was a stalker. *Erg!*

Mumbling miserably to myself, I threw everything back into my bag, shook the powder out of my hair, washed up, and snapped off the light. I had enough happening in my life without worrying about who Romero was bonking. I'd handle my suspicions about Kashi on my own, give a handsome donation to Rueland Memorial once I'd saved up, and live my life to the fullest.

Romero? Ha! Who needed him?

Chapter 4

I pounded back the covers at six-thirty the next morning. I'd had a fitful night's sleep, agonizing over where I stood with Romero. *No more.* I was a woman in control. I had other things to concentrate on. Like this business with Kashi and Lucy. And Max's theories. I climbed down the bunk ladder, grabbed my cell phone, and slid quietly past Phyllis into the bathroom to call my best friend, Twix. I needed a sounding board. And since I couldn't talk to Romero, what were best friends for?

Because it was Sunday and there was no daycare, she'd be sleeping in, letting Tony look after the kids. I didn't want to wake her, but in a few hours, I'd be heading into Nassau, and I had to talk before I left the ship.

"I agree with Max," Twix said, after I shared my Kashi story. "I think you've gotten involved in one too many murder cases. It's starting to cloud your thinking."

"Gee, thanks."

She yawned loudly. "You're the one who phoned me at the crack of stupid, remember? Anyway, why don't you just call that hunk, Romero?"

"Because."

"Because why?"

I filled her in about my attempted phone call and Romero's whereabouts. The more I talked, the more ticked

I became. After I explained about the female voice, an idea struck me. I closed my eyes tight and made a teensy request.

"You want me to *what?*" The way Twix said it, it almost sounded wicked.

I opened my eyes wide. "You think I'm nuts?"

"What, because you want me to drive over to his place, snoop through his mailbox, peek in his windows, and see who he's pumping?"

"When you put it that way, *yes!*" I frowned. "Wait. Forget I said anything. I must be going crazy."

"No, you're not."

"I don't want you snooping in Romero's mail," I said. "He's ten minutes away. Drive by and see if there's any sign of life."

"You mean, see if they're doing the dirty deed on the front lawn." I could see the smile spread across Twix's face. "Quite a change from the I-don't-want-any-men-in-my-life Valentine I used to know. I'm almost afraid to ask what it's like being on a cruise ship with Jock."

Twix was mesmerized by Jock. When she was in his presence, I'd often had to slip her a tissue to wipe the drool from the corners of her mouth.

"Good. Don't ask." I didn't want to visualize Jock and Miss Romania together, and I wasn't going to share any doubts about him with Twix. It was true. I didn't even know myself anymore. And I hated that I sounded desperate where Romero was concerned.

"You could call the station," she suggested. "They'd tell you where he is."

"I'd rather drink a peroxide milkshake with a"—I stumbled for the perfect garnish, then thought of Mr. Jaworski—"maraschino cherry on top."

She snickered. "Cops still ribbing you about your past perm-rod caper?"

"Nooooo." I did a sarcastic tongue click. "They're all adults there. They've moved on."

She sighed. "What the hell. I'll do it. After all, what are best friends for?"

This was what I had to put up with in a best friend? Why was I so blessed?

I showered, brushed my hair, and stroked on mascara. Since my skin was beginning to tan—something I had going for me—I applied only light makeup and picked out pretty sundress number two. Most people would be jaunting around in T-shirts and shorts, but I didn't do T-shirts, and I wasn't sure I even owned shorts. Besides, what could a T-shirt do that a cute summer dress couldn't do better?

I hiked from our air-conditioned cabin to the deck where the hot sea air blew on me in a morning salute. I leaned over the railing and watched crewmen anchor the ship against the dock. Vendors along the pier were displaying clothes, baskets, and sandals. Lure for disembarking passengers.

I turned away from the railing, my thoughts circling back to Kashi and Lucy and my probable misconceived notions about him poisoning her. Twix was right. Those past cases were clouding my thinking. I was on a cruise, for Pete's sake. Nobody was poisoning anyone.

I waved to Sabrina in her jogging suit as she did a lap around the ship. Then Tantig stepped onto the deck in her white Nikes and a fresh polyester, patterned dress, her beautiful hairdo from yesterday looking like it'd been jammed in a wind turbine. It was already eighty degrees, and she was clutching a sweater. She steadied herself, then shuffled off in the other direction.

"Tantig!" I jogged over to her as classy as I could in high heels. "What are you doing up so early?"

"Your mother thinks I need to walk." She blinked heavily.

"Where is Mom?"

"Who-hk cares?" She rolled her eyes heavenward. "I want to watch my soaps and sleep. She says walking is good for my arthritis. That woman is trying to kill me."

I couldn't blame Tantig. She was eighty years old. She'd worked hard as a cook in the old country and lived a tough post-war life as an immigrant to the U.S. She'd earned the right to watch soaps or sleep all day. Wasn't something that enticed *me*, but who knew what I'd be doing at eighty?

She glanced past me at the cruise director wheeling her bag of tricks along the deck. "Are we leaving today?" She stared at the suitcase. "Everyone's got their luggage packed."

"No, Tantig. We're not leaving today. This is Nassau. It's one of the ports of call."

She gave a confused look and trundled off, the sun reflecting on the deck behind her.

I wasn't sure Tantig should be left alone to roam the ship, but after my mother's coddling, she was probably glad to have some freedom. Plus, where could she go?

That thought was still on my mind while I scrounged around in my bag for my sunglasses. I pulled out my Musk perfume and hairbrush, hoping they hadn't crushed my shades.

"A penny for your thoughts," a voice whispered in my ear.

Shrieking, I whipped my brush behind me and spun around, spraying perfume in a frenzy. Typical. Most people jumped and said *ooh!* or *aah!* when someone startled them. I screamed bloody murder and hurled beauty products.

"Brilliant." Max coughed and wiped his face. "So much for *my* cologne."

"Sorry, Max." I gave him a contrite smile.

"It's my fault." He picked up my brush. "I should've known better than to sneak up on you like that. What are you doing up here anyway? Breakfast has already started."

I put my things away. "Just admiring the people and the harbor."

"Uh…" He backed toward the deck chairs. "Can you come away from that railing? You're making me nervous."

We meandered to an inner walkway, secluded from a view of the water.

Max sighed with relief. "Now, what's this 'just admiring the people and the harbor' all about? You sound melancholy. What gives?"

"You want to know? It's this whole business with Kashi and Lucy." Okay, so I couldn't let it go. "No matter how I rationalize it, instinct's telling me there's more to what I saw last night. I'm not looking for trouble, but I don't like the unsettling feelings looming over me."

I also told myself this was only about Kashi and Lucy. My disquieting emotions had nothing to do with Romero. As it was, I had to feed Max tiny doses of Romero or he'd be on my case about Mr. Long Arm of the Law being the love of my life. He'd already pestered me on this trip about Jock being on the hunt and me being the prey. I didn't need to give him more ammunition.

"I had a feeling that's why you weren't at breakfast and why I was searching for you." By the look on Max's face, he was ready to offer more theories.

In that moment, I decided to let it all go. I knew nothing about Kashi or Lucy, and I'd been wrong before. I wasn't going to spend my vacation worrying about other people's affairs. I had enough agony focusing on my own. I cleared my mind of what I saw in Sabrina and Lucy's cabin and pasted a smile on my face. "Forget it. You were right about what you said last night."

Max jerked his head back at my about-face. "I was?"

"Yes. The heat's getting to me. That's all." I took a deep breath. "Now, I'm going to enjoy a lovely day in Nassau, sightseeing and shopping at the straw market. If you're with me, let's go eat."

"Fine by me," he said. "I worked up an appetite falling out of bed last night." He raised his elbow and gave it a rub. "Look at this bruise."

I stared at the mark on his elbow. "What happened?"

He put up his palms. "We must've sailed through a patch of rough waves. The motion kind of threw me when I rolled over in bed."

I pictured him dropping from the top bunk to the floor, and my thoughts turned to Jock lying on the bottom bunk, looking all hunky with a simple sheet covering his semi-naked body. My voice suddenly went hoarse. "Didn't Jock catch you?"

Max gave a lopsided frown. "If you must know, Jock hasn't slept in our cabin since we left Miami."

My eyes got big and round, and Max nodded. "But I'd love to know where he *has* been sleeping. More specifically, with whom."

I swallowed hard, recalling Miss Romania whispering in Jock's ear before the contest winner was announced. Promises for later?

Max leaned in. "And where's he been eating? He's not sitting at *our* table."

"I don't know, and I don't care." Jock could eat on the roof or the poop deck, for all I cared.

I got haughty all over again, thinking of my new lease on life. I wasn't going to be fooled by any man, including Jock de Marco, with his sexy hair and hot body. He could eat where he wished. And if he wanted to sleep with every supermodel on the ship, then more power to him.

Max studied me like my nose might twitch at any second. "Aren't you a teensy bit curious where he's been sleeping?"

I stared right back, steady-nosed. "Not even an eensy bit." I had great self-control when I tried. "Now let's eat. We've got an island to tour."

After a full day in the sun, and getting even more color, I returned to my cabin and took a cool shower. I stepped into my elegant but overpriced Bottega Veneta heels for the captain's Greek-themed Gala and shimmied into a full-length, one-shouldered white gown, perfect for the event.

I stopped sliding the gown over my naked body, thinking twice about going commando underneath. Soft, silky viscose on bare skin was the most delicious feeling…next to the stroke of a man's strong hands. And since I wasn't getting a lot of that lately…Oh what the hell.

I wasn't going to deprive myself of this ecstasy. Plus, wasn't this a beauty cruise? Well, this made me feel like the beauty Helen of Troy.

I fixed my hair into long loose curls, then glanced around the cabin at Phyllis's messy belongings. I hadn't seen her all day, and I tried not to let this worry me. She could be anywhere. My history with murders was haunting me. That's all. I overreacted about Lucy. And I shook off any doubts about Phyllis. She was a big girl. She didn't need monitoring.

Before I locked up, I quickly read through the beauty package to see what else was happening tonight. My gaze stopped halfway down the page. A scavenger hunt? Scheduled the minute dinner finished. All that was required was a bag of beauty tools for cracking clues. Right up my alley and sounded like fun. In addition, I already had my beauty bag. I looked down at myself. White gown. Black sack. Not the greatest fashion statement, but if I took part I wouldn't have time to come back and change. Oh, who cared? I'd take my bag with me and get involved.

I left the cabin, took the elevator to the dining room, and felt the atmosphere there spine-tingling. Everyone was dressed exquisitely. Tables were garnished with olive branches, columns were lit from inside, and the smell of Greek salad and moussaka was tantalizing.

I told myself to have a good time. I looked like a Greek goddess for crying out loud. And I was on a free tropical vacation. What could go wrong?

I watched people vying to be invited to eat at the captain's table. Not me. I had no desire to be up close and personal with the head of the ship. As it was, I regretted not sliding on undies. What if someone could see through my gown? What if I fell, and my dress hiked up? Oh Lord. I couldn't even think about that. I fiddled with the ring on my index finger and got in line to shake the captain's hand.

I inched along, recalling the same greeting ritual a few days ago when we'd boarded the ship. Only, that day, it was interrupted when Lucy and Sabrina had come along, and Lucy had pushed past Max and me.

I swung my bag by my side and surveyed the dining room. No Lucy, or Sabrina, for that matter.

I gave a nervous titter and swiped a fluted glass from a toga-clad waiter's tray. I slugged back the drink, and bubbly slid down my throat into my empty belly. *Mmm.* I momentarily ignored the fact I became an embarrassing drunk on half a cup of booze. Something Romero had made a point to remind me of when he called about California, and I told him about the cruise.

I could almost see the grin twitching the corners of his mouth. "Stay away from the piña coladas," he'd said. "I won't be there to save your fanny when you're flat out on the pool deck, shouting at lanterns." A reminder I'd gotten a teensy bit drunk that night in the Berkshires.

Fine. I wasn't going to have any more than this tiny glass. I took only a sip this time and waited until my brain registered the incoming bubbly. While I was waiting, I thought back to the last few times I'd seen Romero. He'd seemed on edge, preoccupied, unusual for a tough cop always in control. Was this California case weighing on him? Was he already involved with his new partner, Belinda? I stiffened. Was he tired of me? Was this his way of breaking things off?

It was my turn to shake the captain's hand. Outside, I was smiling. Inside, I was working myself into a state over Romero. I felt a zing from my drink, and thankfully my prior thoughts became fuzzy. Still, I did a mental head smack. *Pace yourself, Valentine.*

Suddenly, there was a hand on the small of my back, and warmth seeped into my pores. I knew by the exotic, aromatic smell and the grip rounding my hips, it was either Paul Bunyan or Jock de Marco. Paul Bunyan carried an ax over his shoulder; Jock's tools hung much lower and were presently pressing into my backside.

"What would you say if I asked you to be my dinner companion?" His voice was low, soft.

I tried to turn, but his arms securely held me, facing the captain. I searched for something witty and sophisticated to say, then hiccupped in his ear. "Where would we eat? The poop deck?" I snickered like I'd just told an amusing joke.

He gave me a squeeze, then shook hands with the captain. "How many guests are joining you, Carlo?"

Carlo?

"The table is full." Captain Madera smiled from Jock to me. "Except there is, ah, yes, one seat open, if this *bella donna* would like to join us."

Jock stepped back, allowing me to make the decision. I spun around and gaped at him in his naval white uniform, clad with medals. Hercules goes Navy. Beside the captain in his cruise-line regalia, Jock looked like *he* should've been the one steering this boat.

I didn't know why he was dressed so classy and in naval attire. The only clear thought I had was to rip off his buttons, one by one, with my mouth, down to his sexy, naked, tanned skin.

A faint smile played at the sides of Jock's mouth, as though he knew what I saw pleased me.

An electric charge raced through me, and I pushed down a swallow. "Okay."

Like a prince, Jock led me down the steps into the grand dining room. I managed to retain a somewhat graceful composure, except for one little trip, but I was sure nobody saw that.

"She's going to break her neck one day in those damn heels," Mr. Jaworski crowed off to the side.

Almost nobody.

We passed tall pillars and gawking faces. Max was grinning, ear to ear, from his end of the room, and at the far wall, my mother's eyes were wide. Tantig sat expressionless next to her, looking straight ahead. She wasn't easily impressed.

We carried on the procession to a large circular table in the middle of the room filled with guests. Jock waited for me to sit, then took the seat next to me.

Greek music hummed in the background, and I did my best to schmooze with tuxedoed men and diamond-clad women. But I wasn't comfortable with the *Lifestyles of the Rich and Famous* vibe at the captain's table. I glanced around. Where was Clive? Where was my father? I looked in the direction of the bathroom and saw my dad wander out. As for Clive, I likely should've been searching under the tables.

I clenched my teeth, wishing to slide under the table myself. Everyone seemed relaxed, laughing and sipping champagne. And I was sitting there, bare-bottomed, champagne in hand, Jock's eyes staring into my soul. Great recipe for disaster. I downed my drink, took a deep breath, and when the buzz stabilized in my skull, I snatched a water carafe from the table and poured a healthy dose of water in my glass. That would clear my head.

The woman next to me gasped. "That's our—"

"Shh," her husband said. "Let the girl enjoy herself."

Jock leaned into me. "Don't you think you should slow down?"

I held up my water. "Got it covered."

Right. As long as he was breathing hotly down my neck, his muscular thigh pressing mine, me naked under my dress, I was in trouble.

I chugged back my water, and my throat burned. What the...? Coughing and sputtering, I reached for the carafe and sniffed inside. This wasn't water. Smelled like black licorice. Ouzo?

A loud chime reverberated through the room, making my head spin. The captain stood and raised his glass. "Opa!"

Everyone shouted, "Opa!" Except for me. I jumped and sloshed my drink on my lap.

"Welcome to my Gala," the captain said. "An evening I hope you won't soon forget!"

Hic. I jerked my head up, instantly relaxed, and Jock raised a brow. Not too worried about that, I gave my lap a carefree swipe, then dropped my head onto his huge, padded shoulder. I flicked a medal on his chest, smiling dopily up into his cognac-colored eyes.

"And now," the captain said, "I'd like to present—"

"Here! Here!" I saluted my glass high, smiling all around, then cuddled back into Jock like a kitten, soaking up his attention.

The captain continued, "—our own head chef."

Two men in white rolled out a large cart with a white sheet covering a structure four feet high. Another man with a chef's hat followed. Everyone applauded.

"To my latest creation," the chef announced.

Everyone said, "Cheers!" and the assistants whipped off the sheet.

I stood up—barely—and gasped along with five hundred other guests at the Aphrodite ice sculpture. Inside, staring out at us was a three-foot-high figure, its contorted face pressed against the wall of ice. I squinted to get a better look, but before I could utter a word, Mr. Jaworski dashed to the cart and shrieked, "Lucy!"

Chapter 5

Mass confusion ensued. People screaming. Women fainting. Security blocking exits.

I flopped down on my seat and slapped my face. I was drunk. All I saw was an iced Aphrodite, Greek goddess of beauty. This was a beauty cruise, after all. I didn't see Lucy inside an ice sculpture.

The slap must've brought me to my senses. In fact, I thought I sobered up pretty quickly. I watched the madness in the room, but my mind was back to last night in Lucy's cabin. I tried to think of a connection to what I saw regarding Kashi and the vial, but I couldn't come up with anything concrete. And since I hadn't heard of any fatalities between last night and today, I assumed Lucy was fine after her victory party and had toured Nassau today like everyone else.

If that was true, was she murdered on land and brought back on board as an ice sculpture? Or was there a murderer on board who switched the Lucy ice sculpture with the one intended for tonight?

I grabbed a glass of water off the table, gave it a sniff, and downed the contents, trying to rid the ouzo completely from my system and focus on the events of the evening. I had no intention of butting into the case, but I scanned the dining room nonetheless for anyone who looked shady. I wiped my mouth, and my gaze landed on Kashi. *Hmm.* Talking to a waiter. Didn't seem all that suspicious, but I narrowed my eyes on him just the same.

Jock and the captain had taken up positions by the ice sculpture, and one of the crew got on a podium and told everyone to remain calm. Easy for him to say. It wasn't every day one saw a dead body inside an ice statue. And though I'd had enough bad luck with dead bodies popping up in my orbit, a frozen corpse was a first.

Over the next several hours, passengers were questioned. Jock and the captain had gone into the galley, taking onboard security with them. The melting statue and body had been covered and carted away. Unconscious women were carried out on stretchers, and Max was by my side, counting the bodies rolling out of the dining room.

The ouzo I'd chugged earlier had slowly worn off. I was almost one hundred percent coherent when the captain's crewman got back on the podium and encouraged everyone to carry on with the cruise. Fatalities happened, and the cruise line didn't want Lucy's horrible demise to spoil anyone's vacation.

Despite the crewman's words, the level of hysteria remained. My mother was in the middle of a group of passengers, and from where I was standing I could hear the panic in their voices.

Max and I stumbled over to the group and, after more talk and more questions, everyone decided to hit the piano bar. Emotions were high, but booze was a great antidote for shock or fear. With nothing else left for us to do, we mutely followed the crowd.

Tantig tailgated my parents into the lounge, sat at a small round table, and ordered a ginger ale. The chairs were black and velvety, and the lighting was dim with a bluish-purple glow. Max and I settled on barstools around the grand piano where the pianist was playing a sultry jazz song from the fifties. I wasn't sure how fast word traveled on a cruise ship, but the atmosphere in the lounge was romantic and seductive, and the pianist seemed laidback. I bet dollars to donuts he hadn't heard about the recent tragedy. By the look of the crowd, I was afraid that might change.

My gaze swept to the back corner of the bar where I'd seen Jock talking to the captain on our first night here. The conversation had seemed serious, but they could've been discussing the upcoming contest and Jock and Miss Romania's roles for all I knew. I quickly put that thought to bed and was trying to recall anything else about their meeting when Max accidentally elbowed me, bringing me back to the present.

He joined in some speculation about what had happened to Lucy, while others worried about danger to themselves. I sighed, trying not to eavesdrop on the conversations flowing around me. But everyone believed there was a killer on board, and nobody felt safe. Me included.

Kashi shuffled into the lounge, head down in respect. He pulled up a chair next to Tantig and leaned in to talk. I watched him for a minute through skeptical eyes, then drew a long breath and turned back to the pianist.

Thing was, logic told me Kashi couldn't be Lucy's killer. Sure, he'd slipped something into her drink yesterday—and I still didn't know what that was all about—but that was miles apart from stuffing her in a mold and freezing her. How would a passenger on the ship even have access to a mold? Furthermore, if the drink had killed her, someone behind the scenes would've had to partner with Kashi to accomplish this insane act. But who? I remembered him talking to a waiter earlier, but then again, everyone was in an uproar, looking for answers after Lucy had turned up frozen.

My head was starting to throb from the alcohol I'd consumed. I forced myself to ignore the buzz in the room and stop thinking about poor Lucy. I let my mind flow to the music when the pianist finished his set and stepped away for a break.

One or two people gave a half-hearted clap.

Clive, who was stationed at the bar, saluted with his gauzed arm. "Lovely!"

I threw a tip in the brandy snifter on top of the piano beside a huge arrangement of white flowers.

"Valentine!" my father hollered from across the room. "Play a song. Show that minstrel how it's done."

There wasn't much that affected my father on an emotional level, and his lack of reaction to Lucy's death was proof of that. I gave him a tight smile, hoping he saw the daggers in my eyes. "I'm good, Dad."

I glanced at the pianist who was talking to the bartender, hoping he hadn't heard my father's remark. No luck. He gave my dad a peeved look, then disappeared through a door.

"Go on," my father persisted. "We need something to lighten the mood. Show them how good you are!"

I cringed inside. Now, of all times, my father felt the need to demonstrate his lack of tact. I had to admit the pull was there. Once upon a time, I'd entertained thoughts of becoming a concert pianist or a music professor. I'd settled for playing professionally for a while, and at one time even made a decent living at weddings and in nightclubs. But I chose the beauty route for a lifelong career. Special requests still came my way. However, I mostly played for myself when I needed an escape, or the odd time at the retirement homes when I did hair.

Bad enough my father was embarrassing me from the opposite side of the room, but I could also see my mother's dating radar spinning. It wasn't that my parents were uncaring in the wake of a brutal murder, but they had other concerns that involved me.

I pretended to laugh at something Max said. He looked at me like I'd gone loco.

"Play along." I stared at him with wide eyes. "My mother's on a dating mission, and if she sees I'm deep in conversation, maybe she'll cease and desist."

Max peeked over his shoulder at my mother, and I whacked his arm. "Don't look!"

"It can't be that bad." He rubbed his arm, then ordered a sangria.

I waited until the waitress was out of earshot. "Believe me, it is. Last time I went away with my parents, I wound up on a date with Dieter the Polka King." I grimaced. "I even had to wear a dirndl."

"Think of the positive! You like fashion."

"Why is it you're always so positive when it comes to *my* life?"

He angled his head sweetly. "Because those amber eyes of yours reflect warmth and passion?"

"Flattery's not going to get you anywhere."

I put two fingers between my brows and was applying pressure when my mother marched to my side, unbothered that Max and I were in the middle of a heated discussion. "I've found the perfect man for you, dear." The hysteria from Lucy's death suddenly replaced with more important matters.

When I didn't jump for joy, she swung my stool around so fast I almost toppled to the floor. "Are you listening, Valentine?"

Did I have a choice?

The waitress brought Max his drink, and my father was in the background, going on about me playing the piano. Only now, everyone in the bar was chanting, "Go *on*! Go *on*!"

My mother tipped my jaw back toward her. "I think Mr. Farooq is interested in you."

I blinked. "As in Kashi Farooq?"

"Who else? Look at him over there, handing out his precious 'Get Out of Town' brooches. They're quite beautiful, and he has such a way with people, getting their minds off tonight's tragedy."

Hmm. Exactly what you'd expect a murderer to do. Now what was I to think?

I glanced past my mother—and Max, who was giggling

from behind her shoulder—and spied Kashi talking Tantig's ear off. If I told my mother Kashi could be a possible murderer, she might forget this whole idea. Then again, I thought about my past experiences with her and her matchmaking. If anything, she'd put a positive spin on things. I wasn't sure how, but she'd find a way. I cursed to myself, then silenced Max with my death glare.

"Go *on*! Go *on*!" The chanting got louder, and despite Kashi's efforts, I could see the aftershock of Lucy's murder transforming the crowd from panic to frenzy.

You came on this cruise because…? Because…? I didn't know how to finish that thought except with the blatant answer: BECAUSE I'M AN IDIOT FOR ENTERING A DRAWING!

I struggled to quiet my racing heart. I had to nip this dating idea in the bud before I tackled anything else. "Mom, Kashi hasn't said more than two words to me." I looked over again and spotted my great-aunt hand Kashi a Tic Tac. "If he's interested in anybody, it's Tantig."

My mother gave me a disgusted look. "Bite your tongue."

I charged on. "And what is it with him and the seating arrangements? First, I see him dining at your table, then the next day he's floating somewhere else. And tonight, he was with yet another group. What is he? Mr. Free Rein?"

My mother didn't bat an eye. "Maybe the cruise line was making amends for his lost luggage." She fumed. "Who cares about seating arrangements anyway? I'm talking lifetime arrangements."

There was no winning.

"Go *on*! Go *on*!"

"Oh, for Pete's sake!" Max banged his sangria on the piano. "Will you play something already?"

In desperation, I figured maybe playing the piano *would* distract the crowd from going mad. I had a history with dead bodies, after all. Surely, I could handle *this*.

The bartender gave me a nod, which I took to mean I was free to perform. Swell. I moved onto the piano bench and waited for the pounding in my head to settle and my nerves to calm. Okay. If I was going to do this, I might as well do it right.

I cracked my knuckles, put my fingers on the bottom of the keyboard, and played an arpeggio all the way up to the high notes. After I had everyone's attention, I returned to Middle *C* and began tickling the ivories with the familiar intro to "New York, New York." This got toes tapping and fingers snapping. By the end of the song, everyone but Tantig was on their feet, crooning the last words, "Newww Yooork." I finished with a glissando, sweeping the back of my thumb from the high notes all the way down the keyboard.

Midway through my slide, I looked up and saw Jock stride by the lounge with the captain, conferring about something. The murder? Last time I saw them they were heading into the galley. What did they learn there? Did they talk to the chef? The staff?

The captain squeezed Jock's shoulder and walked away. Jock cocked an ear toward the music, stepped into the lounge, and locked eyes with me.

Adrenaline sped through my veins, and I began sweating behind my knees, wanting, for some reason, to impress him. Amidst that, my mind was still on the murder. I lost all concentration on my big finish and almost swept my fingers off the keyboard. I slid back to the center of the bench and improvised the end of the song, hitting the last chord with command.

I stood up from the piano, and everyone broke out in a cheer. Kashi waved a "Get Out of Town" brooch in the air, and my mother gave me an encouraging nod.

"That wath lovely!" Clive slurred at me from the bar, swinging his glass in the air.

My head was buzzing, and my legs were like jelly. I gave a gracious smile all around and staggered away from the bench, purposely avoiding Jock's applause and heated stare.

The pianist, who'd heard the last half of the song, sauntered back to the piano. "Show-off," he muttered.

Max scowled at him, snatched the tip I'd given him earlier out of the brandy snifter, and stuffed it back in my bag.

I overlooked the pianist's insult, turned a blind eye to Kashi and his "Get Out of Town" brooch, and couldn't have cared less about my mother's interference in my love life. I wasn't even perturbed by my father's lack of tact. He was smiling like a peacock as if he were the one who'd just played his heart out. What the hell. Let him have his moment.

Truth was, the circumstances surrounding Lucy's death hadn't escaped me. In fact, it was weighing on me like a two-ton elephant. And what about what Jock and the captain had learned?

The mood in the crowd had subdued, and now that Jock was in the room, I was glad to be out of the limelight. More importantly, this was my opportunity to question him about what he knew about the murder.

Soft jazz sounds came from the piano, and I heaved a deep sigh. I looked back to where Jock had been standing. A minute ago, he was giving me his intense stare. Now he was gone. Poof. Up in smoke.

I dashed to the entrance and looked right and left, my heart booming so loud I thought I'd explode. Where the heck did he go? His cabin? Since he hadn't slept in the same cabin with Max the past two nights, I doubted he'd be heading there tonight either. What about Miss Romania? Right. I didn't know where she was lodging, and I sure as hell didn't care to find out.

Why was I searching for Jock like a cat in heat? It just added to the pent-up frustration I already felt for the man. I got a hold of my raging hormones and gave myself a reality check. If I found him, I'd simply question him about Lucy's murder. That's what was paramount.

I stepped back into the bar and gave it another scan. No Jock. It was useless guessing his whereabouts. It was even more useless letting it bother me. What made me think he'd tell me anything about Lucy's murder anyway?

Jock was a puzzle. Plain and simple. He might be my employee, but we both knew he was his own boss. Nothing I could say or do would ever change that. Soft prickles ripped along my nape at that, and I shook them away.

Wherever he'd disappeared, I couldn't sit back and play the lounge lizard all evening. I rubbed my aching forehead, hitched my bag over my shoulder, and called it a night.

I took one step outside the bar when Max leaped to my side.

"Look!" He gestured down a long corridor. "Over there."

We put our heads together and watched Jock stride through a set of glass double doors. He stopped, looked at his cell phone, and put it to his ear. After a moment, he slid it in his back pocket, looked over his shoulder, and then vanished.

"Looks like he doesn't want to be followed," Max said.

Yeah. Probably heading to Miss Romania's cabin.

Just then, half a dozen young adults with bags over their shoulders raced by, popping their heads in and out of shops and doorways.

"What's going on?" I asked Max, following the group with my eyes.

"There's a beauty scavenger hunt tonight. Didn't you see it in the package?"

"Shoot. Yes, saw it and forgot about it. Anyway, we have our own hunt. Come on." I forgot I wasn't going to let Jock's elusiveness bother me. I was only human, and I'd had enough cloak-and-dagger where he was concerned. On top of that, I admitted it—I was curious. Was he sleeping around, or was this urgency about what happened to Lucy?

Max yanked me back. "Whoa, horsey. Where do you think you're going?"

"To catch a thief."

Max raised an eyebrow. "What did he steal? Your heart?"

I tugged my arm away from Smartass, my mounting headache giving me an edge of indignation. "Maybe I'm sniffing out a skunk."

"For your information," Max said, "I'm not interested in following that man. If you weren't aware of it, Jock and I have a perfectly good work relationship. I'm not about to ruin that." His voice got high and pitchy. "Have you seen the size of his muscles? He could squash me like Brutus squashed little ole Popeye."

I could tell Max was getting anxious. "Yes." I used my talking-to-a-child voice. "But Popeye ate all his spinach, and he clobbered Brutus in the end." I dragged him closer to the double doors where Jock had exited.

"But look at all the beatings Popeye endured in the meantime." Max wasn't interested in playing the hero. Olive Oyl, maybe.

I hauled us to a stop, my head about to explode from my headache, the turmoil of the night, and the family meddling I couldn't seem to escape. "Okay already! I'm going to see what Jock's up to. If you want to come, fine. If not, stop holding me back."

We stared at each other good and hard. It felt like I was back in elementary school in a staring contest. I'd never lost one of those competitions, and I wasn't about to lose now.

"Oh, fine!" Max jutted out his bottom lip.

I didn't wait for him to change his mind. I jerked him by the collar, and we sped through the double doors. We spotted Jock swaggering past the casino and movie theater. He strode forward, and we acted like double agents, creeping behind him, zipping in and out of alcoves, sliding along walls. We probably looked more like Abbott and Costello than semi-respected stylists, but no one seemed to think twice about what we were doing. Probably just looked like we were taking part in a scavenger hunt. At a T-intersection, Jock turned right and scouted out the pub. We loitered behind a women's clothing rack on the corner.

"This better be good," Max whispered. "He's taking us on quite the goose chase."

I crouched, pressing my bag to my side, thinking once again about Jock conferring with the captain. "It'll be good, all right. There's something going on around here and Lucy's death is tied to it."

Max gaped at me. "How do you know all this?"

"Instinct." I swiveled my head back to the pub. "Do you see him?"

Max wasn't the least bit interested in the search. He plucked a scarf off the clothing rack and flung it around his neck, posing in the mirror. "What do you think?"

Max wasn't exactly a child with ADD, but he could get off topic quickly.

I grimaced. "Am I keeping you from something?"

"Look!" He pointed to a rack with shawls. "This wrap has sequins."

I snatched him by the scarf around his neck and yanked him down next to me. Jock ambled out of the pub, glanced our way, then quickened his pace toward the front of the ship.

Max unwound himself from the scarf and tossed it back on the rack. "Any more ideas?" he huffed.

"Shh." I grabbed his hand, and we continued trailing Jock, staying a good chunk behind.

Jock slowed by a room labeled *Ice Sculpting*. He put his head down like he was considering something, then turned sideways and scratched his jaw.

We sucked in air and flattened into a doorway, hoping he wouldn't turn around. This was one of those moments when I wished to be anywhere but here. Being discovered tracking Jock wasn't exactly on my top-ten list of things to do. And what would I say if that happened? Nice weather we're having? I was such an idiot. Couldn't even come up with a good lie. But I knew he was involved in something. And what about Lucy? Whatever it was, I wasn't about to give up.

Jock did a quick study through the ice-sculpting room window, then swung open the door and strode inside.

I had so much adrenaline pumping through me it seemed an eternity until the door clicked behind him. Finally, Max and I scurried to the same spot and squinted cheek to cheek through the glass.

"Why'd he go in there?" he asked.

"Beats me. With Lucy frozen in an ice sculpture, maybe he's inquisitive about the process." I hiccupped back trepidation at that thought. I'd been a nuisance earlier… and yesterday…and probably the day before that. Maybe he was researching ways to eliminate *me*.

We stared in the window and saw a handful of people. They watched two men in white with shatterproof glasses and lumberjack tools shape chunks of ice into statues.

Max marveled at the spectators. "Suddenly everyone's interested in ice sculptures."

I stretched my neck. "True. But apart from the fascination, the whole scene looks as suspicious as a shopping spree at Neiman Marcus." I scoured the whole room. "The only thing missing is Jock."

Max pressed his nose to the glass. "Nobody disappears into thin air. Where could he have gone?"

"I don't know. There's a door at the right. Maybe he slipped through there."

He eyed the door. "*Now* what do we do?"

"Why don't you try the stairs?" Jock said from behind us.

Max and I screamed and leaped a foot in the air.

Jock put his arms around our shoulders in a friendly hold while we caught our breath. "You weren't following me, were you?"

I stuck out my chin as if we had every right to be there. "Why would we be following you? Just because you look like you know something about Lucy's murder?"

"Is that what you think?" He turned his gaze on Max.

"Don't look at me," Max panted. "I'm only following Simon Says."

Jock nodded, a slight grin on his face meant for me. "And what is it you wish to know?"

"Gee. Just everything. Who murdered her? When was she killed? Was there more than one person involved?"

"Sorry. Don't know the answers to your questions."

"Then where are you going in such a hurry?"

"Can't answer that either."

"Can't? Or won't?"

The grin widened. "Why don't you go back to playing Simon Says. Better still, let Max escort you back to your cabin. And don't forget to lock your doors."

Without another word, he backed away from us, turned, and strode down the hall, slipping through the exit door.

Max clapped his chest. "Boy, that was tense."

Tense. My heart was hammering, and my legs were shaking. Well, Jock de Marco wasn't getting the better of me. I blew out a sigh and got a hold of myself, more determined to find out what he was up to.

Max peered back in the carving room. "I thought they used molds to make those ice statues."

I sliced him a look. "I don't know. You want to go ask?"

He frowned, obviously trying to read my mind. "Didn't you learn your lesson? Jock's on to you."

I drew a thin line with my lips and crossed my arms.

"Oh, no. I don't like that look."

"Come on." I readjusted my bag over my shoulder. "We keep following him. His unwillingness to answer my questions proves he knows something."

"You know what's behind that exit sign?" His voice got high and quivery. "A dark, hollow stairwell. I don't do well in dark, spooky places. I even sleep with my Barney nightlight on."

I rolled my eyes so hard I could almost see my brain— what was left of it. "It's well lit," I said, "and I'll take off my heels so we don't make any noise."

We tiptoed into the stairwell and waited until Jock

exited two floors up. Then we crept up the staircase like mice. At the top of the landing, I squashed my nose to the glass door.

Jock stepped onto the deck, the midnight sky and twinkling stars enhancing the muscular outline of his white uniform—undoubtedly one of the most beautiful sights I'd been privileged to view on this trip. I allowed myself a moment's appreciation when Max elbowed me from behind.

"You're fogging up the glass. What's he doing?" he wanted to know.

I stopped swooning and wiped the door. "Looks like he's going toward the bridge."

"Isn't that where the captain mans the ship? I thought that was off-limits to passengers."

We faced each other, sharing a this-is-Jock-we're-talking-about look. "Right," we said in unison.

Max pulled me back into the shadows. "Maybe he's on some navy mission. Didn't you say he was in special operations once upon a time?"

"Firefighting," I said.

Max sighed. "He's such a hero."

Oh boy. "You don't do on-demand navy work. Once you're out of the navy, you're out."

He narrowed his eyes on me. "How do you know all this?"

I acted nonchalant. "Searched it after I hired Jock." I gestured toward the deck. "Anyway, look around. This is a cruise ship, not a navy vessel."

"True." He stared out at the deck.

"There's no use speculating. Jock's a master at keeping secrets. Sherlock Holmes couldn't decipher the man."

"Then what do you suggest? I vote we ditch the manhunt and go back to the bar or go for a nighttime swim. Or maybe there's still time to join the scavenger hunt."

I ignored his suggestions. "We need to get closer. We can't see anything from here."

He threw his hands on his hips and leaned to one side. "Tiptoeing around like cat burglars might be a flashing sign. And you've already been caught once. I volunteer to wait here in case you need backup."

"Chicken."

"Boc boc boc."

I swallowed the lump in my throat, picked up my hem, and crept toward the bridge. I spied Jock in the brightly lit, glassed-in high-tech room, talking with the captain.

"Do you see him?" Max whispered loudly from the door.

"*Shhh.*" I swept my arm back at him. If I could inch closer, I might be able to hear what they were saying, or at least read their lips. I leaned over the side of the railing and craned my head toward the bridge to take a better look. I angled over too far and dropped one of my heels with a thunk into a lifeboat twenty feet below. Damn!

Now what? I wasn't going home without my four-inch Bottega Veneta heels. I could get two hundred bucks on eBay for these shoes. Easily.

"Max," I whispered hoarsely. I looked up and down the length of the deck. "*Max!*"

Where could he have gone in the span of one minute? He was in my face 24/7, and when I needed him, he was playing hide-and-seek. Great.

I examined the area to see if there was anything that might help retrieve my shoe. Like a fishing pole. Hmm. No fishing poles. Lots of life preservers, though. And while my shoe needed saving, I didn't think a life preserver was the way to go.

I rummaged around in my bag. Surely I had something that would help. Brush. Nail polish remover. Curling iron. Scissors. A few dozen other useless aids. Swell. Unless I wanted to give the lifeboat a makeover, nothing in my bag was going to do the trick.

I gave up and glanced from my bare feet to my shoe below. Was twenty feet such a long drop? I just had to climb over the railing, latch onto the ledge, hang onto the rope, and lower myself down. Rock-climbing in reverse. And if I didn't pay attention to the danger signs or the long descent to the ocean, I'd be good.

I peered up one last time at the bridge. Jock held up his cell phone. The captain looked at it, nodded, and pointed to something on the screen. Then he shrugged at Jock. Jock tucked the phone back in his pocket and turned toward the window in my direction. Oh, no!

Afraid of being seen, I slung my bag over my shoulder, said a prayer, and climbed over the railing. In my haste, I tripped over the ledge, snagged my dress, let go of the rope, and tumbled ass-backward into the lifeboat, landing with a *whump* on top of my shoe.

I bit my tongue so hard to keep from screaming I tasted blood. The lifeboat creaked and swayed under me, my stomach lurching from the motion. Scared of dropping into the sea, I grasped the edge of the boat and held my breath.

Suddenly, I heard footsteps and voices above. Panic swelled in my throat. What if it was Jock? I could shout for help, but I didn't want to look like a fool again, especially after he'd caught me spying several minutes ago. *Pride goeth before a fall, Valentine.* Too late. I rubbed my rear end. Now I'd probably have two bruises—one from toppling on the blow dryer during the contest, and now this. I didn't have time to baby a sore bottom. I had one option. Hide, and hope to get myself out of this.

I searched my surroundings. Not even a tarp to pull over me. I was about as concealed as a brunette in a sea of blonds. Thankfully, my white dress blended in with the boat.

I sucked in the pain, shrank into a ball, and slanted close to the ship. *Please, no one look down.* The voices became louder as if they were right on top of me. Then there was silence. Uncomfortable silence. Except for my heart. It was storming fiercely in my chest.

I held still. Even my hair didn't dare move a strand. *Let them pass, let them pass.* I stayed crouched and, what seemed like hours later, the voices started up again, and the footsteps faded into the distance.

Whew! That was close. I uncurled my body, dusted off my clothes, and took stock of the situation. How was I going to get out of here? I glared up at the railing. Maybe going up wouldn't be as difficult as coming down.

I dug through my bag again and this time yanked out my curling iron. The cord would act as a rope and help in the climb back up, considering the one I'd let go of was too high to grab. I needed to loop my cord on one of those hooks, and I'd be all set. I teetered in the narrow boat, bending to put on my heels. I wouldn't be able to hold onto them while scaling the side of the ship, and my bag was already heavy enough. Plus, my spikes would give me leverage in the climb.

"Another fine mess you've gotten into," I scolded myself. "And this time you've got no one else to blame."

"Oh, I don't know about that," a deep voice said from above. "I'd put a word in to the captain about raising those lifeboats."

Afraid to look up into that cocksure face I knew so well, I clung to the craft and froze, goose bumps covering my arms. How did I explain why I was swinging in a lifeboat, hanging from a cruise ship, alone, at night, after Lucy had been murdered? I swallowed my pride and vehemently raised my lashes to Jock.

"Don't you *dare* talk to me about the captain!" I shouted, glad for the dark night so he couldn't see my skin turn beet-red or witness the steam whooshing out my ears.

He leaned clasped hands on the railing, trying his damnedest to keep from laughing. "May I ask what you're doing down there?" He blinked, totally captivated. "Or would that sound like a stupid question?"

Now wasn't the time to get into an argument. I gulped, worrying at any minute I'd drop into the deep blue sea. Meanwhile, he looked breathtaking in his naval uniform, gazing down at me while a soft breeze blew his hair. I could imagine what I resembled, stranded in this...this raft, like Gilligan.

"Actually, it *is* a stupid question." Evidently, I didn't know when to shut up. "I was admiring the stars when you happened along."

He raised his head, inhaling deeply as he looked out into the clear black night. "Kind of a strange place to stargaze." He tilted his head down at me again. "But I'll leave you to it."

What? I panicked. *Think fast, Valentine. In about two seconds, the only hope you have of being rescued will disappear.* "Wait!" I waved the curling iron above my head like a flag. "I...I need to talk to you."

He raised an eyebrow at the iron. "We can talk later. I don't want to intrude."

Intrude. Any other time, he was breathing his sexy, hot breath down my neck, seducing me like he knew it'd been ages since I'd been with a man. Now he decided he was intruding. Of all the arrogant, sneaky...

Well, I wasn't one to beg. He could go to hell for all I cared. I got myself into this mess. I'd get myself out.

We stared at each other for a long moment, the water below the only sound as it seductively lapped against the ship. He knew the ball was in my court, and his grin said as much. If I'd been twenty feet closer, I'd have slapped him or plastered myself against his hard body and sucked on his full Argentinean lips.

What was I thinking? I was acting like I'd been marooned on a desert island, and Jock was the first sign of life. And if there was one thing I knew about Jock, he was throbbing with life.

Before I could say anything, a large woman, whom I'd seen playing the slots in the casino, propped her wide bosom on the railing ten feet from Jock and screamed, "Man overboard!" She flailed a flabby arm over her head, holding down her wide-brimmed hat with her other hand. "Help! Man overboard!"

Where? I dropped the curling iron in my bag and looked along the row of lifeboats hanging like mine. I didn't see anybody fall overboard. My nest rocked as I leaned and looked over the edge. I didn't see anyone jump.

The woman screamed again. She wouldn't let up, and now she had *me* scared. It was at least a hundred-foot drop to the water, and the night was so dark, a rescue would be hopeless. Fear filled my eyes. One passenger had already died tonight. Wasn't that enough?

The woman shrieked up and down the length of the deck. "Help! She's going to jump! *Hellllp!*"

The ship's horn blared, and about forty people congregated along the railing, gaping down at me in horror. "Don't jump! Don't jump!" they shouted.

Don't jump! They thought *I* was the man overboard? That I was trying to end my life? How did I go from snooping on Jock to being rescued by half the ship? Perfect. I was on a cruise with my family, my mother was doing her utmost to marry me off, I had the world's worst roommate, Romero was God-knows-where with another woman, I just lost the biggest contest of my life, a murder had just been committed, and because I accidentally dropped a shoe in this wretched lifeboat, everyone thought I was suicidal.

Jock looked like he was about to burst. A moment later, the captain pressed through the throng, debonair as always. He spoke through a megaphone as if I were in a raft, floating to Brazil. "Let us help you!" he called in a slow, calm voice.

Jock left his post at the railing and consulted with the captain. The two men shared a smile, and the captain ordered a couple of the crew to help me up.

Jock was having his fun, and I was mortified. I'd give *him* fun if I ever caught him.

One of the crew crawled down the rope and wrapped an ugly white safety harness around my middle like I was a harpooned whale. I boiled with embarrassment. Sadder yet, the harness was void of glitter or frills. I mean, *sheesh*.

Could they not add a few rhinestones or lace to pretty things up in a desperate rescue?

The men hoisted me back up to the platform by a pulley, reeled me too quickly over to the deck, and banged my legs against the top of the railing.

"Yeow!" I kicked my legs in midair, glaring at the guy manning this contraption.

My heels finally hit the deck, and a crew member unhooked me. Everyone cheered. I wanted to die. No, what I really wanted was to come face-to-face with Jock and give him a piece of my mind. I looked up and down the deck, swallowing my humiliation. No Jock. Why didn't that surprise me?

Suddenly, someone yelled, "Watch out!"

I turned my head toward the voice just as the pulley came at me and cracked me over the ear.

"Yee-*ouch!*" I gave my head a shake and rubbed my ear. They really needed to fire that guy.

A man from dinner ran up to me with a large glass of water. "Here! Drink this. You'll feel better."

I chugged back the water, and a second later my throat burned. What the…? Not again. I coughed at the familiar taste of ouzo and felt like I'd been socked between the eyes. I gave myself a moment to get my bearings straight and thought I was doing okay until I took a shaky step forward. The combination of booze and my sore head had me woozy, and I was losing my grip. I went down in a spiral, but before I hit the deck, a strong pair of arms swept me up.

Then I blacked out.

Chapter 6

I pried my eyes open to bright sunlight slanting in through the half-opened drapes. I couldn't hear the boat's constant hum. What's more, everything seemed still. Probably because all the activity was taking place in my brain while a jackhammer drilled my skull. Most likely the champagne and ouzo I'd consumed at dinner last night punishing every inch of cerebral cortex under my scalp.

Wait. *Drapes?* I didn't have drapes in my cabin. I didn't even have a porthole, much less a window. I looked around. This was a suite with *two* windows. It even had a sliding door.

Jock's left arm was wrapped around me, his navy tattoo in licking distance. The life preserver-shaped clock read 7:01, the sheets were a sky blue, and—*whoa!* Jock's arm? Around me? *Aaaaah!* Panic climbed my throat.

Get control, Valentine. It could be worse. I could be in Kashi's bed, or Clive's—or whatever his name was.

I searched my memory, trying to recall how I ended up here. Captain's Gala. Lucy's murder. Piano bar. Trailing Jock. Falling into a lifeboat. Struck by a pulley. More ouzo—oh boy. No wonder it felt like my skull was being drilled. That was a large glass of liquor I'd gulped on the deck. *Way to go, Valentine.* Still didn't explain how I ended up in this suite with Jock.

The top of my ear was still tender, and between that and my headache, I was in great shape. I looked over my shoulder at Jock snuggled behind me in bed. Then I took two fingers and peeked at myself under the blue silk sheet.

"Yes, you're butt-naked," Jock said in a low voice, pulling me against him, his stubble tickling my shoulder.

"Stop screaming." I pressed my ears and tried to wriggle away from him.

Jock moved against me, and fresh panic set in. Big *hard* panic!

I tucked the sheet between us to create some distance, but that proved futile. He draped a leg over mine and slid my hair up on the pillowcase. Then he started kissing my neck. I froze in alarm because when Jock's mouth touched my skin, the sensation sent electrifying jolts of pleasure from my head to my toes.

He smelled delicious, and his warm, hard body was turning me on. But my aching head was reminding me, *No! He works for you!* How did I wind up in bed with Jock? The question was almost out of my mouth when his hand slipped under the covers. His fingers feathered across my stomach, inching up until I didn't trust myself to breathe. He rolled me onto my back, took my hand, and traced my finger across his moist lips. He slid my finger inside his mouth and sucked gently, his tongue teasing, whetting my desire for him.

I was nearing an orgasmic state when he withdrew my finger and caressed my hand, massaging his thumb inside my palm. He stroked my finger up and down, smoothing the ring on my index finger. "Is this a slave ring?"

I could barely breathe, let alone respond.

He purred against my ear. "You want to be my slave?"

Suddenly, there was a knock at the door. I ripped my hand away and tumbled to the floor, taking the sheet with me. Nothing covered Jock but a smile. A HUGE smile. A smile that didn't look like it'd disappear anytime soon. A smile that suggested he wasn't in any hurry to see who was knocking.

I could now safely say I'd seen every inch of Jock's glorious body. And if he ever came at me with a smile like that again, I'd fight my traitorous physique. I wasn't afraid of Jock de Marco, but a smile like that could damn near kill a person.

The knock again.

"Aren't you answering that?" I asked from the floor, trying to keep the pink out of my cheeks.

"Room service," someone called from the other side of the door.

"Room service?" I wrapped the sheet around me tighter.

Jock winked. "Saves me from going to the buffet table and making a hundred bad choices."

Only *he* would see that as a bad thing. I rolled my eyes, and even that hurt.

He swung his feet to the floor, got up, and faced the bed, tossing back the covers and pillows like he was searching for something. Boxers? I stole a look—past the smile, past the scar on his ribs—and *whoa*! What was *that* nasty mark on the right side of his groin? Another navy incident, or some other mystery?

He picked his boxers off the floor, pulled them on, and opened the door. He took the tray from the steward. I crawled on all fours, looking for my dress. My heels were hanging from the ceiling fan, so I didn't waste time on those.

"*Gracias por todo,*" Jock said and closed the door.

Another one of Jock's talents. He was multilingual. A few months ago, I would've said he was showing off. But now, with him standing half-naked in front of me, it was kind of impressive.

He lifted the lid and took a deep whiff. "Want some?"

I peered up from the floor. "No thanks. I don't eat birdseed and soybeans for breakfast."

"Maybe you should."

I was on my feet now, clutching the sheet, shooting him a look. "What are you saying? I'm gaining weight?"

"I'm saying cruises are famous for their rich foods. And the buffets are killers."

I felt my thighs. "If I'm getting so fat, you can stop looking at me like a bear ready to devour a blueberry bush." I sank to the floor again and searched under the bed for my dress. Nothing. I caught him grinning at me, and my head gave another massive throb.

"Your gown is in the bathroom," he said.

Cheeky. I opened a door and stomped barefoot into a closet.

"The bathroom's over there." He gestured to my right, chewing on something that looked like it might've been bread if it'd been half an inch thicker.

I rushed past him into the bathroom, dropped my sheet, and slid on my gown. I avoided looking in the mirror. If I looked as bad as I felt, I was better off not knowing, fat thighs and all.

I put on a bold I'm-your-employer face and charged out of the bathroom, keeping a safe distance from Jock. "What happened to Lucy last night? And why are you always around the captain? And *why* was I naked in your bed?"

He pushed the tray out of the way, enjoying my tantrum. Then he strode toward me with an intimidating look on his face. I stood there in my bare feet, feeling less brave than I did a minute ago. By the time he stopped and towered over me, my breasts ached, and a lump formed in my throat. He ran his fingers through my hair, and I swallowed down the lump.

"Don't you want to brush your hair?"

"No, I don't want to brush my hair," I said, sounding like a spoiled five-year-old. "I want information."

He didn't look put out by my behavior, and this made me all the more angry. He smiled down at me, his hardened nipples staring me right in the eye. I slid my gaze down his ribs. I'd never been this close to the scar from his navy days. I wanted to reach out and touch it, but I controlled the impulse. And while I was controlling impulses, I resisted the urge to ask about the newly discovered scar on his groin.

"Okay." He widened his stance and crossed his arms. "What information do you want?"

I glared up at him. "For starters, how did Lucy die?"

"She was murdered."

"I guessed that when I saw her looking out at me from a frozen statue." Then it set in. Lucy was dead. My drunkenness and all the goings-on last night kept me from dwelling on that fact, but now that I was relatively together, sadness engulfed me. I gave myself a moment to grieve for this feisty woman whom I'd never get to know. Then I met Jock's eyes, my voice soft. "Then how did I end up in your"—I glanced at the bed—"room."

"After you passed out on the deck, I brought you here."

I imagined him carrying me like a sleeping princess, my hair flowing down over his arms, my gown softly trailing behind him. Then I realized how I probably really looked and was thankful he didn't leave me sprawled on the deck like a beached whale. "Noble of you."

"I thought so."

"You could've taken me to my cabin, which is technically across the hall from *your* cabin."

"I wanted to keep my eye on you. Plus, I wasn't about to grope through that sack of yours, looking for your key. And before you say another word...nothing happened." He must've noticed the tormented look on my face because, in all honesty, I didn't take this lightly.

"Are you sure?"

He laughed, showing some teeth. "I've never had that kind of response before. And for your information, it wasn't for your lack of trying."

"*Me* trying!"

"Yes, you." He set his hands on his hips. "You came to and were all over me. You hiked up that almost dress of yours, pushed me onto the bed, and attempted to gnaw off my uniform buttons."

"That's impossible!" Not. That ouzo clearly had a terrible effect on me. It brought to mind that night in the Berkshires—what I could recollect—when I threw myself at Romero in a similar fashion. *Exactly why you didn't drink, Valentine!*

"You know, it's extremely hard to remain a gentleman when a gorgeous woman is throwing herself at you."

I hated the fact that I was probably blushing. "And you're a gentleman."

He grinned at my statement. "Not always. Especially when the lady in question isn't wearing panties."

My lips tingled, and my skin turned hot. How could I have been so stupid? No underwear, all because I liked sheer fabric against my skin. I couldn't decide if I was embarrassed, nervous, or sexually excited. One thing was for certain. Things were becoming too personal.

"Can we change the subject back to Lucy?" I tossed my hair off my shoulders. "How was she killed?"

"They're working on that."

"Who's they?"

"The captain and ship security are working with local authorities in San Juan." He motioned over his shoulder toward the sliding door. "Today's port of call. And fortunately, U.S. jurisdiction."

I let this sink in. "Speaking of the captain, why are you two so chummy? And why were you in a naval uniform last night?"

He took a step back and straddled a chair. "I met Carlo when I was serving. He already had a dozen or so years on me, but we were on the same ship together, worked out of the same naval base."

"I thought he was Italian."

He smiled. "Raised in the Bronx, but he's Italian through and through. His charming accent does seem to impress the ladies."

Didn't impress me. Much.

"About the uniform," he continued, "Carlo asked me to wear it. I complied."

"Nice you obey *someone*," I spouted. Miss Holier-Than-Thou.

He stared at me like he was stripping me back out of my gown, and my face warmed. "After we finished our tour of duty, I went home. He chose to work in friendlier waters. Captain suits him, so does the Caribbean."

"Small world, isn't it?"

He reached for my hand and drew me in. "Getting smaller all the time."

I backed up so I could think straight. "And this is why the privileged accommodations."

"You could say that. When you mentioned the cruise, I gave him a call. You and I could've bunked together, you know. I think I implied that before we left."

"I'm quite happy where I am, thank you." *Liar.*

I mentally stated I wasn't responsible for Lucy's death. Which meant Kashi was not a killer. It just didn't add up. I frowned, wishing I could let it all go, but guilt was a wonderful thing.

Jock rose from his chair as if he knew there was more on my mind. It was true. And sharing what I saw with him would be a huge relief.

I told him how Kashi had slipped something into Lucy's bag at the contest, and the furtive glances between him and Sabrina, not to mention the fact he'd poured something into Lucy's drink. "Something's going on. If Kashi didn't kill Lucy, I'd like to know who did."

Jock rubbed his jaw. "And you think I'm involved in the investigation."

I gave him a smug shrug. He knew I was aware of his involvement—whatever that involvement was. I grabbed his chair, climbed on top, and retrieved my heels from the ceiling fan, not daring to question how they got up there. I waited for him to offer anything further on Lucy's murder, but his silence told me this conversation was over. Dandy. I didn't need him or his help. I marched past him to the door, and he grasped my arm.

"Okay," he said. "There is something Carlo has asked me to look into."

"I'm listening."

He let me go. "It's going to cost you."

I wasn't in the mood for games. "Funny way for an *employee* to talk to his *boss*." I slipped on my heels, feeling braver now that I was taller.

"What if I weren't your employee? I don't think I'd have a hard time finding another job."

Thoughts of Candace sprang to mind and how she'd tried to lure him away. Even *I'd* hired him within five minutes of him strutting through the door. Was I willing to lose him? I avoided his eyes, afraid he'd see the truth.

"All right," I said. "What do you want? Can't be sex. You could have any woman you desire on this ship. In fact, Miss Romania looked like she'd be all too happy to curl your tendrils. *If* you know what I mean."

"I know exactly what you mean. Did you see me put the moves on Ivona, or Miss Romania, as you called her?"

He had me there. In truth, I hadn't witnessed him do anything more than whisper in her ear. It was more a case of predicting the outcome when I saw him with another beautiful woman.

"And not that I cared, but she'd planned on disembarking first thing this morning."

Oh.

He took hold of me by both arms. "Look at me." His tone changed from slightly amused to serious.

The room went still except for the electricity sparking in my chest. His dark, hooded eyes blazed into mine in a way that made my cheeks prickle. "What I want is you. And whether you admit it, you want me." He let me go. "You just need to decide who it is you want more."

My insides tightened, and all logic evaporated the moment he cleverly brought Romero into the equation. Despite his wild track record and tough past, the truth was I'd never wanted a man like I wanted Romero. But I'd yet to reveal this to him—when I was sober.

This was another reason I didn't trust myself around Jock. The pent-up sexual tension I'd built with Romero had, at times, almost erupted around Jock. Whatever Romero's whereabouts or whatever the current status of our relationship, he was always present in my heart and mind.

A little voice reminded me Romero had nothing to do with this. I should stick to the issue at hand, even if I couldn't come up with anything concrete to say. "Ha!" I proclaimed. "I don't need any information from you." I pointed a finger at his chest. "I'm good at finding my own news *and* solving murders!"

He folded his arms across his chest. "Equipping yourself with perm rods and tail combs again, are you?"

I grabbed my bag and almost choked myself swinging it over my shoulder. "I don't need any beauty tools to find a killer. You'll see." What was I saying? I wasn't ready to jump into the middle of another homicide. This might not be Rueland, where everyone knew my unfortunate past, where my life was dissected like a frog pinned to a table. Still, we were on the high seas, and I didn't know the first thing about solving a crime on a ship. But I wasn't going to back down now. I did an elaborate pivot on my heels so he couldn't see the uncertainty on my face. Then I paraded out the door, slamming it hard behind me.

I pressed my thumbs between my eyebrows, attempting to deaden my headache. Everything swam around from last night, right up to my recent discovery of yet another scar on Jock de Marco.

I looked up and down the hall. I had to get out of here, but I had no idea where I was. My floor didn't have any natural light, which told me my cabin was probably three or a dozen decks down.

I hustled down the corridor, all too aware there might be a murderer on board. I didn't know when Lucy was killed, or even where. Since we spent yesterday in port in

Nassau, for all I knew the murderer could still be there and not on the ship. I chewed on my bottom lip. This sounded logical to me. This could've been the job of a random serial killer. Of course, it didn't explain how Lucy ended up in a chunk of ice. And it didn't lessen my unease since my gut told me she was the intended target, and the murderer was in our midst.

I peeked over my shoulder, making sure no one was following me to the elevator. Exhaling my edginess, I waited for the doors to open and glanced out a large window. San Juan. Right. Next port of call. There were dozens of light-colored buildings, hotels, and rows of parked buses at the dock. Probably waiting to take passengers on tours. At the moment, I was only interested in getting back to the safety of my cabin.

The elevator doors opened, and I hurried in, banging into Max, who was running out. I screamed so loud it was a wonder Lucy didn't come back to life.

"Where have you been?" Max gripped my shoulders, looking me up and down in my wrinkly gown. "And why weren't you answering your cell phone. I've been a nervous wreck, looking for you."

I checked my bag for my phone. Not there. I'd been so preoccupied, I must've left it in the bathroom after I talked to Twix yesterday. "I guess it's in my cabin."

"Why's it in your cabin?"

"Never mind that!" I gaped at him. "What happened to you last night while I was spying on Jock? Mr. I'll-Wait-Here-In-Case-You-Need-Backup."

He gave a sheepish shrug. "I thought I saw Tantig shuffling down the stairs. She looked disoriented. I didn't want her to fall overboard."

"How could she fall overboard?" I almost shouted. "The railings are practically up to her neck."

He looked put out by my comment. "Sue me for showing compassion to the elderly."

Oh Lord. "Anyway, Tantig was in the lounge with my parents. Remember?"

He winced. "I said I *thought* I saw her. Why? What happened?"

Self-conscious from my recent remark, I muffled my hand over my mouth. "I fell in a lifeboat."

"What?" He slapped my hand away. "What do you mean you fell in a lifeboat? Aren't the railings practically up to your neck?"

Smart aleck. "Doesn't matter now. I'm fine."

He groaned. "Good. With Lucy dead, I started thinking something happened to you."

"The only other thing that happened to me was that I spent the night with Jock." I shoved my palm in his face. "And before you say anything, nothing happened." I muttered. "That's what I was told."

Max's voice tripled in pitch. "And you believed that hunk of man?"

"Yes!" I gave him my back-off look.

"Works for me." He waited a beat. "So, where's he staying? And why isn't he rooming with me?"

"He and the captain were in the navy together, and since this is the captain's domain, Jock was given a luxurious suite."

"Now everything makes sense."

I gave him a strange look. "Nothing makes sense. It doesn't explain why Jock seems to be involved in this case or why he's been glued to the captain."

"Maybe they've been rehashing their glory days."

I shook my head. "There's more. I can feel it. And whatever it is, Lucy's death is tied to it."

We rode the elevator down to our deck, and Max prattled on about Lucy. "Who do you think killed her? My money's on Kashi."

"Kashi!" I got off the elevator and stopped short. "Weren't you the one giving me theories why he wouldn't have killed her? *Giving her medicine* ring a bell? *Intimate friends*?"

"Okay. Then who do *you* think killed her?"

"I don't know. And I'm going to keep it that way." Not exactly what I told Jock.

"I've heard that before. You forgetting your history with homicides?"

"It's a bad history. And I don't plan on getting involved. Got that?"

Max roamed a cynical eye over my dress where it sagged unevenly off my shoulder. "Know what I think? Jock should've spanked your pretty behind while he had you naked under the covers."

"Who said I was naked?"

Max pursed his lips. "If you spent the night with Jock, you were naked."

Oy! I picked up the pace to hide the tumultuous feelings I'd been harboring all morning.

We walked the rest of the way to our cabins in silence. I was about to insert the key in my door when I heard a muffled voice inside that didn't belong to Phyllis.

Who was in our cabin? Couldn't be the steward. There'd be a cart in the hallway. And where was Phyllis? If she'd been there all night, she wouldn't have let anyone in. On the other hand, it was already after eight. She'd be on land, touring. Bad enough my head was pounding, now a gust of anxiety swept through my veins.

I poked Max and pointed at the cabin. We put our heads to the door, and Max went wide-eyed. "I'll get the pirate skull I bought in Nassau," he whispered, Mr. Courageous all of a sudden.

"What for?" I whispered back. "We're not playing *Pirates of the Caribbean*."

"What if it's the murderer?"

"Why would the murderer be in my room?"

Max shrugged, then a suspicious look crossed his face. "What if it's Kashi? And he's getting ready to kill you next!"

I rolled my eyes. "Thanks a lot."

"If I had my pirate skull, I could conk him on the head with it."

I deliberated quickly. "Fine, go get it!"

He slid into his cabin and came back seconds later, gripping his five-pound wooden skull that had a patch over one eye, a hoop in one ear, and a red bandana tied across its forehead.

In silence, I inserted the door key and braced myself.

Max crashed into the room first like he was 007. He held the skull high above his head and smashed it down on the back of the intruder's crown.

The man, who was dressed in black and had his cell phone to his ear, tumbled headfirst into the bunk-bed ladder, then bounced back onto the floor, face up, cell phone beside him.

We looked down, then at each other.

"Romero!" we cried in unison.

"You killed him!" I dropped to the floor, panic seizing me.

Max tossed the wooden skull on the bed and fell to his knees. We bent close, listening for signs of breathing. I inhaled Romero's Arctic Spruce scent, almost melting from the comforting smell. *Don't be dead, don't be dead.* My pulse roared in my ears.

I squeezed his hand, rubbing my thumb along the platinum band of his Iron Man watch. I took in the scar on his cheekbone, the fine lines around his eyes, his uncontrollable dark, wavy hair.

"Whew! He's breathing peacefully," Max said.

I could *barely* breathe. I stared down at Romero, this tough, stubborn man who, despite his macho image, stood for justice, honor, and integrity. Emotionally, I was aching to the core, but I made myself firm up. "He's not going to like the bruise he'll have when he comes to."

"Which is why I'll be leaving now." Max clenched his pirate skull and flew out the door.

I darted to the bathroom, filled a cup with water, and splashed it on Romero's face.

He didn't jump or stir an inch. Why did it always work in the movies? I didn't know what to do. I knelt beside him and lifted his head onto my lap. I wiped his cheeks with my gown, pushed his dark hair aside, and felt for blood. Nothing tacky, wet, or red. Thank you, God.

My fingers were inches from his five-o'clock shadow, my lips a breath away from his. I gazed into his tranquil face, and it struck me how handsome he was. It also struck me I'd never seen him sleep or been wrapped in his arms at daybreak. Suddenly, the miles that had been spread between us made me care for him more. What an awful moment to realize how much I cherished Romero. If anything happened to him, I...I didn't know what life would be like. I pulled myself together before huge tears plopped onto his face.

He finally groaned and opened his eyes like he was getting his bearings straight. Then he looked up and saw me. "*Merda!*" He jumped a foot back, his gruff voice washing me with relief. "What'd you hit me with? A tire iron?" He rubbed his scalp with the heel of his hand. "No. It had to be a twenty-pound hair dryer or a flat iron."

"Actually"—I winced—"it was Max who hit you."

"You got him assaulting for you now?"

"*Sorry.*" I yanked back my gown. "I wasn't expecting you!"

He eyed my dress. "I can see that."

For a moment, I was taken back to the first time Romero walked into my salon, all self-assured, virile, and arrogant, putting me on the defensive. Well, I'd had about enough of his insults. "And what was that you said in Italian?"

"You don't want to know." He swiped his phone off the ground. "I only say it when I get clobbered." He looked up into my eyes, giving his head another rub. "Want to tell me why you're arriving in your cabin at 8:15 in the morning dressed like that?"

"Not especially." I got off my hands and knees.

This was just like Romero, taking a situation and turning it around. Like *I* was the bad guy here! Who broke into whose cabin? "Maybe *I* have a question or two!" I ignored the murderous look on his face. "Like, what are you doing here?"

He got to his feet. "I'm here because of the homicide."

"The Lucy Jacobs homicide?"

"Are there any others I should be aware of?" He settled his hands on his hips, giving me a stony look.

I glanced around the room, disregarding that self-confident face. "How did you get in here?"

"Phyllis let me in on her way to breakfast."

Great, Phyllis was okay. I didn't need more worries. "That was decent of her."

He lowered his eyes to my breasts and back up, and all I could think was, *God, he looks edible.* The sight of him standing there, looking sexy if somewhat injured, had me wanting to drop my gown to my toes. True, I'd had similar feelings toward Jock less than an hour ago, but there it was.

Romero had an irresistible side to his tough exterior that not only made me nervous, it also charmed me. If I hadn't been so busy acting indignant, I might've told him how much I missed him. Instead, I hooked my thumbs inside my cleavage and yanked up my dress.

He cleared his throat and pulled the cop tone. "I hear you've been looking for me."

Huh? Then it registered. *Twix!* My face stung, and I wasn't sure if it was because of Romero's fiery look or the fact that he was onto me. Either way, I did an about-face toward the bathroom to escape.

He sprang for the back of my dress. "Not so fast. I have some questions for you. Like, why was your friend at my house, standing on a recycling box, snooping through my kitchen window?"

I lost the conviction in my voice. "Maybe she was looking for a recipe?"

"Is that a joke?"

"Are you laughing?"

He glared at me. Hard.

"Well? What makes you think she was my friend, anyway?"

"Let's see. My sister happened to arrive and caught the woman practically cleaning my window with her nose. When Cynthia threatened to call the cops, your friend came clean."

I'd met Romero's sister at her wedding several months ago. She threw me the bouquet and seemed to like me. Now she probably thought I was a loser. Or a stalker.

"Seems your pal's curiosity is worse than yours." He sighed. "If that's possible."

"Okay! I wanted to know if you were back from California. Twix only did what I asked."

"Twix. As in the candy bar?"

"That's right."

He rolled his eyes. "Why didn't you call me instead of sending Nancy Drew, a.k.a. *Twix*?"

Did I admit I tried and a woman answered the phone? Probably Cynthia again. How stupid could I be?

"I only had your home number," I lied. "And no one answered," I lied again. "Anyway, you're here now, and I don't understand any of this."

For the first time since coming to, his eyes softened, and he didn't look like he wanted to kill me. "It's complicated," he said. "Belinda and I finished our business early, and I was ordered to come on board because of a homicide."

"Are you alone, or did Belinda come with you?"

"She flew home. I changed flights and came straight here."

"You do get around."

"It wasn't my idea, but Puerto Rico is under U.S. jurisdiction, and the victim, Lucy Jacobs, had priors in Rueland, New York, and Boston—one investigation in which I'm still involved. I boarded the ship before sunup and escorted the body to dry land."

"Are you going to tell me why you're investigating her?"

His eyes darkened. "Are you going to tell me where you were last night?"

I tightened my lips and folded my arms across my chest. "I guess you'll be leaving now."

"Tired of me already? Or are you afraid I'm going to ask if it's true?"

"Is what true?"

"That you found her dead. Like you have a habit of doing."

"This was different. There were four hundred and ninety-nine other witnesses."

"A world of difference." There was a glimmer in his eyes, and the muscles stiffened around his jaw. I'd seen this look before, like he wanted more from me. I wasn't sure what kind of more, but I felt heat between my legs and a flush on my face.

I smacked my legs together. "I had nothing to do with her death."

"No, but I bet you think you saw or heard something that may have led to it."

Like I was an open book. I wasn't about to tell him—with his ribbing and insults—what I'd seen. Trusting Jock a mere hour ago was currently more than I could handle.

Just as I was about to tell him to kindly leave, there was a firm knock on the door. Glad for the interruption, I swung it open and saw my mother's face, fright drawn in her eyes.

"Tantig is gone!"

Chapter 7

"What do you mean, gone?" I asked. "Heaven gone, mentally gone, or disappeared gone?"

My mother caught her breath and held up Tantig's sweater as proof of her being missing. "Disappeared gone."

Tremors of panic poured in. If she'd announced this twenty-four hours ago, I'd have said Tantig was wandering the ship. But it wasn't yesterday. Yesterday, Lucy was alive and well—at least I'd thought she was alive and well.

"We've reported it to security," my mother said. "But…" She peered past me at Romero and instantly went from looking grief-stricken to looking as if she should kneel before Sir Galahad.

"I'm sorry." She eyed my silky dress, probably noticing the wrinkles, not to mention my day-old makeup and mussed hair. "I hope I wasn't interrupting anything."

"He was just leaving," I said.

"Actually, I can stay a while," Romero said. "Your sister's clearly worried."

My mother dropped Tantig's sweater and gushed, "*Sister.*"

I was toast. Any man using that term on a girl's mother was as good as in. The dreamy look on my mother's face confirmed it.

"Mom? Tantig?"

"Who?" My mother's gaze didn't leave the Knight of the Round Table's face.

Romero brushed past my breast, picked up Tantig's sweater, and handed it to my mother.

"Valentine," she said, "aren't you going to introduce me to this sweet man?"

Sweet? If I knew Romero, he had a gun strapped to his ankle and another under his sports coat at his back. The predatory look he'd given me moments ago had me feeling he'd gone without sex longer than he'd like. Sweet? My breast was on fire where he'd grazed me with his arm. Sweetness had nothing to do with that.

"This is Detective Michael Romero," I said to my mother.

I faced Romero. "And you've now met my mother, Ava Beaumont, the woman half-responsible for this." I pointed to myself.

"Perhaps *you* can find my husband's aunt," she said.

"When did you last see her?" Romero and I asked in unison. Then he gave me a look that said he was the detective here.

"This morning before she went for her walk." My mother was much calmer now, Romero's presence evidently having a positive effect on her. "It's probably another false alarm like the one the other day."

I gaped at her. "What false alarm? When?"

"Our first night here. She wandered off after supper."

I couldn't believe my ears. "Why didn't you tell me this before?"

"Because you were having such a good time meeting new people. I didn't want to worry you, too. And she turned up, uninjured, sitting in a jewelry shop with the clerk, watching one of her soaps on the clerk's computer."

My mother was right. My great-aunt did sometimes wander. Hadn't I seen her roaming the deck yesterday morning before heading into Nassau? True, she was exercising. But occasionally she got lost. Max had even thought he'd seen her ambling around last night. Thank goodness it wasn't Tantig, but it easily could've been. An unsettling feeling tugged at me, like there was something I should've recalled. I couldn't retrieve it, and I wasn't going to think the worst. It did just sound like another case of Tantig touring on her own.

"I don't know what to do." My mother wrung the sweater in her hands. "Your father's chomping at the bit, waiting to see the sights in Puerto Rico. You know your father. Not a care in the world. He said Tantig probably got tired of walking and decided to nap on a lounge chair somewhere."

My father was probably right.

"I'll talk to security." Romero rubbed my shoulder. "Nice to meet you, Mrs. Beaumont."

"Ava, please," she said with a faint smile.

He gave me an I'll-deal-with-you-later look and was gone.

I gulped down a swallow from the look, then turned to my mother. "I'll stay back and find Tantig. You go with Dad. And try not to worry. I'm sure she's fine."

She blinked at me. "If you stay behind, you'll get in trouble like you always do, cutting off someone's ear with a razor or—"

I'd never cut off anyone's ear with my razor. I may have sliced an individual's arm with one, but never an ear. "I promise I won't use my razor, okay? Give me that picture you have of Tantig."

"What for?"

"So I can show it around, see if anybody saw her. What's the name of the jewelry shop she was in?"

"Rugert's." My mother dug in her purse and handed me the photo.

I ushered her to the door when Max burst into the cabin, asking if Romero was okay.

"Oops." He almost collided with my mother. He tore off the straw hat anchored on his head. "Sorry, Mrs. B."

She smiled at Max. "It's all right. I was leaving."

We watched her walk away, head down.

"What was that all about?" Max asked.

"Tantig is missing."

"*What?*" he shrieked, backing me into the cabin, slamming the door behind him. "Where's Romero?"

"Gone."

He tapped his hat in his hand. "Romero's on board. Tantig's missing. And the breakfast buffet was unappetizing. I bet this all has to do with the murder."

"Why do you think that?"

"Woman's intuition."

"You're not a woman."

"Men can have those vibes, too. Anyway, *you're* on the ship. There *had* to be a murder...*and* a kidnapping."

"Thanks a lot. And no one said Tantig was kidnapped." I stuffed the picture in my bag.

He ignored me and put his finger to his chin. "I told you, Kashi's our man. He looks all cheerful and up-and-up, but there's malice in those eyes. And we already know he poured something poisonous into Lucy's drink. He could've killed her, and then lured your great-aunt away with one of his tacky brooches."

Oh brother. "He already gave Tantig a brooch on the shuttle bus to the ship. She didn't look too thrilled *then*. I doubt she'd be any more excited by another pin with hair sticking out. *And* no one knows if Kashi poured poison into Lucy's drink. I'd suggested it, but you yourself said I was probably wrong. Now, if you don't mind, could you tour by yourself this morning?"

"But we were going to buy some top-quality gold today. There're supposed to be a ton of jewelers not far from the dock in Old San Juan."

"Then you go. I'm still in last night's dress."

He grinned. "I can see that."

I pushed him out the door. "Maybe you'll run into Phyllis, and the two of you can spend the day together."

"Very funny. Are you *trying* to spoil my day?"

I shut the door in his face, leaned against it, and took stock of things, ugly as they seemed. I got drunk *again* in front of five hundred people, fell into a lifeboat for a shoe, and woke up naked in Jock's arms. If that wasn't bad enough, Romero was on board, looking all edible and rough around the edges. And he was here because Lucy had turned into a Popsicle, which also spelled murder. Now, Tantig was missing.

I thought this through, uncertain how much worse things could become. Four things were clear. There was a murderer loose, Jock knew something regarding Lucy's death, my anxiety level was climbing, and no one was going to stop me from finding Tantig.

I kept reassuring myself that Tantig was just poking along the deck and we were all worrying for nothing. I looked down at my gown. And if I wanted to start a search, I couldn't traipse around like Cinderella all day.

I found my phone beside my makeup bag in the bathroom, right where I'd left it. I swept my hair up into a messy bun, jumped in the shower, and was soaping up when I thought I heard a tap on the cabin door. I waited a second, but there was no further noise.

I finished showering, toweled myself dry, and did a two-minute makeup job. Then I pulled my hair out of the bun, gave it a quick brush, and gathered a few strands at the back with sparkly bobby pins.

Before I moved on, I called my sister, Holly. Shoot. Battery was almost dead. Well, this wouldn't take long. I filled her in on Tantig's disappearance, pacing the room and slipping into a blue plaid skirt.

Holly was the cool cucumber in the family, next to my father. She'd come up with a logical reason for Tantig's whereabouts.

"I suppose Mom's worried she was kidnapped while Dad's climbing to the top of some ruin."

I fastened the button on my skirt. "You don't think she could've been kidnapped?"

She chuckled. "Why would anyone want Tantig? Don't get me wrong. I love her, but she'd drive her kidnappers crazy with her 'Have a Tic Tac' comments."

"Maybe." The more logical worry was that she was missing because a murderer was killing random passengers, but I refused to go there.

"You know Tantig," she continued. "She gets disoriented and ends up in the strangest places. Sit tight. She'll show up."

"For a cop, you're pretty laidback."

"I've had lots of false alarms. You'll see. Everything will be fine. Now, what's the other thing you called about?"

"Huh?" I gave myself a shot of perfume, my mind still on Tantig.

"I know there's something else, and I bet it has to do with Romero."

Upon hearing his name, I accidentally fired Musk into my mouth. "Blech!" I rubbed my tongue. "What do you mean, Romero?"

"Six-foot-tall male. Movie-star looks. Sexy. Italian. Cop."

I slid into my shoes. "I should go. I only have ten percent left on my phone."

"This won't take long." I could see the amused expression on her face as clearly as if she were sitting in front of me. "You're calling about Belinda, aren't you?"

Terrific. Holly and Romero worked out of the same precinct. Of course she'd know his new partner. "No," I said. "But now that you brought up her name, what's she like?"

"You haven't met her?"

"No." This was one thing about Holly that drove me crazy. She never gave straight answers. Romero possessed this trait as well. Probably part of their clever police training.

She gave one of her throaty laughs. "Oh, little sister. She's everything you're not."

"Meaning?"

"Look," she said. "Belinda's on her way up. This is just

a detour in her climb to the top. I wouldn't worry about her…or who she's sleeping with."

"Thanks a lot." I'd tried to envision Romero's partner as a toothless ogre with dirty hair and a miserable personality. Thanks to Holly, I was seeing her as a Victoria's Secret model.

"If you didn't call about her, you must want information about Lucy Jacobs. I know Romero's on board the Love Boat. And he's good, but he won't always be able to save your hiney. Be careful. Wherever you go, trouble seems to follow."

"That's not true."

"Do I need to bring up your past?"

"Okay, already. My phone's about to die. What can you tell me about Lucy Jacobs?"

"Listen, narcotics investigations are confidential, not something the DEA takes lightly."

"Lucy was a hairstylist! She dealt drugs?"

"I'm only telling you what I'd learned when Romero was on Vice. Drug offenses are subject to federal prosecution, and she was under suspicion for trafficking. She had a few arrests, but nothing we could make stick."

"And Romero was working her case?"

"Yep."

"But he's on homicide now."

"And he probably thought he'd washed his hands of her when he left New York Vice four years ago. But because a past homicide in Rueland was tied to a murder in New York last year, he was pulled back on the case. If you read the paper once in a while, you'd know about the slayings. Her involvement was implied, but the charges were dropped."

Lucy involved in a murder? "You think her death was drug-related?" Maybe she was killed by a dealer. What if she was given a drug overdose? Kashi and the vial came to mind.

"I don't know. But watch your back, okay? And keep your hairspray ready to fire. There's a maniac loose."

She didn't need to tell *me*. I hung up and tried to piece together Lucy's involvement in drugs and a possible murder. Hard to believe.

What about Sabrina's role in all this? Had she worked with Lucy? Or were they simply friends? Was she also involved in these criminal activities?

And what about Kashi? Could Max be right? Was he cheerful on the outside and diabolical on the inside? He detested Lucy at the beginning of the trip. Why the sudden change after she won the contest? Because he'd wanted to lull her into a false sense of security so he could kill her? If so, why? To steal her money? Revenge?

I couldn't see Kashi as a cold-blooded murderer. It'd be too easy an answer. Plus, he was genuinely kind to Tantig on the bus. How could someone that nice be so crazy?

I decided to grab something to eat, then start my search at the jewelry store. Knowing Tantig, once she found a quiet spot to watch her soaps, she'd be there the rest of the week, especially if she could escape my mother's fussing.

I gripped my bag and tossed my phone inside. What would be left from the morning buffet? Jock and his room-service breakfast popped to mind. Then my mind shifted to what we were doing before breakfast. *Yikes*. I almost gave myself to him, wrapped up in a pretty bow. Now Romero was here, pulling me in like a moth to a flame.

I clapped my hand to my chest to stop the thundering inside. I had to calm down. I had more important things to think about.

I twisted the doorknob, walked out into the hallway, and *Crunch*!

What? I glanced down at the Tic Tacs container I'd speared with my right heel. Tic Tacs like the ones Tantig always carried. I looked up and down the hall. Nobody. Had she been here, looking for me? Was that who'd knocked on the door when I was in the shower?

I lifted my heel and unpierced the container when my

phone chimed in my bag. Damn thing. Forgot to leave it behind to charge.

It was my mother calling, asking if I'd found Tantig.

I turned toward my cabin and dropped the Tic Tacs in my bag, deciding against telling her about them just yet. "I'm leaving the cabin now. I'll let you know when I find her."

I stepped back inside the doorway to charge my phone when a large hand came from behind and smothered me while the other hand wrapped tightly around my waist. Fear blindsided me, stifling all my senses. The only thing I could do was stomp down on my captor's foot. I stabbed my heel on top of his shoe with little impact. A second later, I was dragged back into my cabin, kicking and wriggling, the door banging behind us.

"*Shh!*" came a soft whisper in my ear just as my phone chimed again.

"Mmmfmm," I muttered hysterically, the phone slipping from my grasp to the floor.

"I'm going to remove my hand. Promise you won't scream."

Deaf to everything but my pulse pounding in my ears, I nodded up and down. I'd do anything to get free so I could yell and holler at the top of my lungs. I slid a shaky hand in my bag and rooted around for something that might help me. I felt a smooth bottle that narrowed at the top. Nail polish remover! I clenched it with my fingers and one-handedly flipped open the lid. My assailant released me, and I turned around, screaming, squirting acetone in his face.

"*Aaaaah!*" he hollered above my shrieks.

"Oh, no!" I stopped dead in my tracks. "Jock!" I ran to the bathroom for water while he clawed at his eyes.

"Are you crazy?" he shouted.

"I thought you were abducting me!" I dabbed his eyes with a drenched cloth.

He pushed me aside with one arm and dove into the bathroom for the shower hose.

I picked up my phone, which had stopped ringing, and placed it on the little table in our cabin. Then I stood in the middle of the room, watching Jock like a scared child who'd just set her house on fire. He bent over the drain with tense shoulders and aimed the nozzle at his face. Water poured down his neck as he worked furiously bathing his burning eyes.

A few minutes later, with a towel draped over his massive shoulders, he stood in front of me, hands on hips, chest heaving. In my closet-sized cabin, Jock seemed tremendously imposing. There wasn't anywhere else to look but up into his patchy red eyes that were darkening by the minute.

"I was trying to prove a point about being careful," he finally said.

"What? You scared me half to death to prove a point?"

He exhaled. "With a killer on the loose, you can't stand in your open doorway where anyone could drag you back inside your cabin. There's already been one murder. Now Tantig's missing."

I narrowed my eyes. "How did you know Tantig was missing? I only found out about an hour ago." Then I realized, not much got by Jock. When the world comes to an end, he'll know a day before everyone else.

"I was talking to security when your mother rushed in with the news. After some discussion, it seems your great-aunt has taken off before without your mother's knowledge, once already on the ship. It's likely she's roaming around on her own again." He gave me a stern glare. "I don't want you imagining all kinds of horrible scenarios." He paused at that. "I know. Dumb idea."

I cut him a surly look. "You could've told me this instead of suffocating me."

"I'll remember that next time. Just so you know, Rugert's and all the other stores have been notified in case your great-aunt decides to look for more places to watch her soaps. As of right now, she hasn't visited any of them. But we'll keep an eye open."

I was touched.

I didn't know why, but I had a sudden vision of Tantig at one of my piano recitals when I was twelve. I looked up during my performance of Mozart's "Sonata in C Major" and saw Tantig slouched in the front row beside my parents, fast asleep. After the recital, when I came off the stage, she woke up, looked at the stranger next to her, and said in a dry tone, "That was my grrrreat niece."

The man had replied, "She's very gifted."

Tantig had given him her chin-up and slow blink. Her way of saying *yes*, or *thank you*, or about a dozen other terms she couldn't be bothered to utter.

Tears formed in my eyes, thinking back to all the times Tantig had been there. My piano concerts, ballet recitals, graduations, even at the little funeral I'd had for my beloved cat Pusso. Tantig was a big part of my family, and now she was missing.

"I—" I blinked back the tears when my phone rang for a third time.

Jock reached for the phone and handed it to me.

"Am I ever glad I caught you!" Twix said. "You're not going to believe what I unearthed about Romero. I drove over to his house, like you asked, and—"

I was trying to pay attention because I wanted to hear Twix's version of what happened. But Jock's serious stare was intimidating me. What was he doing here anyway? Other than proving a point.

"—so by the time I noticed the sports car in the driveway, I was halfway up the kitchen window, and this gorgeous blond tapped me on the shoulder, asking if she could help me."

I coughed and almost choked on my spit, worried that Jock could hear Twix's every word.

"You okay?" Twix asked. "What's wrong? You haven't said a thing."

"Sounds wonderful," I mumbled into the phone, turning a shoulder away from Jock's prying eyes.

"*What?*" Twix was having a fit. "*Wonderful!* Did you

hear a word I said? You were right to worry. The things she said about her and Romero? Whew. No doubt, that woman was his lover—"

Buzzzzz. The battery died before I learned anything else.

I let out a breath and collapsed on a chair. I had enough going on without wondering why Twix was mistaken about the blond's identity. The woman was Cynthia, Romero's sister. He'd told me that himself. Why would he lie? I thought back again to the last few times I'd seen him and how he'd been preoccupied, almost distant. I wanted to believe it was the case he'd been working. But what if it was personal? What if there *was* another woman in his life, and *she* was the woman at his house? Was he lying to me to save face? Was he going to come clean after the cruise?

My stomach was rumbling, I was on the verge of passing out from hunger, and my mind was racing with a dozen other concerns. What did I care about Romero? I sniffed, all indignant. He could have a *hundred* lovers for all I cared.

I rammed the charger into the phone and heard Jock clear his throat. I got to my feet and whipped around fiercely, my anger getting the best of me. "What are you doing here anyway? Other than scaring me to death."

His eyebrows shot up in surprise.

"Yeah, you heard me! I woke up *in your bed* with a major hangover, Tantig is missing, Romero's joined the Love Boat, and I haven't had as much as a bowl of cereal. Why are you here?"

He pulled my earrings from last night out of his jeans pocket and dangled them in front of my nose. "You forgot these."

There was a sharp rap at the door, interrupting us for the second time this morning. I grabbed the earrings and opened the door.

Romero's frame filled the doorway. He looked from me, to the earrings in my hand, to Jock, and he didn't look happy. Romero and Jock in the same room produced extreme and tangible electricity. But as a hardened cop, Romero displayed immense restraint.

He assessed Jock's red eyes, gave him a nod, and slid his hands into his pockets. Meanwhile, I felt like we were at the OK Corral, and at any moment there was going to be a gunfight. What's more, I couldn't have cared less. I wasn't too thrilled with Jock at the moment, and as far as Romero was concerned, he was a lying cheat. He had some nerve coming back here like he owned the place.

I swallowed hard, waiting for someone to make the first move.

Romero glanced one last time at the earrings, probably wondering what he'd walked in on. A muscle tightened in his jaw, and he straightened as if deciding to move on. Wise of him.

"I spoke to ship security." His gaze fastened on me. "There's no sign of your great-aunt anywhere. The Coast Guard's been notified, and the police in San Juan will put out a missing persons report after forty-eight hours."

"Forty-eight hours!" I snapped, flinging the earrings on the table. "She could be in grave danger." I ripped open my bag, snatched the Tic Tacs, and planted them in Romero's palm. "These were outside my cabin door when I got out of the shower earlier."

Romero held up the mints and looked from me over to Jock. "A broken container of mints?" I could've sworn I saw grins tug at their faces.

"They're not just mints." I gritted my teeth. "They're Tic Tacs. Tantig's Tic Tacs."

"Aren't you jumping to conclusions?"

"No!" I gave him a dirty glare. "Tantig has carried Tic Tacs on her for…forever. She's always handing them out. Someone could've kidnapped her and dropped them at my door as a threat."

"A threat about what?"

"I don't know! *You're* the detective here."

He rubbed his neck, which he often did around me,

like he was aggravated. Too bad for him. It wasn't *his* great-aunt who was missing.

"Was there a note?"

"No."

"Phone call?"

"No."

"Okay, I'll check it out." He looked at Jock, and it was as if I'd become invisible. "Tell me what you know," Romero asked him.

Jock widened his stance. "The captain suspects one of his crew is involved in a drug run. He's maxed out his security officers and has asked me to investigate."

"Do you think there's a tie-in with the murder?"

"Could be. I'm still exploring leads."

Exploring leads? Tie-in with the murder? "Hold on a second." I tilted my head up at Romero. "Why are you asking Jock questions? He's not Batman. He's not even Bruce Wayne." Although I was beginning to wonder. "He's a hairstylist and an ex-navy firefighter."

"Also, a master-at-arms."

"A what?" I gaped from Romero to Jock.

Jock gave me a part-amused, part-questioning grin.

"You heard me," Romero said. "I imagine that's why the captain's asked him to investigate."

"Is *that* what you imagine!" I was full steam ahead, not sure who I was angrier with. Now I understood Jock's encounters with the captain. Seemed everyone but me knew about his gripping past.

I fixed my gaze on Jock. "Anything else you'd like to tell me about your background? Like maybe at one time you were a lion tamer? Or in the CIA? Or maybe you're one of those guys who removed land mines."

Jock folded his arms and winked. "Never done that." I thought he was referring to my last comment. But how could I be sure of anything where these two were concerned!

"I have to go," Romero said. "I'd love to see how this plays out, but I'm expected in New York tonight with the body." He tipped his chin down at me. "Let me know when you locate Tantig. In the meantime, I'm sure Jock will help you." He gave a last glance at Jock's irritated eyes, then sniffed the air. "My first guess was perfume. Then I thought hairspray, but it doesn't smell like either."

"Try nail polish remover." Jock rubbed a fist in his eye.

Romero gave me a stern look. "Why doesn't that surprise me?"

I folded my arms across my chest in a huff. Why the assumption I was the reason for Jock's red eyes? He could've gotten soap in his eyes! Chlorine! Sunscreen! And about a dozen other things.

Romero flicked my chin with his finger, settling his piercing blue gaze on me. Once again, my heart melted at his Mediterranean coloring and thick black lashes. How was having blue eyes this intense even possible? But I was ticked off. I wasn't going to be won over by good looks.

"You've got my cell number," he said. "Probably better using it than calling Nancy Drew to hunt me down."

"Don't expect me to call anytime soon," I said, nose high, frustrated at so many things, I couldn't count.

He slammed the door behind him, and I stuck out my tongue like a teenager who'd been dumped by a double-crossing boyfriend. And what was up with him and Jock? Last time he saw Jock, there were silent daggers being thrown. Now, he was unconcerned. *I'm sure Jock will help you?* What kind of love interest offered a woman on a silver platter to another man? Especially one who looked like a Greek god? Obviously, Romero didn't care. This was his way of cutting ties. I tapped my finger on my bag, hurt and anger slicing me inside.

"You okay?" Jock asked.

I spun around. "That's what this is all about. You think someone's smuggling drugs."

"That's the short of it."

"Anyone you have in mind?"

"I've got my eye on a couple of people."

"Care to share?"

He walked to the door and turned around. "Nope."

"May I ask why not?"

"Because I don't want you involved." He wrapped his hand around the doorknob.

"With Tantig missing, I'd say I'm already involved."

"You're overreacting. People get lost wandering the ship all the time. This isn't unusual."

And with that he was gone.

Chapter 8

The dining room was empty of passengers. Everyone had eaten and was already well into their day. Waiters were gathering plates and removing serving bowls from the buffet stations. I showed Tantig's photo to a couple of the cruise staff, taking a chance someone had seen her. Nobody had.

This didn't discourage me. Despite my outburst at Romero, I was holding onto the notion that Tantig's disappearance was a false alarm and that she was simply wandering around the ship.

Needing something to eat before I looked for her, I asked a nearby waiter if I could grab a few things off the buffet before it was all removed.

"Sure, senorita," he said. "Help yourself."

"*Gracias.*" Jock wasn't the only one who could reel off Spanish.

First, I poured a glass of tomato juice for my hangover and downed it. Then I grabbed some fresh fruit salad, a hard-boiled egg, and a croissant. I thought twice about the calories in the croissant, put it back, and snatched a seven-grain piece of bread. Damn Jock and his *buffets are killers*!

The room was quiet except for the clatter of cutlery and dishes being piled into heaps. Then the galley doors swung open, and a couple of local police walked out of the kitchen and exited the dining hall.

The rest of the ship seemed abuzz with the news of Lucy's death. Passengers murmured in the halls, local officials questioned guests, and everyone seemed on guard.

I didn't want to get too comfortable, so I ate standing, meandering toward the galley. One of the waiters gave me a friendly nod, then banged his hamper on wheels filled with soiled tablecloths out through the double doors. The breakfast rush was over. He was probably wishing I'd vamoose so he could finish his job.

I polished off my fruit salad and refocused on Tantig. I'd seen her taste-testing a piece of baklava from the dessert table last night after Lucy's death. She'd rolled her eyes and put the hunk back down. I knew what she was thinking. Dry.

Maybe she found her way into the galley this morning to show them how to saturate the dessert with a syrupy sauce like the Armenians soaked its counterpart, paklava. I wouldn't have put it past her. I glimpsed at the galley doors. Talking to the chef might be a good place to start.

I peeked through the window on the door and saw a dozen or so people in white, scurrying around the steamy, stainless-steel area, banging pots, stirring sauces, and chopping vegetables. An industrial-sized production line of sorts. *Here goes nothing.* I pushed through the doors with a smile on my face, taking in the aroma of cinnamon and warm custard. Everyone stopped what they were doing and looked up.

"Excuse me," I said in my sweetest voice, realizing I'd stepped on sacred ground. "May I please talk to the chef?"

"Roy!" one of the cooks called, wiping his chin on his shoulder while kneading dough. "Someone else here to see you."

Roy? I expected something more exotic, like Chef François. But okay. Chef Roy.

He came out of the walk-in fridge, tall white hat on his head, frazzled look on his face, mustache twitching.

"Where are my chives? I can't do anything without my chives!"

A petite woman with a net over her head tramped past Roy, dove into the walk-in fridge, and a second later shoved a large bag in his hand.

He smacked the bag on a chopping block, then inspected me teetering at the kitchen door. "Another cop?" He scowled.

"No," I said. "I was at dinner last night and was hoping I could ask you a few questions."

"What is this? *Murder, She Wrote?*"

"It has to do with my great-aunt."

"What's she got to do with it?"

"She's missing." I started to tremble.

Roy must've noticed the look on my face because he shouted orders to his sous chef, then took me by the arm and whisked me out into the dining room.

"Talk." He pulled out a chair for me.

"My great-aunt—Tantig—is gone." I dropped on the chair. "She may just be lost, but I'm concerned, especially after last night's murder."

"The frozen spectacle?"

"Yes." I showed him Tantig's picture.

He sat in a chair across the table from me and studied the photo. "Look, who are you?"

"My name is Valentine Beaumont. I came on board for the beauty cruise and—"

"Wait a minute. Did you say Valentine? You run a salon in Rueland, Massachusetts?"

"Yes?" Oh boy. Here we go.

"My godmother lives in Woburn. Comes into your salon or did until one of your clients was strangled. You sure have a reputation."

So I've heard.

"But I like you, kid. Anyone crazy enough to go after a murderer with a perm rod has got to have chutzpah. How can I help you?" He handed me back the photo.

"Have you seen my great-aunt?"

He shook his head. "My days are spent in that galley right behind you. I come out for air occasionally, or when I need to explain to my staff how I want things set up in the dining room. But I rarely see passengers. Except, of course, when there's a big unveiling, like last night."

Last night had changed the course of the cruise. A little person had been frozen inside a statue and put on public display. Not only that, but there was a drug smuggling on board. Now, Tantig was missing. I wasn't sure if any of this was tied together. And I wasn't going to worry about what Jock *or* Romero had to say on the subject. Just because I wasn't a master-at-arms or a macho detective didn't mean I didn't know anything. I knew plenty—even if I didn't read the newspaper religiously. The more questions I asked, the more I might find out about what could've led to Tantig's disappearance.

"Then what *did* you see? How did Lucy end up frozen in an Aphrodite ice sculpture?"

"Damned if I know," Roy said. "We poured water in the mold Friday night after the midnight buffet, flipped on the switch, and forgot about it."

I recalled the men working in the ice-sculpting room. "I thought ice sculptures were carved by hand."

He rolled up his sleeves. "You know how many ice sculptures we display on the ship? About twenty a day. It's much easier to use molds than to carve each form. The smaller ones, yes, are hand-done."

"Did you check on Aphrodite at any time?" I asked.

"Didn't need to. It takes up to forty hours to set—almost two days for the bigger molds like Aphrodite, and we place the molds in an ice machine that freezes the water slowly." He frowned, tapping his chin. "Hold on! I did check it Saturday morning. I ordered Aphrodite for our theme night, and as it was a new mold, I wanted to make sure the casings were snug. Everything looked fine that morning. Then I didn't see it until the unveiling. By then, Lucy was frozen stiff."

Which meant Lucy had to have been dumped in the mold sometime after Friday's midnight buffet when the water started to freeze, and before Sunday's unveiling when it was totally frozen. And since Lucy was still alive Saturday night when I left her cabin, her murder and entry into a partially frozen mold must've taken place soon after. I thought about this some more. "Maybe one of your assistants saw something."

He shrugged. "Nope. And since the mold was pulled out from under the sheet seconds before leaving the galley, *we* didn't even see the body inside the statue until the unveiling."

The waiter who'd left with the soiled tablecloths came through the swinging doors, whistling to himself.

"What about the dining staff?" I asked.

"If anyone had seen something strange, they would've reported it. And if I suspected criminal behavior in any of my staff, that'd be the end of them." He chuckled, smiling in the direction of the whistling waiter. "Some are a bit scraggly, like Devon over there, but as long as they keep their hair in a ponytail or under a net, I'm happy."

I looked over at Devon, a fair-haired guy, about five-ten, now polishing silverware. "Is there a high turnover with staff?"

"Sure. But some have been here forever." He grinned. "Devon's one of the funnier ones, always with a joke to crack."

I nodded and looked back at the galley. "Could someone have broken into the kitchen during the night?"

"The galley's not under lock and key, mostly because there's usually someone here preparing one meal or cleaning up from another. You might have a quiet hour around three a.m., but after that, we start winding up for the next day."

"Then it's possible someone could've brought Lucy here in the wee hours of the night when everything was quiet and placed her in the mold."

"Yes, it's possible. Like I said, it takes up to forty hours to freeze the water solid. I'm sure a little person would've even put up a fight from being stuffed inside. And there were no signs of a struggle in my kitchen." He shook his head sadly. "No. If Lucy Jacobs was tossed in the mold, she was already dead." He pushed his chair away from the table. "Look, I just want this cleared up. I've never been so embarrassed. This is a terrible blow to Chef Roy's spotless reputation."

He stood and gazed down at me. "Sorry about your great-aunt, kid." He patted my shoulder. "If I hear anything, I'll let you know." He disappeared back into the kitchen.

I sat there for another minute, trying to understand things. If Chef Roy didn't see anything suspicious, and the staff was as honest as he professed, then how did Lucy end up in the mold? The answer had to be here somewhere, and once I found Tantig, I'd make it my goal to find out.

I questioned a few more people, checked Rugert's and several other stores for myself, and after coming up empty, I decided to go on land after all. Maybe Tantig had gotten off the ship and was rambling around the dock.

I showed her picture to security at the gangway before I disembarked, and they assured me she'd already gone ashore for the day. I couldn't believe what I was hearing. "Are you certain?"

"Absolutely," one of the guards said. "Scanned her ID and everything. I think she was headed for the straw market."

Relief flooded me at such a pace I almost felt giddy. It *was* a false alarm. Tantig was fine. She just went touring on her own. That's all. I'd track her down at the straw market and bring her back to the ship.

I walked away, reaching in my bag for my cell phone to call my mother. I dug around but couldn't find the thing. Where the heck was it? I retraced my steps and—right. Died when I was talking to Twix earlier this morning. I groaned. It was charging. Yay, me, for remembering that much. I snapped my bag shut. What was I doing trying to call my mother anyway? She didn't own a cell phone. "I'm always home if you need me," she'd say. Great. Weren't we a pair! I'd just have to surprise her when I found Tantig. Maybe I'd even run into her here if she accompanied my father off the ship.

I relaxed a little, keeping my eyes peeled for my family while I wove among hot, sweaty tourists strolling under colorful tents and storefront awnings. Forgetting to bring something for my head, I bought a huge Babajaan straw hat at one of the stands. Then I ran into Max.

"You're here!" He bounced by my side, my faithful Labrador, happy to be on dry land, panting at the prospect of shopping for 22 karat-gold jewelry. "Where should we go first? The gold shop or the diamond shop?"

After losing the contest money for the hospital kids, I wasn't in the mood to spend much.

"You go ahead." I wiped my sweaty brow. "Security saw Tantig leave the ship this morning. She's probably here somewhere. I'm going to show her picture around."

Max disappeared in the crowd, and I talked to tourists and locals. Nobody had seen an elderly lady wandering aimlessly. I bought a bottled water and roamed to an alley corner between stalls to cool off. Feeling invisible among so many people, I chugged my water and watched vacationers of every shape and size haggle with the locals.

I was playing with a cloth marionette in front of a store when I spotted Molly and Polly inside the store, dressed for the beach as usual. Then something caught my attention. A man came out from behind the counter, led the girls into a backroom, and began talking to them.

I darted inside the store and ducked behind a beaded curtain separating clothing racks. I peeked through the beads at the backroom, shadowing my face with the brim of my hat.

Molly and Polly didn't look alarmed or scared. In fact, it all looked rather friendly, but also secretive. Polly looked over her shoulder a couple of times, obviously making sure they weren't being overheard.

The man handed them a small baggie holding something white and powdery. It was hard to see past Polly, but she angled enough that I saw her slide her long pinky fingernail, palm up, in the powder and hold it under her nose. Then she smiled from ear to ear and nodded at Molly. Molly dug into her canvas bag and handed the man money. He counted the bills, folded one back up, and stuffed it down Molly's bikini top. What was that? A refund?

I held still, making sure I didn't crinkle my water bottle. What was I to do with this new development? I didn't want to get anyone in trouble, but I wasn't comfortable hanging around, witnessing a drug deal either. At least, it smelled like a drug deal—more specifically—cocaine. And if it was, was it tied to the drug smuggling Jock had mentioned? And possibly Lucy's murder?

I crept out of the store and ran like the devil. I looked over my shoulder to make sure no one was following me and saw Molly and Polly zip inside a florist shop. What were they up to? I took a corner and slammed into Mr. Jaworski, knocking his straw fedora off his head.

"Valentine Beaumont!" He picked up his hat, shaking his head disgustedly. "What's the rush? You're going to break your neck one day in those damn heels." He slanted his hat on top of his head.

"I'm looking for my great-aunt." I let out a heavy breath and peeked around the corner. No Molly or Polly.

I stared down at Mr. Jaworski and took out Tantig's picture to refresh his memory. "Have you seen her?"

He barely glanced at the photo. "Can't say as I have."

I slid the photo back in my bag and told him I was sorry about Lucy. "I thought you might have already gone home."

"Gone home? What for?"

"Because of Lucy's, uh, murder?"

He shrugged. "This is my vacation, too. Do you know how long it's been since I've had a real vacation? 1972."

I couldn't close my gaping mouth. Was this my landlord who came on the cruise to be with his *little Lucy*? His *lovely niece*? *A real joker*? For a second, I wondered if he could've been responsible for Lucy's murder, but I dismissed the idea as ridiculous. Mr. Jaworski was cheap, self-absorbed, and insensitive, but he wasn't a killer. "So, you're not leaving."

"Not on your life. I just might do a little investigating myself. If the cruise line's responsible for Lucy's death, there could be a lawsuit here."

Bingo. The truth always surfaced.

"I talked to my brother early this morning," he continued. "He agreed I should finish the cruise. They're waiting for the results of the autopsy. The funeral won't be until next week at the earliest."

I bet Romero would know more before then.

"In the meantime, I'm going to live it up. Do you know I haven't had a vacation like this since 1972?"

"Yes, you mentioned that."

"And it wasn't nearly this fabulous, well, except for Lucy dying. You sure didn't get an all-you-can-eat buffet or those tasty mai tais." He shook his head. "But you gotta tell them about the maraschino cherries."

I never had a migraine before, but this feeling of pins being stuck in my eye made me feel I was getting close.

"And I'm not too happy about the tours. You know they want you to pay extra for those damn things? When I came on this cruise, I was told it was an all-inclusive. No extra fees. Didn't I tell you that? I said I was on an all-inclusive cruise with my niece." He grunted. "*Another* problem. And if my brother wasn't such an egghead, he wouldn't have spoiled her rotten when she was growing up. Where did it get him? Kid was always in trouble. Lying. Cheating. Stealing."

This was really none of my business. I only wanted to find Tantig and get back to the ship.

He squinted up at me. "You're probably wondering what I'm talking about."

"Me? No. I'm just looking for my great-aunt."

He wagged a finger in my face. "Yes, you are. You're wondering why Samuel H. Jaworski would say something so harsh about his niece. Hmm?"

In the beauty industry, I'd learned to let people talk. My opinion was rarely asked, and for that I was grateful. One Phyllis in the salon was enough. "Okay. Maybe I'm wondering a little."

He dragged me over to a bench. "Lucy was like that blasted kid in the story of the prodigal son. You know that story?"

"Yes." We sat, and I put my water bottle and bag at my side.

"Kids today don't know their Bible. Out stealing hubcaps and spraying graffiti on bridges." He sucked on his teeth, shaking his head. "It's the parable about a man with two sons, one a hard worker, the other dissatisfied with his lot in life."

"Yes, I know it."

"And the dissatisfied son asks for his inheritance, and then squanders it."

"Yes, I remember the story."

"Lucy was like the no-good brat in that story. She blamed my brother for everything from her personal problems to money problems, and she caused him endless grief. She finally moved to New York—thank the Lord— but demanded her parents give her her inheritance now." He pursed his lips. "Can you imagine? He should've tanned her hide when he had the chance."

I recalled Holly's news about Lucy's involvement in drugs. Was it possible Lucy was financially hard up? As pathetic as it was, I almost felt sorry for her and how she'd led her life. "So, what happened?"

"My brother isn't a total loser. He works hard and wasn't about to watch his money vanish. He made a deal with Lucy. She wanted to take the cruise so she could win the contest and turn her life around. He agreed to give her half the money on one condition. She had to stay close to me, let me keep my eye on her. No Samuel H. Jaworski. No money."

His brother probably figured if his daughter survived one week with her uncle, she deserved an inheritance.

He blinked sadly. "Things just didn't turn out for anyone."

I had a feeling somewhere deep down in Mr. Jaworski's soul, guilt was gnawing away at him. Maybe if he'd stayed closer to Lucy, she'd still be alive. I patted his shoulder, said I was sorry again for his loss, and gathered my things.

I was still no further ahead at guessing who killed Lucy or why. While I had my doubts about Mr. Jaworski, my biggest suspect was still Kashi. I wanted to rule him out because he seemed harmless, but what did I know? Looks could be deceiving. Of course, if he'd poisoned Lucy, he wouldn't likely be waving a flag.

Added to the mystery was Molly and Polly's secret exchange. If this was drug-related and had something to do with Lucy's death, I was yet to find out. And once I located Tantig, that was exactly what I intended to do.

After hours of searching the island for Tantig, and two people telling me they saw her with another couple heading back to the ship, I hurried to the dock, convinced she was safely on board with my parents. My mother obviously found her and was probably at this very moment ushering her into the cabin, gently scolding her for leaving the ship by herself.

First thing I planned to do was head to my parents' cabin. Make sure everyone was okay. I stepped onto the deck when Molly and Polly came up from behind, slipping their arms through mine.

"We were just talking about you," Molly said, an orange flower tucked behind her ear.

"You were?" I looked from her to Polly who had a

yellow flower tucked in her cleavage. Flowers from the florist shop they'd entered earlier?

"Yes." Polly glanced over her shoulder like she didn't want to be overheard. "We saw you at the market this morning. Tried to catch up to you, but you disappeared."

I kept my expression neutral, but inside I was gasping. "There was so much to see. Felt like I was running all morning." No lie there.

"I know what you mean. Hardly seems fair to be enjoying ourselves when Lucy is no longer with us." She shuddered. "And what a way to go. I'd hate to be frozen in a block of ice, even if it was a beautiful statue of Aphrodite. But she was small. Maybe for a little person it wasn't so bad."

I couldn't believe we were having this conversation. As they listed all the terrible ways to pass on—not once mentioning drug overdose—I listened with half an ear. What I really wondered was how Lucy truly died. Chef Roy said she had to have been dead when she went into the mold. If this were true, were the two blonds messing with me? Pretending they didn't know Lucy had been murdered before she'd been frozen?

I rewound things to last night. In my drunken state, I didn't see Molly and Polly at dinner. Was that planned? If they'd killed Lucy, did they think their absence from the dining room would guarantee they wouldn't be questioned or be suspects? Then again, what would their motive be for murder? As far as I could see, the only thing Lucy did to annoy them was win the contest. Not something a reasonably sane person would kill over. Unless this was all tied to drugs.

People were hustling past us, heading toward the high-in-the-air obstacle course. If I wanted to question Molly and Polly about Lucy, it'd have to be in private. I didn't want to put off checking in on Tantig and my mother, but I was certain Tantig would be resting by now. I looked at their beach garb, and an idea struck me.

"Want to join me in the steam room? I was just heading there."

Molly stared down at my plaid skirt and high heels. "You're not even in a bathing suit."

Polly gave Molly a flippant wave and tightened her grip on my arm. "No need, Molly. Where we're going, she won't need one."

Molly pulled out a pack of spearmint-flavored gum on our way to the steam room. "Boy, am I dry. Want one?" She held out the pack toward me. "I usually carry Tic Tacs, but I can't find them anywhere."

Tic Tacs? I coughed and almost swallowed my molars.

Molly whacked me good and hard on the back. "You going to live?"

I gulped back a breath. "Yeah, thanks." I took a piece of gum and chewed the life out of it, telling myself lots of people carried Tic Tacs. Probably five percent of the people on this ship carried Tic Tacs. With a ship this size, that was a lot of people.

We arrived at the steam room, not a soul in sight. It was as if everyone was having a siesta or up on deck climbing the high ropes. All the better. Relaxing harp music played in the background, and a stack of white towels sat on the counter along with a sign asking guests to drop dirty towels in the wooden box next to the door.

We stripped in the dressing rooms around the corner. By the time I tiptoed into the ten-by-ten steam room, Molly and Polly already had their heads back in relaxation mode.

I hated these suffocating soundproof steam boxes. Sweat bubbled on my lip, and I'd only just stepped inside. If it wasn't something I thought they'd enjoy, I wouldn't have suggested it in the first place. Better make this quick.

I clicked the narrow door on the magnetic catch behind me. My towel was draped tightly around my body, my bag wrapped inside another towel by my side. Silly to bring a purse into a steam room, but the truth was, I didn't trust these two. And my bag of tools gave me a sense of security.

I settled on the tile bench across from Molly and Polly, chewing my gum, pretending to be as relaxed as them. I let out a heavy sigh. Polly cracked an eye open at me, blinking through the fog, and I thought this was my chance to see what they really knew about Lucy's death.

"This is the first time I've tried the steam room." I leaned my head back against the wall. "Lucy had suggested using it the first day we boarded the ship." That was a fib, but I needed to say something to steer the conversation back to the murder. "Guess she enjoyed them."

"Could be," Polly said. "She was full of surprises."

I nodded. "Speaking of surprises, it's like she disappeared after the contest Saturday." Another fib since I was with her in her cabin for the post-contest party. "Did you see her Saturday night or yesterday morning when we were in port in Nassau?"

"Can't recall seeing her around." Molly shrugged. "But it's a huge ship. Hard remembering who you've bumped into."

"True. What about before the contest? Did you see anything that looked out of the ordinary? Maybe Lucy was involved in an argument, or someone was threatening her?"

"Ha!" Polly barked. "Lucy was always arguing with someone. If it wasn't a waiter, it was a passenger, or a steward, or anybody with two legs."

She had a point.

Molly scooted onto the bench next to me. "What did you buy at the market today?"

I wasn't sure why the sudden change in conversation, but I decided to make nice. "Not much. A few souvenirs. My hat. How about you?"

They gave each other a quick glance. "Same thing. Shopping...for souvenirs."

Polly slid on the other side of me. "We California girls

like to sniff out rare souvenirs whenever we can." She ran a bead of sweat off my neck. "Know what I mean?"

I gulped down my gum, sensing the tables had just turned. Why were they dropping hints regarding their drug activity? Were they expecting me to spill the beans about what I'd seen earlier? I was good at playing dumb. I could pretend I didn't see them making a drug deal. I'd even pretend I was the Queen of Sheba if it'd get them to back off. A steady stream of water trickled down my spine, and I wriggled my shoulders in discomfort. "Sure."

"Good!" Polly said.

Molly jumped to her feet. "Time's up for us. It's still early, and we've got to see more of San Juan before we head out to sea!"

They pranced out of the steam room, securing the door behind them.

I closed my eyes, glad for the peace, though still unclear whether they were involved in Lucy's murder. If Lucy had been under suspicion for trafficking and these two were making their own deal in San Juan, could there have been a connection in all this to Lucy's death? Suppose the beach babes also did some dirty dealings in Nassau and arranged for a hitman to come on board to kill Lucy. Then suppose the killer arranged to have Lucy dumped in the mold and got off the ship once we docked in San Juan. Or suppose he disembarked before we even left Nassau. It was a lot of hypothesizing, and I had no idea if there was merit to any of this.

I'd give them a minute to dress, then I'd quickly throw on my clothes and see if they were going ashore again. Shoot! I opened my eyes. Tantig! I couldn't sit around here or follow Molly and Polly back to San Juan until I knew Tantig was fine.

Thick steam clouded the room, and it was getting harder to breathe. I squinted through the dense fog at the control panel on the wall but couldn't make out numbers. I darted over and found the heat cranked up to one hundred and forty. Probably Molly and Polly playing a joke on me, turning up the control outside. The joke was on them. I wasn't staying here a moment longer.

I grabbed my bag and sprang for the door and fresh air, but the door wouldn't budge. I yanked on the handle. Nothing. I stepped on my tiptoes, rubbed the safety glass, and peeked out. Nobody there.

Suffocating temperatures made me panicky, and my pulse surged. I wasn't sure how much longer I could take the steam. Sweaty and shaking all over, I reached for the dial and accidentally loosened the hard-plastic cover. The cover broke in two, jammed the dial in place, and sliced my palm. Blood oozed out of the gash while the intensity of the steam snowballed around me.

I nabbed the towel that had covered my bag and wrapped it around my hand, wincing from the pain of the stinging cut. I was now beyond panicky. The walls were getting smaller around me, and my head was throbbing from the heat.

"Help!" I pounded on the door with my good hand. "Anyone out there?"

Okay. Calm down. Nobody's going to hear you. You've got to help yourself.

Yeah? I couldn't get myself out of a locked laundry room at work. How was I going to manage it in a sauna or steam room—or whatever the hell this was—on board a ship with no one around? Hot tears spilled down my cheeks. When I'd been trapped in the laundry room a few months ago, Jock had been by my side. Where was he when I needed him? Suddenly, I didn't buy Molly's story about the lost Tic Tacs. Worse, I began thinking about Tantig and where she might be.

I recalled the tapping sound I'd heard this morning when I was in the shower. Maybe Molly and Polly had taken Tantig, locked her up, stolen her mints, and dropped them on my doorstep to taunt me. But why? Did Tantig stumble upon the two of them in Nassau the other day? See something she shouldn't have? Perhaps more drug dealings such as I'd witnessed today?

None of this made sense because several people saw Tantig today head back to the ship with another couple. Another couple! Oh, no! What if that couple wasn't my parents? What if it wasn't even Tantig?

I was getting worked up. I could barely focus. Through the blur of tears, I looked down at my bag. *Your phone, stupid.* Message Max, or Jock, or someone. I dumped my bag on the floor. Where was my phone? Darn it all. No phone. Right. Dead battery.

I delved through my heap of supplies. Perm rods, scissors, combs, gel. Blow dryer. *Yes.* I clutched the butt of the dryer and lunged at the tiny window. *Bang.* Nothing. *Bang. Bang.* Zilch. Damn safety glass. I flung more tools and bottles around. It was no use. I had nothing. Who was I kidding? I was a dumb beautician with good skin who was going to die in a boiling sauna.

Fighting dizziness, I unwrapped the towel from my body, wiped the sweat and tears off my face, and stuffed the towel in one of the steam vents. So I was naked. It was a hundred and forty degrees, and I was alone. Now wasn't the time for fashion or modesty.

I swiped my hair off my back, twisted it in a bun, and went to secure it with the bobby pins I'd fastened earlier. Bobby pins! I ripped one out of my hair and wheedled it around the magnetic latch. It always worked on the bathroom door at home when Yitts accidentally locked herself inside. I jiggled and rattled the door, whipping my wet hair out of my face.

"Oh, come on! How hard can it be?" The more frantic I grew, the more bent out of shape the bobby pin became. My towel unraveled from my hand, and blood smeared everywhere. I gave a loud *err* and banged my fist on the door.

"I'm screwed!" I slid down to the floor, light-headed and exhausted. "Wait! A screw!" That's it! I plunged through my mess of products, glanced up at the door and back down again. It wasn't an especially thick door, nor was it wide. If I loosened the screws on the hinges, I might get out of here.

"Aha!" I gripped my nail clippers and unwound the sturdy arm. I started with the bottom hinge, working it loose. The clippers slipped out of the socket time and time again, stabbing my hands, cutting my skin. I did a haphazard job of rewrapping my palm and finally managed to twist out the pin, but I grew more desperate and sloppy in my one-handed approach. My whole body was slick with sweat like a turkey basting in oil. Blood trickled down my fingers, and tears rolled down my cheeks. None of that mattered. I had to escape.

After an eternity, I freed the second pin. I stepped back from the door, swiped my toweled hand across my mouth, and was about to start on the third pin when the door banged open, broke off its last hinge, and crashed to the ground. A rush of steam whooshed out.

"*Aaaaah!*" I shrieked, leaping for the towel covering the vent.

Captain Madera, Jock, and a handful of the crew stood, heads angled inside the door frame, gawking at me like they'd never seen a naked woman before.

Jock turned off the steam and held up a clean towel in front of me, his face carefully devoid of expression.

I snatched the towel, realizing how this probably looked.

"Bella," Captain Madera said, "you look in the strangest places for entertainment."

"I...I..." I swaddled myself and looked from my toweled hand to my tools strewn on the floor. My bottom lip began to tremble, my head woozy. *Don't cry. Don't you dare cry.*

I closed my eyes and took a huge breath. Everything was going to be fine. I kept telling myself this because it was the only way I wouldn't lose control.

Chapter 9

Despite my best intentions to stay alert, I must've blacked out. I came to in the ship's infirmary and looked up into Jock's face. No doctor in sight. Only Jock, a mix of worry and exasperation etched in his blotched eyes.

I frowned and tried to roll off the table.

"Easy." He pressed down my bare shoulders.

I glanced at myself, relieved I was still covered in a towel. My hand was wrapped in a white bandage, my clothes were on a nearby chair. Someone must've gathered my stuff. I looked up at Jock, knowing who that someone was.

"I'm fine." I struggled to sit up.

"You got pretty dehydrated in there." He handed me a paper cup. "Here, drink this."

I peered into the cup and didn't ask questions. I was bone dry. "Yuck!" I sputtered. "What's in this?"

"Electrolytes."

"Blech!" I made a sour face. "I need a Diet Coke."

"You're not getting one. Doc insisted you drink that before getting off that table. And I'm here to make sure you do. Think of me as the enforcer."

I dragged my gaze from his healing corneas and looked over my shoulder around the white sterile room. "I want to see the doctor."

"He's out on a call. You're not the only person who needs regular saving. Speaking of which, how's the bruise on your backside?"

"What?" Then I recalled my several falls. "When did you see—"

"When you were butt-naked in my bed." He grinned. "I'm glad everything else looked okay."

"*O-kay!*" How much roving did he do when I blacked out? "I thought you were a gentleman!"

"I said *not always*."

I put up my nose. "I'm done talking to you. I want to see a nurse."

"This isn't *Grey's Anatomy*. The nurse had to join the doctor, so you got me. Your blood pressure lowered within minutes of getting you out of that steam bath, and your heart rate is normal. The nurse took your pulse before you came to." He raised his palm. "And before you ask for the captain, he's gone back to the bridge to look up your history. He's curious about Valentine Beaumont."

He folded his arms and raised an eyebrow. "Now, while you're sipping on that, do you want to tell me what you were doing, digging your way to China with nail clippers?"

I felt a tantrum coming on, but it wouldn't get me anywhere with Mr. Mighty here.

"I was locked in." I threw back my drink in one swig. I coughed, made another acidic face, and extended my empty cup to him. "Happy?"

He scrunched the paper cup between two fingers and tossed it in the garbage. "How'd you get locked in?"

"I didn't lock myself in, if that's what you're thinking."

He fought to keep the grin from spreading up his cheek. "I wasn't thinking anything."

"Yes, you were." I balled up my good fist. "You were thinking how ridiculous I looked, sweating and helpless in that sauna."

"Steam room," he corrected, his eyes lowering to my loosening towel. "And believe me, that's not what I was thinking. But I will tell you the handle was busted and jammed tight. I'm assuming this wasn't accidental. Someone wanted to keep you in there."

"Aha!" I scrubbed up the towel, knotting it under my armpits, not daring to let myself be taken in by his heroic deed. "What were you and the captain doing there anyway?"

He gestured to the discarded bloody towel that had covered my hand. "A spa employee went down to get dirty towels from the steam room. She discovered the broken handle on the door and saw someone moving around inside. She quickly notified the captain—who I happened to be with—and he didn't waste time addressing the situation."

"He could've knocked first, you know." Stupid thing to say since I was in a soundproof room.

"I'll pass that on."

My blood pressure may have been back to normal, but heat rushed to my face. "Since you're on such good terms with the *Grey's Anatomy* team, maybe you want them to look at that scar on your groin. It looks pretty nasty."

His laugh was short but genuine. "You're talking about this morning."

I did a pleased "Mmm-hmph," crossing my arms while I was at it.

"I didn't think you were looking at my scar."

My voice faltered. "Well, I did, uh, see it—the *scar.*"

He bent forward, his breath a soft whisper on my neck. "I bet you're dying to know how I got that scar." He grinned in that sexy way that made women melt. Then he backed up a foot. The humor faded from his eyes, the weight of what he was about to say resting on his shoulders.

An unexpected lump formed in my throat because I didn't want to hear anything bad. But I had a feeling it was too late. I swallowed tensely while his dark eyes focused on mine.

"I was part of a Latino gang," he said, "when I was eighteen. And I got knifed." His fist tightened for a split second, and a trace of regretfulness crossed his face. "I'd been helping my mother in her salon and was trying to stay clean while my father was away working. But life isn't always easy." He took a breath like he was remembering the past. "After that incident, I decided I was either going to survive and become something or die in a street fight and devastate my family. Being knifed to death didn't hold much appeal."

"So that's when you entered the navy and became a master-at-arms?"

"The time frame's a little broader, but yeah, you got it."

"That's a little different from the dream-to-be-in-the-navy story you gave me a few months ago. *An urge to see the world at twenty. Big ships enticed me.*"

He nodded. "That's all true. The slashing incident made it clear. I came to the States, got my head straightened, then after a few years, I enlisted."

My muscles relaxed. Jock's life was like something out of a suspense novel. Hard to believe three days had passed and I'd seen him little more than half a dozen times. And what I had seen always made me question who he was.

I gave him a reluctant nod. I was relieved to hear his story. But I had to focus on finding Tantig. If I hadn't been so engrossed in Lucy's murder, I wouldn't have gotten sidetracked in the first place.

I rolled off the table and headed toward the chair where my clothes were laid out. I turned my head over my shoulder. "Do you mind looking the other way so I can dress?"

"You weren't this modest last night."

I shot him a lethal glare, not trusting myself to verbalize what I was thinking.

"Turning," he said, palms up.

I flung on my clothes and slapped on my hat, not trusting his roving eyes. "By the way"—I whipped around with my good hand on the doorknob—"as for who locked me in the steam room, you might want to put Molly and Polly down as a couple of suspects."

"Molly and Polly?" he said thoughtfully.

"Yes. Buxom blonds? Wear only bikinis? They took part in the contest, and if you haven't noticed them yet, you'd better have your eyes checked." I held up my bandaged hand, feeling like Quasimodo, physically battered and emotionally bruised. "They're the reason I'm in this state."

It wasn't an Oscar-winning performance, but it was as good an exit as I'd ever made.

I went straight to my parents' cabin, hoping to find my mother and Tantig inside. I knocked on the door and waited. I called their names. I tried the doorknob. Nobody was there, and I couldn't stand around doing nothing.

I did a lap around the ship in the hot sun, looking in every nook and cranny for any member of my family. My scare in that steam trap had me imagining all kinds of horrible things, but if I was being rational, I'd admit it *was possible* Molly and Polly hadn't taken Tantig or locked me inside the steam room.

I thought about our conversation and the girls' illegal activities that I—and perhaps Tantig—had witnessed. But even if Tantig had seen them dealing drugs, I couldn't come up with a good reason why they'd abduct her. She was an elderly lady. How much of a threat could she pose?

The handle on the steam room door was another thing. It could've been temperamental to begin with, and when they shut the door, the action could've jammed and locked it. Or maybe someone else happened along, bumped into it, and broke it.

I took a deep breath, sorting this all out. Assuming Tantig wasn't with my parents, she wasn't senile. She wouldn't do something crazy like get locked inside a steam room. Or fall into a lifeboat. I looked heavenward. *Thanks for that thought.* But the truth was, she was aging and forgetful. I had to accept it was a possibility she could've walked off the ship and not returned. Or if she did return, she may not have been with my parents. All I knew was if Tantig came through this ordeal, her forgetfulness would be a blessing.

I continued my search, opening and shutting every door I could find. Then, just in case she had wandered too close to the edge, I rushed along the length of the ship with my head hung over the railing, scrutinizing each lifeboat below.

My clothes were plastered to my body; I was sticky, sweaty, and headachy from the steam room; and my hand was aching. I slurped back a pink lemonade from a passing waiter and decided I'd be in a much better frame of mind once I showered off the filth and sweat from today.

I marched into my cabin and found the beds newly made, fresh-cut flowers in the vase, and mint chocolates resting on both pillows. The smell of acetone still hung in the air. Cringing at the memory of nearly blinding Jock, I dug out my Musk and freshened the room. Then I stripped and jumped in the shower, taking care not to soak my bandage.

After I lotioned my arms and legs, I tugged on a short flowered skirt and top. If I'd had an extra twenty minutes and a hand that wasn't sore, I could've done something fabulous with my hair. But I didn't worry about perfection. I wanted to get back to searching for Tantig.

I stuffed my charged phone in my bag, plucked a pink flower out of the vase, snapped off the stem, and tucked the blossom over my ear. I stopped for a moment and thought about the flowers Molly and Polly were wearing and their visit to the florist shop in San Juan. Was there a link to this and the drug deal I'd witnessed? Or was I overthinking things? With no time to deliberate on it now, I slid into my open-toed white stilettos with bows on the sides and rushed out of the cabin.

I found myself heading toward the dining room, probably because of my rumbling stomach and the smell of nachos and salsa pulling me in. Colorful piñatas hung from the ceiling, waiters wore ponchos and sombreros, cacti and red hibiscus sat in corners, and a Mexican trio strummed their guitars to a well-known Mexican tune.

I pushed my steam-room episode to the back of my mind and showed Tantig's picture at several tables, asking if anyone had seen a white-haired woman in Nikes roaming around. No one had.

Deflated, I shoved the photo back in my bag, thinking if I grabbed a bite to eat off the early-afternoon buffet, maybe my mother and Tantig would stroll in with the same idea. Also, I hoped it'd dull the persistent ache from worry in my stomach.

I spotted Sabrina sitting alone in a corner of the room. I carried over my plate that I'd filled with a nacho dish and a quesadilla and asked if I could join her. She said, "Be my guest," and complimented the flower in my hair.

"Housekeeping hasn't finished cleaning our floor," she said, tissue in hand, a half-eaten burrito in front of her. "I'm allowed back in our cabin since the police said they were finished processing everything."

"You okay with staying in the same cabin?"

She sighed. "I think so. While housekeeping's still at it, I was deciding whether to take one of the San Juan walking tours or go gold-hunting."

I bit into my nacho dish, and she looked at me as if she was expecting a barrage of questions. "Aren't you going to grill me?" She blew her nose. "Like everyone else? Because I knew Lucy?"

I licked my lip. "No. I'm just hungry." That was part of the truth. The other part was I saw Mr. Jaworski weaving through tables, looking for a place to sit. I hated to see an elderly person eat alone, and I could've invited him to join us, but I wasn't up for more talk of the prodigal son and maraschino cherries. In all honesty, I'd had enough of my landlord for one day.

Sabrina looked in the same direction, and we watched Mr. Jaworski plant himself at a table. The other five people at the table smiled at him, then shifted a few inches in the opposite direction.

"Yep. Uncle Sam." Sabrina smiled and wiped her nose. "He used to drive Lucy nuts."

"Did she talk about him much?"

"Hardly, except to say he was coming on this cruise, and it wasn't her idea."

I dabbed my mouth with a sombrero-shaped napkin, my bandaged hand catching Sabrina's eye.

"What happened?" she asked.

I put down my napkin. "I had a run-in with a wall." Half-accurate.

"Sprained?"

"A cut."

She frowned like she was trying to figure me out. "Is it true what they say about you?"

"That I'm beautiful, sexy, and smart?" I batted my eyelashes.

"No." She gave a polite smile. "The other thing."

Oh. "That depends. People have a way of embellishing the truth."

"But you've solved murders."

"*Solved* is a complex word, and one usually avoided in association with my name."

"Then you're not trying to solve Lucy's murder?"

"I just want to find my great-aunt." I took a sip of water.

"Your great-aunt?"

"Yes." I pulled Tantig's picture out of my bag. "Have you seen her?"

She took a good look at the photo. "Not much since the contest. But I'll keep my eye out for her." She glanced around the dining room and quivered. "I hope she's okay. It's been eerie around here since Lucy's murder."

Tell me about it.

"How did you know Lucy?" I asked.

She pushed away her burrito and patted her mouth dry.

"I worked for Lucy. She had a salon in New York City. Shortcuts."

"Good name." I recalled Holly's news about Lucy's arrests and her possible involvement in a homicide. I wasn't sure if I should take this questioning to the next level. "Work there long?"

"Six years."

"You must've been fairly close."

"It wasn't a partnership, if that's what you mean."

I didn't know what I meant, but I was getting a feel for their relationship.

"We were doing pretty well, too, until all of a sudden customers started leaving."

I knit my eyebrows together. "Too much competition in the Big Apple?"

"You could say that." She rolled her eyes. "One rival in particular. Kashi."

"Kashi?"

"Yes. His salon is down the street from Shortcuts. He's a real snake in the grass." She flattened her lips. "Do you know he was responsible for the dead skunk?"

I scrunched up my nose. "Dead skunk? As in one got hit on the road in front of the salon?"

She shook her head in a thoughtful manner. "Nooo. More like one was delivered in a hair box with a message saying it was free hair extensions."

"You're kidding."

"That's what Lucy said when she opened the box."

"And you think Kashi delivered it."

"We know he did. It came with a nicely decorated card, saying so." She gave a disgusted head shake. "Word traveled fast about a dead skunk in the shop, and with dozens of salons nearby that people can patronize…well, business hasn't been great. When Lucy saw the ad for the cruise contest, she decided this was what we needed to make a comeback."

"And she won," I said, trying to find the bright side in all this.

"Yeah. Some people have all the luck." She zeroed in on me. "I can tell you one thing. Kashi disliked Lucy with a passion. He'd do anything to remain top dog in New York's hair world."

"Anything?" Like come on the same cruise and murder Lucy?

She gave me a direct nod, a nod that said she was nailing Kashi to the cross.

Was he the snake in the grass she made him out to be? Was I trying to convince myself he was innocent when he was a ruthless murderer? I scratched my chin, deciding how to broach the subject of Kashi and the vial of liquid and what happened in their cabin Saturday night after Max and I left.

Then out of the corner of my eye I spotted Tantig leave the dining room.

I leaped from the table and called an apology over my shoulder to Sabrina for deserting her so abruptly. But I didn't want to lose sight of Tantig. Sabrina called out it was okay, that she was heading ashore anyway. Then she shouted my name.

I screeched to a stop, turned around, and found her standing there waving my bag in the air. "You forgot this."

I dashed back to the table, grabbed my bag, said thanks, and hitched it over my shoulder. Then I aimed for the exit. By the time I got there, Tantig was gone. I looked right, then left, then forward, then back. I didn't know where she'd gone or whether she'd stepped into the elevator. I whipped out her photo and asked a young couple coming into the dining room if they'd seen her. They weren't helpful. Okay, the elevator it was.

I rode down to her floor, figuring she was finally heading back to the cabin. I got there in record time, but still no one answered my knock on the door. Nonetheless, it was a relief knowing she was on board the ship and safely trundling around. She was probably glad for the independence.

I retraced my steps, thinking maybe Tantig took the elevator but got off on the wrong floor. Maybe she ended up on my floor. Couldn't hurt to check.

I rode the elevator to my floor, walked the hall to my cabin, and didn't see any life. I kept walking and before I knew it, I ended up in Lucy and Sabrina's wing.

It was the conversation about Kashi that had me stupefied. More than ever, I needed to see if I could find any clues about what was in that vial. If I could search Sabrina and Lucy's cabin, maybe I'd find a drop of potion left in the glass that Kashi had spiked and I'd knocked over. I didn't think a dirty glass from Saturday would be lying around, especially after the police had examined and bagged everything, but it wouldn't hurt to look. Plus, there could be other clues as to why Lucy was killed. All I needed was the key. And since housekeeping was still making the rounds, and Sabrina was heading ashore, this was my chance. It would only take me a few minutes. Then I could get back to locating Tantig.

I saw a cabin steward with his cleaning cart parked in their hallway. I approached the steward and hummed a ditty. "*Buenas tardes*," I chirped.

"*Buenas tardes*." He slipped a master key in a door, then hung it back on the corner of the cart. He took an armload of towels, glasses, shampoo, and mint chocolates, and slid into the cabin without another look back.

I took a deep breath. I wasn't a pickpocket or a thief. I was borrowing a key and taking a friendly look in a murder victim's room. If I could even just find the vial Kashi had used, I'd be in and out before the steward finished making up the beds. In theory, my plan worked great.

I whipped the key string off the cart, darted across the hall to Sabrina and Lucy's room, slipped the right key in the door, and magically it opened. I tossed the string back on the corner of the cart and dashed into the cabin.

I flicked on the lights and double-locked the door

behind me. *Whew.* I took a look around the freshly made-up room. Darn. The police obviously did a thorough job processing the cabin. Almost looked too empty, which seemed odd. But what was missing? I opened and closed several drawers. Sabrina's clothes were neatly folded along with a few small souvenirs. Nothing screamed *peculiar.* I slammed the last drawer shut. Everything looked the same as the night of Lucy's win, except now her belongings and big blue suitcase were gone.

I took a moment to absorb this, and my heartbeat slowed down. As mean as Lucy was, she left her mark on many people. The cabin didn't even have the same vitality to it. I glanced at the nightstand where the photo sat. It too was gone—probably sent home with Lucy's other belongings—and replaced by a fashion magazine, pen, and pad of paper. The only glasses in the room were clean and sitting upside down on paper coasters.

I crouched and looked under the bunks. No glasses, wine bottles, or signs of a vial anywhere. And the carpet was spotless. Now I'd never know what Kashi poured in Lucy's drink—not that it mattered since I'd knocked over the glass before she drank from it. Unless Kashi spiked Lucy's drink again after we'd left, and the substance somehow showed up in the autopsy report. Of course, there was a fifty-fifty chance of Romero revealing what was in that report. But it was logical to think Lucy could've ended up in the ice mold after being poisoned or drugged. If that was the case, she really could've frozen to death.

The bigger issue was that I worried Kashi was guilty and I was unwilling to rat him out until I investigated more in case I was wrong. On the other hand, if he was innocent, I needed proof to reassure myself. Best not to jump to conclusions until I gathered more information.

I took a quick look in the bathroom. Nothing outstanding. Clean glasses there, too, plus a fresh papered bar of soap.

I picked up the soap and sniffed. Mmm. Herbal. We had lavender in ours. What gives?

Suddenly, a voice came over the speakers. My heart jumped in my throat. I squeezed the soap so hard it plopped into the toilet. Wide-eyed with disbelief, I looked from my bandaged hand to my good hand. Now what? One thing was certain. I wasn't plucking it out.

The voice continued. "Valentine Beaumont, please report to the purser's desk. Valentine Beaumont."

Why was I being paged? They didn't page people like this. It had to be about Tantig. Did they find her? Was she okay?

I cracked open the door. The cleaning cart was in the same spot. Dirty sheets lay in a bundle on top, and a stained lampshade sat over everything. The cabin steward was nowhere in sight.

I stepped out into the hall at the same moment the chief steward and his cohorts rounded the far corner, deep in conversation. Guilt filled my bones, and out of fear I grabbed the lampshade, plunked it on my head, and sprinted in the opposite direction.

"Wait! Senorita!" one of the men called. "You dropped your flower!"

I felt the side of my head. To heck with the flower. I kicked up my heels and kept running until I turned a corner and crashed into my mother. The lampshade tumbled to the ground, and I screamed for my life.

"Valentine!" My mother clapped a hand to her heart, trying to remain on two feet.

There was no time for chitchat. I grabbed her hand and whirled her around. Neither one of us spoke until we were safely inside an elevator, going up.

"What's going on?" she panted. "Why are you running?"

I put my palm in her face while I caught my own breath.

"And why was your name called on the speaker?"

She obviously recuperated quicker than I did.

"What happened to your hand? And why were you wearing a lampshade?"

"Mom!" I gasped. "Let me have my heart attack here, will you?"

She pressed her lips together and waited, which was quite a feat.

"Okay." I swallowed and collected my thoughts. If I told her I'd committed a B&E, she'd drop to her knees and ask God where she went wrong. All things considered, I thought I'd better modify my story.

"I was taking part in one of the beauty cruise games—lampshade hide-and-seek. I didn't expect anyone to be in front of me." I gave an exaggerated *whew*. "Boy, are they going to be mad when they can't find *me*."

She folded her arms. "You're playing games while Tantig is missing?"

"About that—"

"Why are you wearing a cast?" She glared down at my hand. "I don't see you for half a day, and the next time I do you have your hand in a cast."

"It's not a cast. It's a bandage. I got a few scrapes in the steam room."

"How does my daughter end up with scrapes from a steam room?" She looked around the empty elevator. "Somebody tell me! Mary Ubeniwitz has a steam room, and her skin looks lovely. *You*. You come out with bandages."

I had so many things on my mind I could hardly think straight. My mother grilling me about steam rooms and casts was the last straw. The elevator doors opened, and I click-clacked to the main lobby with her on my heels.

"Where are you going now?"

I stopped and spun around. "Mom, what are you doing on the ship? I thought you and Dad were going to shop in San Juan."

"What kind of person would I be, shopping and living it up when Tantig is missing? Your father went off by himself in search of cigars while I've been turning this boat upside down." She put her hand to her forehead. "First there's a murder. Now this. What if she fell overboard? Had a stroke? What if she was *kidnapped*?"

"She wasn't kidnapped," I said, trying to calm her.

"And I know for a fact she didn't fall overboard. I ended up disembarking this morning to look for her in port. Security at the gangway told me Tantig had left the ship. Showed them her ID and everything. She must've found her way back on board because I saw her myself about an hour ago."

"You did? Why didn't you tell me?"

"Because I couldn't find you. If you had a cell phone, I could've reached you." Never mind mine was in the cabin charging.

"If you saw Tantig, where is she?"

"I don't know."

She exhaled loudly. "You're not making sense. Did you see her or not?"

"Yes, but I sort of lost her. I think that's why they're paging me. They've probably found her."

"Why would they page you and not me? I'm responsible for her. It's all my fault," she said. "Tantig wasn't keen on walking, but I made her go anyway."

"You were doing what you thought was best. Don't beat yourself up." I was a great one to talk. I couldn't rid myself of the misguided guilt I felt over Lucy's death. I sighed. "Let's go to the purser's desk. Tantig is probably there."

The corners of her lips turned down, and worry lines framed her eyes.

"We'll find her," I said in a gentle voice.

She swallowed back further conversation and tramped in my shadow.

Minutes later, we arrived at the grand atrium that had the appeal of a glittering European plaza and spanned several decks. Perfume boutiques, diamond jewelers, a leather store, a wine-tasting salon, sushi bar, Internet center, bistro, bakery, and an art gallery were all encompassed in this huge plaza trimmed in gold. I gaped for several seconds like I'd landed in Oz. I seriously had to get my head examined for missing out on all this.

My mother gave me a shove.

"Huh?"

She tilted her head toward a huge, ornate desk. "The purser?"

I turned my back on the shops, found the purser, and gave him my room number and ID. Then I asked what the problem was.

"Your friend is Max Martell, yes?" He held out the phone to me. "He's in jail."

Chapter 10

"How did you end up in jail?" I asked Max, phone tight to my ear.

"Never mind that. What took you so long? I kept trying your cell phone."

"It was in my bag. It must've gotten switched off."

"Why'd you have it switched off?"

"Gee, I'm sorry. I forgot I was supposed to rescue you from jail today. Next time I'll let the battery run dead so I can be ready for your call."

"I'd appreciate that."

I rolled my eyes so far back I saw home. "Do you want to tell me what happened?"

"It's a long story," he said. "I'm lucky the warden's letting me use the phone. He's kind of cute in an ugly Billy Bob Thornton way."

My mother had her ear pressed to the backside of the phone. "Ask him if he has clean underwear."

I gave my mother a strange look and repositioned the phone to my other ear. "I'll be there as soon as I can. Do you need anything?"

"No. Just get here!"

I hung up and asked the purser for directions to the jail.

"I'd better come with you," my mother said. "You never know what kind of felons they have in jails down here. They steal your money and that's not all." She leaned in. "You know they do funny things to men, not to mention beatings and stabbings. Max is probably scared stiff being around those sickos."

"He sounds fine," I said. "And the jails down here don't have the monopoly on sickos. Sickos are everywhere."

"The sickos down here are on drugs, and they're desperate for money."

"Mom, the sickos down here—" I clamped my mouth shut. Why in the world was I defending Puerto Rican sickos to my mother? I had better things to do with my time. Like make sure Tantig was okay once and for all. Find out more about Kashi. Call Twix. Bail Max out of jail.

I left my mother behind and took a cab to Max's holding cell. The ride there was not an experience I wished to replicate. The taxi resembled Fred Flintstone's car with a big hole in the backseat floor. Every time we went over a bump, I braced myself, straddling the hole, afraid if the cab gave birth, I'd be the newborn.

We finally arrived at the correctional facility, a four-story white building with a barbed wire fence wrapped around the entire yard. Mild deterrent in case an inmate had a hankering for Ben & Jerry's ice cream in the middle of the night. The jail sent a chill down to my painted toenails, which I stared at inside my open-toed heels. My gaze traveled up my tanned legs and short flowered skirt. Perfect outfit for springing a criminal. I'd probably get arrested for indecent exposure. Boy, what I didn't do for Max.

The driver squealed to a stop, and I almost flew over the front seat. "Senorita want out here?"

"*Si. Gracias.*" I thanked the Lord I was still in one piece, then handed over money.

The inside of the jail, though old, had been updated. But fresh paint and stucco didn't erase the overwhelming stagnant and oppressive smell. Vomit that hadn't been eliminated. Urine that hadn't been washed away.

The plan was I'd go up to the front desk, ask to speak

to Max, explain that this was all a mistake, and take Max back to the ship. I didn't have a plan B.

I noticed Billy Bob right away. He was leaning against a desk, talking with half a dozen other men in gray uniforms. He leered at me from his pockmarked face, then rose to his nearly six-foot height. Likely not too happy to be pulled back to work.

Hiding my revulsion, I sent him a smile meant to look sincere, one that said I was an upstanding, polite American citizen. Even if I was trembling on the inside.

I asked to speak to Max Martell, then waited an hour while Billy Bob and his cohorts consulted with each other in Spanish, grinned at me once in a while, and then came and went from sight. Everything but bring Max out or lead me to him. Beads of sweat stung my upper lip, and my patience wore thin. I asked again if I could speak to Max, but no one was in much of a hurry to honor my request.

Finally, Billy Bob led me down a hall and into a small room furnished with a table, two chairs, a clock on the wall, and a threadbare couch that looked like it was home to a few cockroaches. I sat at the table, and a second later he ushered in Max.

"What took you so long?" Max said when Billy Bob left the room.

My impatience got the best of me, and I almost shouted my words. "They were asking for wallpaper suggestions! I don't know what took so long! We're in Puerto Rico. Everyone breathes in slow motion."

He pulled up a chair. "Have I got a story to tell you!"

I sighed, not sure I was ready for one of Max's stories. "You don't seem too broken up that you're in a Puerto Rican jail…with a bunch of sickos."

"You're overreacting. They said I'd be released as soon as the paperwork was done."

"That could take until Christmas."

"Then you have lots of time to hear my story."

I sat back in my chair and folded my arms. "Okay. Shoot."

"Your arm!" he gasped. "What happened?"

"I'll save that story for marshmallows by the campfire. Let me hear yours first."

"If you're sure."

"Wild horses couldn't keep me from hearing how you landed in jail."

He gave me a pointed look. "You know you're starting to sound a lot like Mr. Long Arm of the Law." He wriggled his tushy on the chair, refocusing. "Remember this morning when I came to hunt for gold? It's true, Puerto Ricans make the best jewelry. Twenty-two-karat gold! You can't buy twenty-two-karat back home."

I tried to suppress a loud yawn, but it got the better of me.

"Anyway," he said, tight-lipped at my interruption, "I came out of a jewelry store this afternoon and caught a glimpse of Molly and Polly tiptoeing into a florist shop with a big duffel bag."

Now he had my attention. I sat up, recalling my sighting this morning of the beach babes scurrying into a florist shop.

"I was about to call them, but something held me back."

"What?"

"A man with a gun."

"You got held up?"

"Not exactly," he said. "A few minutes before that, I was minding my own business, trotting along the counter in this one store, eyeing their elaborate selection of gold chains, earrings, and diamonds. Lovey, you should've seen the diamonds."

"Max! I hear shackles in the next room. Get on with it!"

"I was pricing a gold *M* charm when this sweet, bumbling old lady lost part of her diamond necklace. It was dragging on the floor behind her, and then broke off entirely. I wouldn't have normally reacted the way I did, but I thought it was Tantig, so I grabbed the necklace and rushed out into the street to give it to her, and that's when nasty security came and stuck a gun in my ribs."

I shook my head, trying to make sense of his story. "They thought you were stealing?"

"Yes. Can you believe it? And here I was being a good Samaritan, returning an elderly lady's jewels."

"And it was then you realized the lady wasn't Tantig."

"Yes. They handcuffed her and brought her back into the store. You should've seen the loot in her purse!"

"And you explained all this to the police?"

"Yes, when I finally had a chance to speak to someone who knew fluent English." He leaned in. "Funny thing was, I'm sure it was the same lady I followed shuffling down the stairs last night."

"What stairs?"

"On the deck. Remember? You were spying on Jock. I told you this morning I left you there because I thought I saw Tantig."

I mentally rolled my eyes at that scene and the memory of falling into the lifeboat moments later. But part of me wondered if this could've been the same woman tourists mistook for Tantig heading back to the ship earlier today. Heck, could she have been the lady disembarking this morning that gangway security said was Tantig? No. Couldn't have been. Tantig had shown them her ID.

"What about Molly and Polly?"

He shrugged. "There was something fishy going on with them."

"Maybe it wasn't them. Maybe you mistook them for two other blonds."

"Lovey, cataracts wouldn't stop me from recognizing the bounce on those babes."

He had a point.

"I can tell you this much. They were up to no good. They came back out of the florist shop a moment later with a black-haired, ponytailed guy, covered in tattoos. And they were *without* the duffel bag. Before the gun hit my back, I saw the guy count a wad of money and stuff it in his shirt pocket. Real slick."

"Maybe Molly and Polly just bought a huge bouquet of flowers, and he was making sure they didn't cheat him."

"Maybe. But do you normally shake hands with your florist after *you* buy flowers?"

"No."

"And does your florist look like a hitman?"

I thought of the sweet elderly couple who owned Dilly's Florist in Rueland. "No." I grinned. "But you can't base what you saw on the florist's looks. Not everyone resembles Tom Hanks in *Forrest Gump*."

"If they're selling flowers, maybe they should."

Uh-huh. I didn't need to further the questioning. The tingles spreading across my shoulders were a good indication of what transpired between Molly, Polly, and the ponytailed man. I agreed with Max. There was more to what they were doing in port than buying flowers. But what was in the duffel bag? More money? More drugs?

"Let's get you out of here," I said.

"Can we make one teensy stop first?"

By the time we made our jailbreak, it was almost five. We raced back to the jewelry store so Max could purchase his gold charm before the ship took off without us.

Thankful that everything had turned out, I led him to the ship's gangway, half listening to his happy prattle, half thinking about today's discoveries.

"This is my best souvenir yet," he said, head down, admiring his *M*.

"It must be special." I hiked up the walkway. "You haven't noticed the water once."

He looked up, pale-faced. "Did you have to mention that?" He gripped my arm until it turned blue.

"Sorry." *Darn.* Where was my head? "Uh, Max? You're squeezing my arm a bit tight."

He closed his eyes, legs quivering. "I can't go forward. I can't go back. They'll have to sail without me."

"Come on," I begged. "My feet are killing me. And we're already late."

"I can't!"

"Look," I said, "this hasn't been the most amusing day of my life. I woke up in a spoon position in Jock's bed with Jock as the ladle. I had another round with Romero—who showed up unannounced before you almost killed him. Then I discovered Tantig was missing, almost blinded Jock, learned Romero has a lover, had to endure another five minutes with Mr. Jaworski, was locked in a steam room, cut my hand, committed a felony, *and* I had to travel into a hot, sweaty Puerto Rican jail to save your ass. But not before I was leered at by Billy Bob Thornton. I know I'm forgetting stuff, but that's the kind of day it's been. Now, if you think I'm leaving you behind, *think again*!"

The whole time I ranted I was dragging Max along the gangplank. By the time I finished my speech, we were safely inside the ship.

"Romero has a lover?" Max turned pink again.

"So I've been told."

"See? You should've jumped him the first minute you laid eyes on him. Honey, men like Romero don't drop out of the rainforest every day. All that wild dark hair and thick lashes. And I'd kill to have a muscular body like his."

Max was perfectly toned in the body department, but he had to play the drama queen once a week.

"Now see what's happened?" he went on. "Some other woman has her hooks into him. And I bet she doesn't have your eyes."

"I'm not interested anyway," I lied. "I've got too much on my mind to worry about who Romero's sleeping with."

"Mmm-hmm. Keep telling yourself that, and you'll be fine."

Chapter 11

Max pranced off to take in a live performance, and I found my parents on the lido deck with a hundred other passengers. They were standing amid spread-out deck chairs behind a roped-off circle staked with burning torches. A Jimmy Buffett tune played in the background, the smell of mesquite barbeque sauce filled the air, and all eyes were on the cruise director who stood in the ring, a megaphone in one hand, two foam swords in the other.

I walked over to my mother and asked if Tantig had shown up.

She gave her head a shake. "A few passengers thought they'd seen her, so I wanted to do one more lap around the ship before talking to the captain. Then I got trapped by this beach party, of all things, and Julie McCoy introducing a sword competition."

"Her name's not Julie McCoy. Julie McCoy was on *The Love Boat*."

"It's the only way I'll remember her. And why did they take that show off the air? I loved that show. I had something to look forward to every Saturday night. Now we have reality TV. I have enough reality every day looking after your father and Tantig." She clapped her mouth like she realized she shouldn't have uttered that.

I felt her pain. "And you haven't spotted her?"

"No. But since you did, I know she's got to be here somewhere."

What worried me now was that I wondered whether the elderly lady I spotted in the dining room was actually Tantig. She got away so quickly, maybe it was a look-alike. A Tantig twin. Best not to alarm my mother any further. Tantig would show up. Probably when we weren't looking. She just had to.

"Captain Madera's been so helpful," my mother said. "He even gave us free passage for another cruise because of our suffering. Wasn't that nice of him? You know, I don't think he's married." She tapped my arm. "Valentine? You're not listening."

She was right. I knew where this conversation was leading. So far, my mother had considered suitors in the form of a funeral director, a car salesman, a neighbor's grandson, the minister's nephew, a retirement home senior, Kashi, and now the ship's captain. All that were left were the butcher, the baker, and the candlestick maker. Was it any wonder I was still single?

"Where's Dad?"

She nodded to the poolside bar. "He's over there, having a drink with Clive."

I could smell the rum in Clive's glass from where I was standing. He was in his usual spot, hanging half off his barstool. Beside him was a tousled-haired man two days past shaving, wearing a casual shirt over rolled-up pants and flip-flops.

I blinked wide. "That's Dad? He hasn't shaved! And his shirt isn't tucked in with a belt around his waist." I gaped down at his flip-flops. "What happened to his fear of getting athlete's foot?" My jaw hung loose, but I couldn't snap it shut. "And why is his hair sticking up all over?"

My parents could look after themselves, but I kept their hair styled and my father's nose hairs trimmed. It was hell being a perfectionist.

"He's getting into this cruise thing."

"That still doesn't explain why he looks like one of the

Beach Boys. And why isn't *he* looking for Tantig? She's *his* aunt."

"Your father? The king of carefree? He roamed the deck for half an hour, searching for her. Said she'd show up before we all went to bed."

Sounded like something my father would say. I gawked at him taking a slug from his drink.

"He's been on this Blackbeard kick since Nassau," my mother said.

"Blackbeard?"

"Yes. Legend says Blackbeard used to light his beard to scare off merchant captains."

"An-n-nd?"

"And he's growing a beard."

"A beard. To scare off merchant captains."

My mother raised her palms. "You know your father. Anything for attention. And he's thinking of piercing a gold hoop through his ear."

I shook my head, sure I didn't hear right. "A gold hoop."

"Yes. Like Max. Stella Bartola said her Frank went through a similar period. Dressed up like Gene Simmons from KISS. Bought platform shoes and everything. Stella said he walked around town like that for a week before his rheumatoid arthritis started acting up."

"My father. Blackbeard, with a gold hoop." My life as I knew it was over.

The cruise director called out for volunteers, and our gazes swung back to the ring. We heard a distinct cry, and a second later, Kashi bounced to the stage.

"Yes! I, Kashi Farooq, will take the challenge!" He bowed. "In my country, we are proficient at sword-fighting. The khanda is a weapon of great prestige."

"That's uh, lovely," the cruise director said, a vague look crossing her face like she hoped she hadn't welcomed a knife-wielding closet terrorist into the ring. She raised her eyebrows at the crowd. "Anyone wish to take on Kashi?"

"Valentine will! Yoo-hoo! Julie McCoy! Over here!"

"No!" I backed up from my mother and ducked.

My mother grabbed my arm and hauled me to the front. "This is the perfect opportunity to get to know Kashi. You said yourself he hasn't said more than two words to you."

"That was at the beginning of the cruise. Since then we've said *hi* and *nice day.*"

"*Hi!* What does *hi* tell you? Nothing."

"I'm okay with that." There was no point telling her he was a murder suspect. She'd only come back with *everyone's innocent until proven guilty.* I grasped at straws. "My hand! It's in a cast!"

"You said yourself it was a scrape."

"What about Tantig? I should keep looking for her."

"She's not your responsibility anymore tonight." She gave me a shove. "Go."

I tripped into the ring in my white heels and short flowered skirt. Everyone cheered me on.

The cruise director gave us both a foam sword and said to play clean. What was clean? I didn't know a thing about sword-fighting, or fencing, or whatever it was called.

"And if you can't play clean"—she snickered—"play dirty!" Then she blew a whistle.

I stood there, red with embarrassment, waving my purple toy sword like a wand.

Kashi bowed from his side of the ring, a fiendish look on his face. He gave a blood-curdling scream and lunged at me with his green sword like he was about to spear a bull.

I shrieked and scooted in my stilettos to the opposite side of the ring, narrowly missing being jabbed by his sword. What was I doing here? I liked romantic dancing and glittery tutus. Not sword-fighting. I wasn't Holly. *She* was the one who liked boxing and beating up on boys.

We parried each other, me avoiding getting lanced while Kashi did his own rendition of the "Mexican Hat Dance."

"Boooo!" The spectators shouted. They weren't interested in us tap-dancing around. They wanted blood. The volume doubled and was enough to work up my courage. I had nothing to be embarrassed about. I'd been through enough today to stand up to a lifetime of humiliations.

I puffed out air and looked at Kashi with new eyes. He was a mealworm. A guppie. A flea on a dog. Nobody I should be intimidated by or scared of. At least not in such a crowd. I was mentally reinforcing myself of this as I got the hang of poking and prodding, shuffling my own jig around my opponent.

Sweat rolled down my temples, and my heels pinched my feet. My dance probably looked more like a chiropractic nightmare than that of a professional fencer.

"What is it with you, woman?" Kashi did the *en garde* thing. "You have no talent with such a weapon. You are a worthless opponent."

This wasn't what I needed to hear at the moment. I'd spent the first half of this cruise on edge. I wasn't going to take it from Kashi Farooq. I narrowed my eyes at him, threads of steam escaping my ears. Suddenly, I pictured him pouring that vial of blue liquid into Lucy's drink, and all the fury I had building inside me exploded. I went on the attack and clocked him on the side of the head with my sword. *Ha!* Take *that*!

His head rotated in a circle from the blow, and he lost his balance. The crowd cheered. Things were picking up.

I whacked at his legs until I took him out. He landed with a thump, and I jumped him, losing my shoes in the process. We rolled around on the ground, me bending my sword around his scrawny neck, him trying to beat me off like a horse.

"Why did you kill her?" I cried in his ear.

"What are you talking about?" he shrieked, his wire-rimmed glasses askew on his face.

I got on top of him, straddling his stomach, my skirt fanning out around me. "Don't play dumb with me." I tightened my hold around his neck. "I saw you!"

"You saw me?"

"Yes. I saw you pour something in Lucy's drink. You poisoned her!" True, I wanted to deem him innocent, but the moment and the fright of a killer on board was getting to me.

"I, Kashi, would not hurt a tick!"

"That's *flea*!" I smacked him again with my sword. *Smack. Smack. Smack.*

"*Aaaaah!* Get this beautiful crazy woman off me!"

"This is great!" the cruise director cheered. "You two know how to have fun!"

The crowd whistled and applauded. "More! More!"

"You heard them," she sang. "Round two!"

"Round *two*!" Kashi cried. "I will need an ambulance after round one."

I ground my teeth at him. "Tell me what you poisoned Lucy with."

"It was nothing. Honestly! It was only blue food coloring."

"*Food coloring.*"

"Yes." He straightened his glasses. "If you let me live, I will tell you all about it."

"Not until you tell me what you did with Tantig!"

"Who? Why is Kashi responsible for everything? I do not know any Tantig!"

"Five-foot-nothing. White hair. Pasty skin. Ring any bells?" My hands were trembling. "You gave her a brooch, and...and"—tears swelled in my eyes—"she's missing!"

"I know nothing! *Please.* I liked that pasty little woman. I wouldn't hurt a"—he dared to look in my eyes—"flea!"

I swiped away tears with my unraveling bandage while someone peeled me off him. Two long feet in flip-flops told me it was my father.

"Valentine," he said, "you're embarrassing your mother and me."

I shoved away from his grasp. Gee, I wouldn't want to humiliate Blackbeard.

"And we have a winner!" the cruise director said. "The lady wins the Saber Cup."

I accepted the two-inch toy trophy, gave her a wan smile, then fixed my skirt and pulled my tangled hair out of my eyes.

I collected my heels from the edge of the ring and saw one of the white bows had been torn off. Fabulous. I stuffed the bow in the toy trophy and slid on my scuffed stilettos. Then I seized the back of Kashi's shirt.

"Aah!" he yelped.

"Let's go," I said. "Over there. I need a drink."

We settled ourselves at a table for two and gave a waitress our orders.

Kashi removed his glasses and wiped the perspiration from his eyes. "I am humbly sorry," he said. "I did not know about Tantig."

I rewound my bandage, staring at him, not sure if I should give him the benefit of the doubt.

"You really do know how to beat butt." He dabbed his neck with a napkin.

"You mean kick butt."

He slid on his glasses. "That too."

The waitress brought Kashi a banana daiquiri and me a cranberry cocktail.

"So, what's the story?" I asked, after she left. "Why'd you pour food coloring in Lucy's drink?"

"First, you must understand there is a long history between Lucy Jacobs and me." He removed the orange umbrella from his glass and took a swallow of his drink. "I have a successful hair boutique in New York. Lucy was my greatest competitor."

Same thing Sabrina had told me, but I'd hear him out.

"If I ran a special on tanning, Lucy would top that and give away tanning products with their special. I'd run a buy-one-get-one-free. Lucy's sale would be buy-one-get-two-free. It was continual."

Sounded like the same tricks Candace Needlemeyer pulled on me. The witch.

"That little spitball was constantly undermining Kashi's marketing genius. And that's not all. Sometimes she would do nasty things like deliver a dead skunk in a hair box with a message saying it was free hair extensions."

Huh? Wasn't this what Sabrina had said Kashi had done? Who was telling the truth? "Are you sure it wasn't the other way around?"

"What?" he squealed. "Why would I do something so distasteful? I love all animals. I would never hurt another living being."

I sipped my drink, my eyes narrowed on him.

"Another time, she delivered a box of chocolate Turtles with clipped fingernails sticking out of the chocolates."

I spit my drink back in my glass.

His eyebrows went up. "You see? Devilish."

"Okay, you and Lucy weren't the best of friends."

"That is to put it coolly. So I decided to pull a Kashi prank on her." He twirled the orange umbrella in his fingers. "Actually two."

"Two?"

"Yes, two pranks." He took another shot of his drink. "The first was after Lucy won Saturday's competition. That little imp detested my 'Get Out of Town' brooches. Said they looked like beetles, and she hated beetles." He shrugged. "I made a tiny brooch for her and snuck it in her bag. I told Sabrina to please not tell, as it was harmless. At most, Lucy would scream her fool head off. Sabrina nodded and told me to go nuts." His eyebrows creased. "I took that to mean have fun—not the Cashew reference Lucy bestowed on me."

I gave a small grin. "I'm sure that's what she meant."

He nodded in earnest. "Prank number two came after you spilled Lucy's drink, then left the party. I slipped more food coloring in her wine bottle, and I took a picture of her holding her check. I said in my congenial fashion, 'Smile,' and she gave the brightest, bluest smile you ever did see."

He laughed and slapped his knee. "I tell you, sometimes I outwit myself. She had no idea how ridiculous she looked. My plan was to post her blue face on social media and send it to the newspaper, announcing my wonderful friend's win. But then she died, and I did not have the heart to go through with such a farce."

He slumped in his chair, twiddling his umbrella. A moment later, a tear slipped down his cheek. "It is almost as if I did kill Lucy Jacobs. That was the last time I saw her, and here I was being Mr. Comedian."

He sighed, looking up at me mournfully. "It seems there may have been others who had a bad relationship with Lucy."

"What are you talking about?"

"About a year ago, there was a dead body. I'll never forget it. I was on my way to work one morning, and I saw a corpse hanging on their salon awning. As I got closer, I realized it was a man."

I guess I wasn't the only stylist who discovered dead bodies. "Did you know him?"

"It was kind of hard to place him with half his features missing. But I heard he was tied to a drug ring. A note had been pinned to his clothes that said *Happy Halloween*."

"And you think Lucy was involved?"

"That is what I suspected. The police came, and in a flash, half of New York was gaping at the scene. Photographers. Media. It was crazy. Lucy was taken in for questioning. I heard two stylists quit shortly after, and people shied away from the salon after that."

Hmm. Was this the real reason Lucy lost business? If so, why didn't Sabrina tell me this instead of pointing the finger at Kashi? Was she trying to protect Lucy's reputation? Or protect someone else?

Kashi stared down at the table. "I never should've left her room that night. Maybe she'd still be alive if I'd stayed."

"Why? What else happened?"

"Nothing noteworthy. Another friend showed up at Lucy's door. By then, it was very late. I was tuckered in and decided to hit the hatchet. I left as he came in."

"Who came in? Who was it?"

"Don't ask Kashi. I did not make his acquaintance. His

head was down, and he wore a ball cap and had an ugly snake tattoo on his arm."

"A *tattoo*. Did you share any of this with security?"

"Yes, when they questioned everyone after they found Lucy's body."

All I wanted was sleep, but after I finished with Kashi, I saw my mother talking to the captain. By the intense look on her face I knew it was about Tantig, and it didn't look good. I approached the two to find out what was going on.

The captain said the ship couldn't leave San Juan because Tantig's disappearance occurred while we were docked at a U.S. port. My mother argued that Tantig was on board, but the captain was adamant. He assured us they were working with the police in San Juan, and he'd let us know of any developments.

My parents went back to their cabin to see if there was anything they could find among Tantig's things that would explain her disappearance. I stumbled back to mine, wondering if Tantig really was on land.

I wobbled off the elevator, blisters stinging the backs of my feet, my hand throbbing, my head sore. The latest news from Kashi didn't make me feel any better either. If security knew about the tattooed man who'd entered Lucy and Sabrina's cabin, I bet Jock and Romero knew, too. And getting anything out of those two would be futile.

I put them out of my mind, stopped outside my cabin door, and wondered what Phyllis had been up to. My day wouldn't have been complete without some type of confrontation. I knew I shouldn't have expected the worst, but with everything else that had happened today, it was a safe bet.

I opened the door, and my gaze swung from Phyllis, combing through our suitcases, to the tornado-swept room. Clothes and toiletries were strewn everywhere. Yesterday's gown was in a heap on the bathroom floor, bras hung on doorknobs, and Phyllis's vitamins and souvenirs were scattered on the rug.

My first thought was that we'd been robbed. But even a burglar wouldn't make the mess Phyllis could. The backs of my eyes bled red, and nasty words brewed to the surface.

I inhaled, counted to three, and before I blew up, I took a good look at Phyllis. Her shades sat on top of her head, her feet were badly swollen, and huge blisters covered every inch of exposed skin. I looked half-dead, but Phyllis looked barbequed. I exhaled my rage and climbed the ladder to my bunk, asking with a gentle voice about her day.

She moaned, arms out, zombie-like. "If you didn't notice, I got burned to a crisp." Her sunglasses slid down over her forehead, and she tossed them on the bunk, flinching in pain from the sudden movement.

"And if that wasn't bad enough, I went on one of those tropical tours of a rainforest. El Yunque. What a mistake that was." She slapped down the flap on her suitcase, sank to the floor, and ripped off her sandals.

I was going to be sorry for asking, but I was a beggar for punishment. "Why was it a mistake?"

"Because I hiked twenty miles in these flimsy things." She hurled her sandals under the bed and rubbed her foot. "I knew I should've bought those hiking boots last time I was at Target. The trails were full of lizards, or whatever they call them down here, and there were stumps and stones all over the place. Not only that," she griped, "eerie-sounding birds swooped down around us. One even landed on my shoulder. What a pest. Everyone was snapping pictures like they'd never seen a bird before."

I refrained from rolling my eyes.

"And to top off the day, a snake slithered by and scared the bejeezus out of me. Then some idiot knocked into me because *she* was scared, and I slipped down a slope of rocks. And the tour guide didn't do a thing." She reached for her makeup bag and fished around inside.

"What do they pay these Pablos down here anyway? I should phone the parks and recreation people and get him fired. Because of him, I got pummeled under the waterfall. Now my neck is sore, and my blisters are breaking open. And I can't find my ointment anywhere." She abandoned her makeup bag and started searching through mine. "Did you take it?"

I was trying to pay attention to her when a white plastic bag on my pillow caught my eye. I scooped up the bag and peered inside at dozens of containers of Tic Tacs. Wisps of fear crawled down my neck. "Phyllis?"

Phyllis nattered on, absorbed in her search.

"Phyllis!" I shouted. "What's this?" I held up the bag.

"Oh yeah. Tic Tacs."

"I can see they're Tic Tacs. How'd they get here?"

"I don't know. The bag was hanging on the doorknob when I got back. I looked inside, saw the Tic Tacs, and figured you'd hung them there."

"If I was this close to our cabin, why wouldn't I bring them inside?"

"I don't know." She shrugged. "Why didn't you?"

"Because I didn't put them there."

"Then who did?"

I wrapped my hands around the bunk post and whacked my forehead on it three times. I looked at Phyllis, taste-testing my lip gloss, and gave my head another whack.

I climbed down from my bed and snatched my lip gloss from her hands. Then I stormed into the bathroom, scooped my dress off the floor, and stuffed it, my bra, and half a dozen other worn items back into my laundry sack.

"Let me see your shoulder bag," Phyllis said.

I swiped it from under her nose and sealed it tight. "You are not going through my beauty bag."

"But I need my ointment. These blisters are killing me."

"Use aloe vera. There's a bottle in the bathroom."

"That stuff gives me hives." She gawked at my bandage. "What happened to you?"

Thanks for *finally noticing*. "Nothing. Don't worry about it."

I continued to clean up her mess and found her tube of ointment under her bed. "Here." I thrusted it under her nose.

"What'd you put it there for?"

Oh brother. I swept my makeup bag from her grasp and escaped into the bathroom.

"What are you going to do with all the Tic Tacs?" she hollered.

I flung open the bathroom door. "Phyllis, I should tell you, Tantig is gone."

"Where'd she go?"

"I don't know. She's missing."

"Huh. Maybe she fell off the boat and drowned. Or maybe she was killed. You know they found that rude little woman dead. Cut up into a thousand pieces."

"Who told you that?"

"Clive."

"What time of day did he say this?"

"I don't know. What difference does that make?"

"I wondered how drunk he was when he fabricated that story."

"Don't underestimate Clive," she said. "He's not as dumb as he looks."

"Phyllis, Lucy was frozen inside an Aphrodite ice statue."

Her eyes got big and round. "Then there *is* a murderer on board."

"Would seem so. And why weren't you at the Captain's Gala last night?"

She put up her nose. "I ate at the bistro by the Internet center. Greek food gives me gas."

I was momentarily stunned. Who knew there were foods that disagreed with Phyllis?

"What are you doing about it?" she said, bringing me back to the conversation.

I shook my head. "I just want to find Tantig."

"Don't expect me to waste my time looking for her. I get my fill of old people every day of the week. This is my vacation, too."

I bit my cheeks. I wouldn't want to ruin Phyllis's holiday.

After the cabin was in order and Phyllis was slathered in ointment, I decided to poke around the ship some more. Maybe the captain was onto something. Maybe Tantig *was* in San Juan, and I was wasting my time searching the ship. The bag of Tic Tacs was telling me something, though. I just didn't know what. And I couldn't rid myself of the anxiousness until we found Tantig.

I cleaned my tear-stained face, made myself respectable, and came out of the bathroom ten minutes later to find Phyllis snoring through her nose and whistling out her mouth. I was tempted to stick cotton balls up her nose. Instead, I heaved a frustrated sigh. Phyllis had had her own tough day. I couldn't blame her for my problems. I just had too much on my mind.

My bandage was unraveling again, so I did a better job securing it, suddenly thinking about the picture of Lucy and Sabrina in their room. Again, who was the third person who'd been cut from the photo? Could it have been the friend who came to Lucy's door as Kashi left that night? Kashi said the guy had an ugly snake tattoo on his arm. If I was correct, the squiggle in the photo could've been a tattoo. But there were thousands of people on the ship. Where did I begin to look? And who knew if the person from the photo was even on the ship?

Kashi also said the guy wore a ball cap. I'd seen lots of men with ball caps. Most of the football sports jocks watching the mega-screen the first day at the pool wore ball caps. My mind went back to that day. I'd seen tattoos on several of their arms. But did any of them know Lucy or Sabrina? I hadn't kept tabs on the girls, but I couldn't recall seeing either one of them with a man. I'd seen

Candace with several of the football guys. Maybe she'd know something.

Once more, I started thinking about Lucy's body encased in ice, and this got me thinking about Tantig disappearing into thin air. If she wasn't on land and she didn't fall overboard, where was she? There must've been countless nooks and crannies on a ship this size. What if she was hurt? Or worse, dead? What if she was also stuffed in ice? My throat went tight as a fist as tender memories of Tantig rushed to mind. I swallowed hard. I had to pull myself together. I couldn't bear to think of Tantig frozen in an ice statue. That was ridiculous.

Where did that leave me? As I saw it, I had two options. One, leave it to the professionals to find Tantig. Or two, keep digging. I glared at the delivered Tic Tacs and decided on option two.

I grabbed my bag and headed for the door when the phone rang.

"We found Tantig," Romero said after I answered.

"You did?" Relief penetrated my bones, hearing those three words. "Where?"

"The market area in San Juan."

"Thank God." At the same moment, I felt a shift from under me and heard the ship's horn give a long blast. "Wait a minute. Why are we moving?"

"Likely, you're heading back out to sea."

"Not without Tantig!"

"Tantig's safe but in need of care. She got into a bit of trouble on land today, and she's dehydrated. They're keeping her in the hospital overnight."

I dragged the phone out into the hall, looked cautiously both ways—thanks to Jock—then started pacing. "She might be scared. She needs one of us 'there with her." I stopped short. "Hold on. I thought you went back to New York with Lucy's body."

"They decided to do the autopsy here. There may be ties to Lucy's murder in San Juan."

None of this made sense, and I still hadn't forgotten I was mad at Romero. But I cleared my head of romantic matters and concentrated on Tantig. "I've got to let my mother know she's all right."

"If the ship's moving, she already knows. And she's probably also been told they can pick up your great-aunt in a few days when the cruise ends in Miami. I'll personally make sure Tantig is delivered to you there."

Tears stung my eyes, threatening to spill. "Have you seen her?"

"No. I haven't had the pleasure of meeting her yet. I'm at the station right now." He muffled the phone, said thanks to someone in the background, then came back on the line. "I have to go."

"Wait! You didn't say what kind of trouble she was in."

"It'll be in the report."

"Report! What report?"

"Look, they're paging me. She's in good hands. Don't worry."

We disconnected, and I gave myself a second to take this all in. A shaky breath left me, relief that Tantig was fine. Then I thought about Romero, and I didn't know what to feel.

Maybe he'd fallen for another woman, but he'd still shown concern when it came to my family. If nothing else, I needed to be sure the woman Twix had seen at his place was his lover. My best friend liked to exaggerate. Well, no more guessing or snooping. In the morning, I'd call Twix and get the story straight.

I gave my mother a quick call before turning in. Though we were both ambivalent about leaving Tantig behind, we agreed she'd receive good care. That was what was most important. If they threw in a room with a TV, she wouldn't mind if she didn't see us at all until Christmas. Since there was nothing else we could do now, we said goodnight.

I crept back into the cabin, locked the door, and put the phone on the toadstool table. Phyllis gave a loud snort that all but loosened the screws on the bunk. I got ready for bed, ripped open a package of complimentary earplugs, and stuffed them in my ears.

Within seconds, I was deaf to the world.

Chapter 12

I woke Tuesday morning, feeling relieved yet blue. Tantig was alive and well, and for that alone I should've jumped out of bed, ready to start the day. But when I thought about the cruise almost being over, I felt disappointment.

Such a large ship, and I hadn't even had the full benefit of enjoying what it had to offer. I hadn't taken in any nightly shows, hadn't played the casino, tried the waterslide, high ropes, golf simulator, rock climbing, or even gone for a swim. My ass-backward plunge into the pool the first day didn't count. Jock was partly responsible for that. I'd spent all my time getting into trouble, avoiding trouble, and saving others from trouble. Some holiday! Oh wait. I did win the Saber Cup thanks to my swordfight with Kashi. What was I complaining about?

Stop crying over spilled milk, an inner voice said. You're ticked because you can't get Romero off your mind. I went to yawn and jammed my jaws tight out of frustration. Couldn't even have a decent yawn because of Romero.

I stretched my arms and legs, deciding to get on with the day despite the fact my blisters were killing me and my bandage was gray and unraveling again. I peered over at the bag of Tic Tacs I'd tossed on the floor last night. Right. I hung my head over the bunk. Where was Phyllis? She usually slept until…

I glanced at the clock. Eeks! Nine-thirty. How could I have slept so late? Why didn't I hear Phyllis get up and leave? I wiggled my ears. *Darn*. Earplugs. I tugged them out and leaped down the ladder.

Not sure what to do first, I looked down at my hand and finished unraveling my bandage. Instantly, I was back to another time when I was a kid and I'd scraped myself. I'd been riding my bike on a gravel road, had taken a corner too fast, and wiped out. My parents weren't home, and when I dragged my sorry butt into the house, Tantig wordlessly cleaned my palm and stuck a bandage on my hand. Then she'd patted my shoulder. "You're going to be all right." Her tone was dry, and there wasn't a lot of power behind the pat. But she was there. And that was comforting.

I swallowed a lump in my throat while I gaped from my clean wound to the used bandage. I didn't need this clumsy piece of cloth anymore. And I sure didn't need to keep looking at these Tic Tacs. There could've been any number of logical reasons why they were hanging on the doorknob in the first place. However, this no longer concerned me.

I swiped them off the floor, tossed them in the garbage, and decided to forget about them. Since Tantig was okay, I planned to do some sleuthing today into Lucy's background. Maybe I'd even find time for a swim.

I showered, then stuck a small bandage on my palm to keep it protected. While I was at it, I did the same for the backs of both feet. Today was going to be slip-ons all the way.

I applied my makeup, shimmied into a green sundress, and braided my hair down my back. I ordered breakfast from room service. Then I called Twix.

"It's about time you got back to me," she said. "I've been trying your cell forever. I keep telling you to leave that thing on you."

"It's on me when I need it." Usually.

She sighed and moved on. "I don't want to worry you, but…"

I didn't like the sound of that. "But what?"

"That blond at Romero's. Dressed to kill, all slinky and sexy. And she had this silky voice and protective attitude, like she owned the place."

I wanted to give Romero the benefit of the doubt on this, but Twix's insistence on the woman being his lover was making it hard. "He told me the woman was his sister."

"Ha! I've never known a man's sister to act so possessive. When I pulled away from the curb, I saw her open the door and waltz right into the house."

"Maybe she was checking up on the place."

"She was checking up on something, sweetheart. I'm just not sure what."

Twix could be a drama queen like Max, but she never failed to pique my curiosity.

If it wasn't Romero's sister, then who was this woman? Possessive airs. Silky voice. Hold on a minute. I knew that silky voice. I'd heard it with my own two ears. Suddenly, it became clear. *Belinda.* Didn't Romero say they'd finished up early, and she'd flown home while he came to Puerto Rico? She sure didn't waste time moving into his house.

I looked down at the mile of bandage I'd left in a heap on the table. Feeling abandoned inside, I gripped the wad and threw it at the wall, watching it hit the floor and unwind. Romero was no different from all the other creeps I'd dated. In fact, he was worse. *Taking things slow.* Making me believe he cared. Boy, was I dumb.

I heard whining in the background.

"Listen, toots," Twix said, "I've got to go. Laura Panetti's kid is here this week. Remember Laura from ballet class? She used to suck on her ballet slipper ties, and when she tired of that, she switched to her hair. Her kid sucks on everything he gets his hands on, mostly his middle three fingers. Drives me up the wall." I could see Twix raising her palm to the sky.

"I'm thinking of dipping his fingers in jalapeño sauce. Give him something to taste." She chuckled. "By the way, you didn't tell me how the contest went."

True. And I didn't feel like talking about it now. "Lost."

"Are you kidding me? You're the best stylist I know. What kind of sorry-ass judges did they hire not to see your amazing talent?"

"They didn't announce it, but I think Jock was one of the judges."

"Oh." I heard her gulp. "His ass is anything but sorry. Probably would've looked fixed if he'd chosen you."

"I would've been okay with that."

She sighed in agreement. "What are you going to do about the children's wing?"

I shrugged my shoulders as if she was sitting beside me. "I haven't figured that out yet. I don't know why I aim for unreachable goals. I must be stupid."

"You're not stupid. And you'll figure it out." She hung up.

Right. *I've got no money to donate, but I'll figure it out. Maybe I'll figure out Romero, too.* I'd been taken in by his good looks and charm. Who hadn't? But I wasn't going to obsess over him anymore. I didn't need Romero. I'd get along fine without some macho cop in my life.

I pitched the phone back in my bag and walked over to the corner. I picked up the bandage, wrapped it in a ball, and tossed it in the garbage on top of the Tic Tacs. Then I took a good hard look at myself.

I wasn't stupid. I'd solved murders, hadn't I? Plus, I'd sat at the captain's table. What kind of stupid person did that? I'd even won the Saber Cup, sword fighting. I must've shown *some* brawn and intelligence! I grimaced at my wrecked bow still cradled inside the trophy. Well, nobody was perfect.

Room service delivered my breakfast and saved me from any more self-pity. I ate everything down to the last bite of egg, then put my tray outside the cabin door.

Devon, the tablecloth guy, was wheeling a cart down the hall, picking up discarded breakfast trays. He was dressed in a flat-topped white hat and a white buttoned-up jacket, the sleeve smeared with shiny brown grease. Now that I saw him up close, I noticed he had a skinny goatee and a Fu Manchu mustache that hung limply from the corners of his mouth. The rest of his blond hair was pulled back in a neat ponytail.

He smiled at me as he rolled by. "Gotta snag these trays before those hardy iguanas eat all the leftovers."

My eyebrows hiked up to my hairline. "Iguanas?"

"Yeah." He shrugged. "Those creatures are everywhere. Don't know how they get on the ship. When we find them in the kitchen, we throw them in the soup."

I must've paled because he gave me a toothy grin.

"Kidding!"

"Ha. Funny." Grinning back, I closed the door, remembering Chef Roy's remark that Devon always had a joke to crack. At this point, I could use a good laugh.

I brushed and flossed my teeth, applied a coat of lipstick, and thought again about digging into Lucy's background. What was her involvement in that homicide at her salon? Who were her enemies? How was she tied to the drug world? I reached for my phone to start a search but chucked that idea. I'd rather leave my cramped room and use an actual computer at the Internet center. And maybe I'd get to see some of the ship while I was at it. With renewed purpose to my day, I slid into my green heels, swung my bag over my shoulder, and sprinted out of the cabin.

I took the elevator to the grand atrium and stepped out into the glorious plaza as if I'd walked onto the red carpet. I knew I'd seen a computer center somewhere. I meandered around, going in and out of boutiques, distracted by all the unique things to see. Jewelry. Clothes. A leather store. What the hell. I was on vacation. I could afford a bit of time to window-shop, couldn't I?

An hour later, I'd worn out the lady in the diamond store and tired out the salesclerk in the leather shop. But it had been fun. No one watching or judging or complaining. It was just me.

I strolled past the bistro where Phyllis had dined Sunday

night and finally ambled into the Internet center. The lighting was soft, and private computers sat on desks divided by partitions.

I asked the lady in charge if I could use a computer. She led me behind a partition, typed in a code, and told me to let her know if I needed assistance. I thanked her and turned my attention to the screen.

The drug-related murder outside Lucy's shop had happened about a year ago. What did Sabrina say the salon was called? Shortcuts? Yes. I typed *Murder outside Shortcuts Hair Salon, New York City*, pressed ENTER, and waited.

There it was, spread across a half page in the *New York Post*. DRUG RING CENTERED AROUND NEW YORK SALON. Interesting caption. Photograph and everything. I scanned the article about the drug dealer who was found dead and thought Lucy was implicated more strongly than Kashi had suggested. She wasn't arrested for the murder, but this had to have hurt business. I now understood her reasons for wanting to win the contest.

I looked at the picture again. Several people were lowering the dead man off the awning. I blinked and studied it closer. What? I zoomed in. There it was! The snake tattoo on a guy standing at the sidelines. Too many people in the picture made it hard to get a clear view, and enlarging the newsprint only created a blur. I checked the *Post*'s online site, but the picture wasn't much clearer.

I swallowed hard and fell against the back of my chair. Who was this tattooed man? And was this the same guy Kashi saw at Lucy's door? Seemed like a huge reach. Lots of men had snake tattoos. And this shot was taken in New York City—hundreds of miles away from here. But something told me my suspicions weren't so bizarre.

If the tattooed man knew Lucy and had possibly been involved in the drug dealer's murder, and there was a drug-smuggling ring on board the ship, who was to say he wasn't here right now? Maybe I was grasping at straws, looking for something that wasn't there.

I was also suspicious of Molly and Polly's dealings, and

I wasn't sure where that was leading either. But I had a gut feeling there was a connection in all this to Lucy's death.

If I could've trusted Romero, I'd have shared my findings and asked more questions. But I couldn't trust him. And what about Jock? He knew something was going down. He was a master-at-arms after all. Why bother sharing any more thoughts with him? So he could have a wee laugh? The only answer was to keep digging on my own. One way or another I'd get to the bottom of this.

It was one o'clock by the time I'd finished my Internet search. I was hungry but wasn't in the mood for the noisy buffet dining room. I ambled over to the bistro and ordered a bowl of squash soup with half a bacon and tomato sandwich, a peanut butter cookie, and pomegranate juice. The bistro was quiet. Only a couple staring starry-eyed at each other over a cappuccino, and a business suit reading the newspaper while devouring a bagel. I took a seat, happy to be in my little nook all by myself, eating my lunch, staring out at the plaza.

I was blowing on my soup, gingerly swallowing each hot spoonful, when I spotted Sabrina. She walked by hand in hand with one of the sports jocks who'd been slugging back Coronas and laughing at football bloopers playing on the mega-screen that first day by the pool. He had perfectly cut brown hair, a square jaw, and he was dressed in shorts and a red football jersey with a white twenty-three across his chest. They kissed on the friendly side, then Sabrina hurried to the glass elevator, and the football guy moseyed into the bistro.

I all but dunked my head in my soup as he strode by, not sure why I was acting silly. I guess I didn't want him to think I'd been ogling them. Or staring at his biceps.

The hunk ordered a BLT, chicken noodle soup, and a Mountain Dew, then sat at the next table, facing me. Lovely. Now I had nothing to look at but this six-foot-tall glorious creature. No book. No magazine. Not even a menu. And my cell phone was in my bag. Wouldn't that look brilliant, whipping it out, looking all self-important, focused on some app. Nope. I had salt and pepper shakers and a feature card standing on my table. That would have to do.

I munched on my sandwich and nabbed the card, feigning interest in the slice of Rocky Road cake that was on special for eight-ninety-five. Fascinating. I nodded and flipped the card over, reading the same thing on the other side.

"Excuse me," Football Guy said from his table. "May I borrow your salt?"

"Salt? Be my guest."

He rose from his chair, approached the table, and reached out for the salt shaker. I went back to slurping my soup. Then I saw it. The snake tattoo on his arm.

Chapter 13

I coughed and spit soup back in my bowl—all class—grabbing my napkin to wipe my mouth.

Football Guy gave me a puzzled look. "You okay?"

I coughed some more and fanned my face. "Soup's… hot."

He sat down again, and I tried not to gawk at him. Who was this guy with the snake tattoo? And why had he kissed Sabrina? Was this the man who came to their room the last night Lucy was seen alive?

I was boiling from the inside out, looking around as if I'd come face to face with a murderer, yet I couldn't scream for help. *Calm down. You said yourself lots of people have snake tattoos. Oodles of people. They were everywhere.* Right. To date, I'd seen, um…exactly one, belonging to Football Guy.

Maybe I had it all wrong. This guy came on board with a pack of jocks. I saw them by the pool. But maybe this guy wasn't from the pack. Maybe he was here on his own, and he happened to wear a jersey, looking all big and hunky. And naturally, I placed him with the sports fanatics. But if he was Sabrina's boyfriend, he had good reason to stop by their room the night of the party. Just a friendly celebration, right? Oh boy. This wasn't helping. I was getting confused.

"How 'bout them Patriots." He salted his soup.

What? Was he from Boston? "Yeah." I smiled warily. "How 'bout 'em." If he was going to talk football, I was outta here. I never caught on to the football craze, maybe because when I was in high school and most students were having fun cheering for the team, I was playing the clarinet in the marching band with the other nerds, hashing out "The Star Spangled Banner."

"First place in their conference," he said. "Some would say they're due for a beating."

"Yeah. Nothing like a good beating."

He gave me a strange smile and dug into his soup. Probably sorry he tried to make nice.

That was fine with me. I didn't need to talk sports to humor some jock, or worse, a possible murderer. At the moment, I could barely focus on anything but his tattoo. Once again, the New York photo came to mind. Was he the guy on the sidelines? Was he part of a drug ring? Had he killed Lucy?

I tightened my jaw, deciding what to do with all this when I heard a commotion out in the corridor. I scooped up my cookie bag and drink and edged to the entrance of the bistro. I heard a breathy female sigh. Then two. I knew without looking, Hercules was approaching. I peeked to my left. Yep. Jock de Marco in the perfect flesh, sauntering down the corridor, leaving panting women in his wake.

Just my luck. I didn't feel like bumping into Jock or his harem. I ducked back into the bistro and stationed myself at a corner table until the coast was clear.

Football Guy turned and watched my dance. Big deal. I came back in to eat my dessert. He gave a slight eye roll, then swiveled back to his lunch.

I ripped open my pastry bag and chomped down on the peanut butter cookie. I chewed slowly and watched Jock walk by the bistro. He headed to the purser's desk where the captain appeared from an inner room. They spoke for a minute with the purser, then leaned casually against the desk like they were waiting for something to happen.

I poked my head up, trying to see all angles of the plaza. Who were they waiting for? People were moving about. Nothing looked suspicious. But something was about to happen. I was sure of it. I shoved more cookie into my mouth, crunching furiously, sitting on the edge of my seat.

"Have a nice day," Football Guy whispered over my shoulder.

"Aah!" I dropped my cookie bag on the floor. *No! He couldn't leave.* I needed to see where he was going. But what about Jock and the captain? Something was in the works. I couldn't just get up and go.

I caught my breath. "Uh, you too." I picked up the bag and watched him walk out the bistro down the corridor from where Jock had just come.

It took everything inside me to stay riveted to the table. I dug my heels in the ground, bit into my cookie, and resumed staring at Jock. A moment later, Molly and Polly bounced out of the leather store draped in brown leather jackets, matching shorts, and high-heeled boots that rode over their kneecaps to their thighs.

A chunk of cookie dropped out of my mouth onto my lap. I ignored it because I was trying to swallow without choking. Earlier, I'd had on the exact jacket and had delicately handed it back to the store clerk when she told me it was on sale for three thousand dollars. And here Molly and Polly were each wearing one. Holy Doodle. Where'd they get their money?

They wiggled their way over to Jock and Captain Madera. I didn't like the possibilities forming in my mind. Had I missed something? Was this a double date? A proposition?

I searched my mind for what I knew about Molly and Polly so far. They were from California, had very little wardrobe, and from what I'd just seen, expensive taste. In San Juan, Max and I had both witnessed them doing something that screamed illegal. Added to that, they'd trapped me in the steam room. I didn't want to get ahead of myself, but were they also responsible for the bag of Tic Tacs hanging on my cabin door? If so, what purpose did that serve?

I tapped my fingers on the table, deep in thought. What did any of this have to do with Captain Madera and Jock? Maybe this rendezvous was related to the drug smuggling Jock had mentioned. He must've been onto them, though he certainly played dumb when I mentioned their names yesterday after the steam-room incident. Like he didn't know who they were.

I narrowed my eyes on Jock, waiting to see his next move.

Captain Madera opened his arms to Molly and Polly. The girls were all smiles. Jock's gaze dropped well below their smiles. Probably wondering which one floated better. His grin already told me he knew their cup sizes. *Animal.* Didn't look like he was taking them in for questioning. Seemed like the furthest thing from his perverted mind.

Hang on! Maybe Jock didn't know about the San Juan drug deal. I glanced at my hand and scowled, recalling our talk in the infirmary. All I'd insinuated was that Molly and Polly were responsible for my hand being bandaged. I didn't tell Jock I'd seen them on land or say anything about the drug deal. As usual, I was too busy defending my pride, such as it was. So what did all this mean? Was he cozying up to them because he didn't believe my story? Or did he have his eye on them, trying to gather evidence?

Captain Madera led Molly and Polly to the glass elevators. The ladies swayed enticingly in front of Jock, who followed, head down. I didn't have to guess what part of the anatomy he was scrutinizing now.

I threw my cookie bag in the garbage and tossed the juice bottle in the recycling. I lingered at the doorway, pretending to look at a stand loaded with coffee bags. Like I was a connoisseur. I did a mental shrug. Okay, so I didn't drink the stuff. Didn't mean I couldn't start. I picked up a bag and sniffed the hickory-roasted beans. Then I gave a casual look toward the elevators.

Captain Madera, Jock, and the girls stepped inside an elevator, and Polly placed her hand on Jock's butt. What? I stepped toward them to get a better look, and *pish*. The coffee bag caught on the stand's sharp edge, and an instant burst of hickory filled the air as coffee beans scattered on the floor. I looked up from the beans. *Darn*. The glass elevator doors closed, but not before Jock's hard stare met mine. The elevator went up three floors, then disappeared.

The lady from the bistro ran out with a broom and dustpan, giving me a tight smile.

"Sorry." I bent to help gather beans. "I don't know what happened."

"It's okay," she said. "I could see you had more on your mind than just beans."

I was still trying to process what this meeting between Jock and the captain and the girls was all about when my cell phone chirped in my bag. It was my mother, and she was frantic.

"I just spoke to Tantig," she cried, "but it wasn't Tantig."

I found a quiet spot outside the bistro and turned my back on the noise. "What are you talking about?"

"I told the captain I wanted to speak to Tantig today to make sure she was okay."

"And?"

"When I heard her voice, I knew right away they had the wrong woman."

"What do you mean, *wrong woman*?" I replayed my conversation with Romero. He'd disclosed that Tantig had gotten into a bit of trouble on land. "Romero said Tantig was safe but dehydrated. If the woman wasn't Tantig, who are they holding?"

"Another woman! She stole Tantig's purse and ID sometime yesterday morning and walked right off the ship with it. Probably no one paid much attention to an elderly lady shuffling about. Then, once she was on land, she tried to rob a jewelry store."

I straightened. The robbery Max had witnessed! This was likely the bit of trouble Romero was referring to. Even Max had mistaken the lady for Tantig. "What did the captain say?"

"They're still working with the police in San Juan. They think Tantig could still be on land."

I pressed my lips together. "How? If she didn't have her purse or ID?"

"I don't know how!" my mother almost shouted into the phone.

"Okay. Listen, I'll start looking for her again."

"What's the point, if she's in San Juan?"

"There's a chance she could be on board, right?"

"Yes, but it sounds unlikely."

"Won't hurt to look then. Between them searching in San Juan, and us scouring the ship, we'll find her." I tried to put my mother at ease, then hung up and instantly envisioned the bag of Tic Tacs again.

As much as I wanted to let that go, there was a reason they were placed on my door. And I was afraid that whoever had put them there had also taken Tantig. But if someone had kidnapped her, why would they have drawn attention to themselves by delivering mints? Unless it was some kind of warning. Warning for what, though? To stop looking for my great-aunt? To stop digging into Lucy's murder? Were the two even linked? Up until a few minutes ago, we believed Tantig was back in San Juan. Did that factor into a potential kidnapper's plan? Or were they waiting for that misunderstanding to be cleared up so they could issue another warning?

I wasn't going to jump to conclusions. Maybe it did sound like Tantig could've been kidnapped. But I was positive I'd seen her leave the dining room yesterday during the Mexican buffet. There was a distinct possibility she'd found a cozy place to hibernate, and we simply hadn't discovered where that cozy spot was.

I rubbed my arms, suddenly chilled from the air-conditioning. Why not take my search outside? I'd been indoors long enough today. Maybe the heat and sunshine would give me a new perspective.

I started at one end of the ship and hurtled along the deck, showing Tantig's picture to anyone who would give me the time of day. I snooped in and out of doors, ducking through alleyways, often coming back to where I started. I continued showing her picture to everyone I passed. I may have even asked some guests twice if they'd seen her. Several passengers showed genuine concern. Others gave me a put-out look like I was ruining their cruise. Far be it for me to spoil anyone's vacation!

Wiping my brow from heat and frustration, I walked by the pool and squinted from the sun's reflection off the water. An old country tune hummed through the speakers, and people were soaking up the last days of the cruise, splashing, lounging, and playing games.

I spotted Max, lying in the shade, water wings on his arms, sunglasses on his nose, tall glass in hand, a stack of magazines by his side. I strolled over and dropped onto the foot of his lounge chair, tossing my braid over my shoulder.

"Hey!" He bounced up with a start. "Where have you been?"

"Looking for Tantig." I grabbed the glass out of his hand and took a swig. "Mmm, what is this?"

"Fruit punch."

I smacked my lips and took another sip. "Yum."

He plucked the glass out of my hand. "You've had enough."

I huffed. "You wouldn't give a dying person a drink of punch."

"A dying person, yes. You, no." He sipped his drink and set it on the magazine table away from my reach. "And what do you mean you're looking for Tantig? I thought you said security saw her get off the ship in San Juan yesterday morning. Didn't they find her?"

"It's a long story. First, they thought they found her. Then they realized they hadn't."

Max looked confused.

"Remember that woman trailing diamonds out of the jewelry store yesterday? Ends up she stole more than just diamonds. She stole Tantig's purse and ID from the ship."

Max sat up. "What does that mean?"

"For one thing, that woman was a thief. For another, I'm back to searching for Tantig."

I looked around the pool and saw Phyllis at the bar, making wild hand gestures to Clive. She was wearing a scarf-type hat spilling with fruit, and a sarong and matching bikini top splashed with every color under the rainbow. Her stomach was Eskimo-white, her shoulders and arms, devil-red. "What's Phyllis doing talking to Clive?"

Max glanced at the bar. "You mean Carmen Miranda? She thinks he has something to do with Tantig's disappearance."

"Come again? I just told you she's officially missing."

"Phyllis has obviously believed it all along. Don't ask me to figure her out. You hired her."

I rolled back to last night and remembered telling Phyllis about Tantig's disappearance. Of course, that was before Romero had called with the news that they'd found her on land. And since Phyllis had fallen asleep before I could deliver *that* news, she was running with the former. Which in the end happened to be the most accurate since Tantig's reappearance was a case of mistaken identity.

I watched Clive in his black Speedo duck away from Phyllis's sweeping gestures. Then I glanced back at Max. "Who's Carmen Miranda?"

He whipped out his phone, tapped the screen, and held it out to me. "Brazilian singer-actress from way back when, known for her fruit-salad hats."

I stared from the photo of the actress to Phyllis. Another costumed masterpiece.

I shook my head and went back to thinking about her

statement that Clive wasn't as dumb as he looked. "Clive can barely stand on his own two tiny feet. How does she suppose he could've abducted Tantig?"

Max reached for a magazine. "Lovey, I'm trying to enjoy my time by the pool. Up until a minute ago, I was doing just that."

"Oh, so I'm being a pest."

"Not a pest, but you do seem peeved. Care to share?"

Share? Did I tell Max how anxious I was over Tantig's disappearance? My fears about Molly and Polly? Or the football guy who had his lips glued to Sabrina's face and who happened to have a snake tattoo, the same snake tattoo that appeared in the *New York Post* at a crime scene in front of Lucy's shop? And that was just the half of it.

Did I reveal that I planned to tell Romero to hit the road once the cruise was over? Was that even what I wanted?

My stomach tightened into a knot at the thought of saying goodbye to the man I once called Iron Man, but it was for the best, *my* best. I wouldn't stand on the sidelines while Romero had his fling with his female partner, even if she *was* climbing her way to the top. I had standards, too.

No, I didn't feel much like sharing. "Another time." I targeted my stare at Phyllis—another worry—nose to nose with Clive. And when did she start caring about Tantig? Last night she was fed up with old people. Today she was Florence Nightingale.

The country song died in the background, and the cruise director stood on her platform and held a hand in the air. Everyone was getting good at following her lead, and instantly there was silence.

"What's going on?" I whispered to Max.

"Julie McCoy's playing Name That Beauty Tune with the crowd. They're mostly old hits from way back when." He smiled. "So far, Clive's answered all five wrong. I can't wait to hear what he slurs this time."

"All right, everyone." The cruise director had an optimistic smile in place. "What was the name of the last song? And *who* was the artist?" She asked this like it was the million-dollar question. I even thought I heard a drum roll.

Clive swung his stool away from Phyllis and threw his limp, gauzed arm in the air, ice cubes clinking in his empty glass. "Thath eathy. 'Jumpin' Jack Flash' by the Rolling Stones."

The crowd snickered. Max snorted punch through his nose.

"Uh, no sir," the cruise director said, probably wishing Clive would go drown himself. "It was 'Stand by Your Man' by Tammy Wynette."

"Clothe enough!" Clive saluted. "That song don't even have the word beauty in it. What do I win?"

"Uh, let's try another," she said.

Another oldie piped through the speakers. Clive cocked his ear, nodding harmoniously, his bandaged arm resting on the bar, finger waving in the air.

I watched him for a moment, then turned back to Max, curiosity getting the better of me. "Know why Clive's wearing a bandage on his arm?"

Max shrugged. "Nope. Haven't gotten close enough to ask."

I bit my bottom lip. Probably a cut. Or maybe he had stitches or had a mole removed.

"Boy, is she a sucker for punishment," Max giggled, shaking his head at the cruise director.

"Speaking of"—I hoisted myself off the lounger—"I better go see what Phyllis is up to."

"Aww. And spoil the fun?"

I looked down at Max and, for a second, saw double. Probably the hot sun. I needed my own punch. I gave him a smile, then went up to the bartender and ordered one.

"What kind of punch?" he asked.

I whirled around and pointed to Max, who was holding up his glass in a toast to me. "One like the guy over there is drinking. With a twist of lime, please."

The bartender craned his neck past me. "The guy with the yellow trunks and water wings?"

"Yes."

"The guy with the stack of magazines and a rubber duckie?"

"*Yes.*"

"Lady, that's not punch. Your friend's drinking a Long Island Iced Tea. And judging from your size, a punch is exactly what it'll do to you if you drink one. Kapow! Right between the eyes, followed by you crashing to the deck."

"I'll have one."

His eyebrows went wide.

"Without the liquor."

I glared at Max, and he gave me one of his looks that said *What?* Mr. Innocent.

A moment later, the bartender handed me a drink. "And here's your twist of lime." He spread a wedge of lime on the rim of the glass.

"Thanks." I took a sip. "Hey! This tastes like cola."

"Exactly. Without the vodka, gin, rum, tequila, and triple sec, that's what you've got."

I did an eye roll and slapped a tip on the counter. Then I slid over to Phyllis and Clive.

"Hey there." I clinked Clive's glass, trying not to look at his gaunt little frame, sagging pecs, or, God forbid, anything lower.

"How are ya?" He gave a simple smile and scratched his head. "Have we met?"

"Yes. I'm Valentine Beaumont."

"Nice to make your acquaintanth."

I nodded at Phyllis. Her feet were puffy, a nausea patch was stuck behind her ear, and her shoulders were peeling in long, blistery strips. True, I'd fallen in a lifeboat, almost died in a steam room, and endured a swordfight with Kashi, but Phyllis was a walking disaster. Better take it easy on her. "What's up, Phyllis?"

She tapped her toe like she was a prosecutor in a courtroom. "I'm asking Clive what he knows about Tantig and the murder."

Clive smiled dopily from Phyllis to me. I turned my

back slightly to him. "I think you should leave him alone."

"I thought you wanted to find her."

"I thought you didn't want to be bothered."

"Well, I couldn't sleep last night because of it."

"You? Couldn't sleep? Who was setting off the earthquake in our room?" So much for taking things easy.

"Maybe I slept a little. But I got to thinking about Clive and how he was dancing with Tantig in the lounge the other day."

The hairs on my neck stood on end. "What? When was Clive dancing with Tantig?"

"I don't know. The other day."

"What other day? Saturday? Sunday? Yesterday?"

"Lemme see. Lemme see. It was after I got back from the tour of Nassau. I stopped to get a bottled water and peeked into the lounge. Tantig and Clive were holding each other up on the dance floor."

I bit my lip, processing this. "That was Sunday."

"Okay. Sunday."

Clive had lost interest in eavesdropping. Smart man. He'd swiveled back toward the bar and ordered another drink.

"So, I put two and two together," Phyllis continued, "and figured Clive was guilty."

"Tell me how you came up with that 'cause you lost me." I sipped my drink, thinking I was in for a long explanation.

"After they were done dancing, he persuaded Tantig to go back to his room where she's now handcuffed to a bed, stark naked."

Cola spritzed through my mouth and sprayed onto Phyllis.

"What the—" She wiped soda off her arm and threw her hands on her hips.

"Phyllis, do you hear yourself?" I grabbed a napkin off the bar and dabbed my lips.

"What! Dr. Phil had a guest last week, and she was a victim of date rape, like Tantig."

I looked at Clive, arms flattened on the bar, head barely up. It'd be a miracle if he walked a straight line, let alone led Tantig into a cabin, stripped her naked, and tied her to a bedpost. And from what I'd already seen of our shrunken friend, I didn't want to visualize him in anything less than a Speedo. I already knew I'd have nightmares from that image.

"Tantig didn't go back to Clive's room, Phyllis. She was with my parents at the captain's dinner that night. And my mother sent her for a walk the next morning. That's the last time she saw Tantig."

"If she didn't go back to Clive's room," Phyllis said, "then who could've taken her?"

"I don't know." I looked down at my cola. "I'd need more than a virgin Long Island Iced Tea to figure that out."

"I know who took her," Clive piped. Then he stared at me with a slobbery grin. "How are ya? Have we met?"

Phyllis yanked Clive's willowy beard. "She's Valentine!"

"Thought she looked familiar." He hiccupped.

"Clive," I said. "Who took Tantig?"

"It was that beautiful Rita Hayworth doll."

"What's he babbling about?" Phyllis asked.

"Rita Hayworth," I said. "Redheaded actress from the forties or fifties." I motioned for the bartender to bring Clive a coffee. Then something struck me. I was trying not to get ahead of myself, but panic was beating me to it. "Do you mean Sabrina?" I asked Clive. "The redhead from the contest?"

"Could be." He breathed out alcoholic fumes, and I backed away. "I'm not too good with names."

Or faces. The coffee came, and I cajoled Clive into sipping some.

"Blech!" He sputtered. "Whaddya trying to do? Kill me?" He cranked his head to the bar and held up his glass to the bartender. "Fill 'er up."

The bartender followed orders.

"Okay, Clive." Impatience tickled my neck. Much more

of this, and I was afraid I'd lose my cool. "How 'bout you answer my questions, and then have another drink."

"Whas in it for me?"

"If you answer my questions"—I took a frantic search around for an incentive, my gaze stopping at Carmen Miranda beside me—"Phyllis will give you a kiss."

Clive gave Phyllis and her fruity hat a frightening look. Phyllis dropped her jaw.

Okay, dumb idea. "If you answer my questions, I'll, uh, buy you another drink."

"Deal!"

"Now, what makes you think Sabrina took Tantig?"

"I saw it with my own two eyes."

I peered into his bloodshot, bleary eyes. And I was considering anything he had to say as gospel? "When did you see this?"

"The other day."

Here we go again. "What day?"

"Yesh-terday."

Without looking, he reached out for his fresh drink, but I slid the coffee cup in his hand instead. He took a hearty slurp and choked it back up. "Hey, that wath nasty."

"You promised to answer my questions."

"Whaddya wanna know?"

Brother. "Clive, what did you see?"

"I was lying right over there on one of those lounge thingys, waiting for the bar to open." He gave a peaceful smile. "I like to get a head shtart on the day."

"And?"

"And that's when I shaw her. Rita Hayworth. She came jogging down the deck with all that glorioush red hair bouncing in the breeze, and she met up with Tantig. I shaw them talk, then Tantig shuffled off with Rita."

Something was wrong with this picture. Sabrina jogged by the other morning right before I saw Tantig scuffing her feet aimlessly. But it wasn't yesterday. Yesterday was Monday. I was in bed with Jock on Monday. Anxiousness swirled in my stomach at that thought. I rolled back another day and saw it clearly in my mind. Sunday morning, early, before everyone had disembarked for Nassau, I was walking the deck when I saw Sabrina and then Tantig.

"Are you sure it was yesterday, Clive? And not Sunday?"

"Yep."

Phyllis crossed her arms, eyes on Clive. "How can you be so sure?"

I glared at Phyllis playing the heavy cop.

Clive leaned off his barstool. "I got a lot more going on up here than you think." He tapped his skull at Phyllis like he wasn't going to take her abuse. A second later, he did a nose-plant to the deck. Whump. Out cold.

I grabbed his drink and splashed his head. Nothing. Then I dumped my drink on him. Finally, he stirred, hoisted his tiny butt in the air, and attempted to get up. Phyllis and I scooped him under his armpits and heaved him to a standing position.

"Thath better." He shifted himself onto the stool and gave me a blurry-eyed stare. "I shaw them Sunday, too. *Hic.* Kinda liked watching Rita's routine."

Maybe Sabrina knew *Tantig's* routine, and she'd decided on a good time to nab her. But why? What possible reason could she have had to abduct Tantig? On top of that, unless she'd hidden Tantig in her cabin—which she didn't because I'd already searched it—she would've had to hide her somewhere where no one would find her. And this would require knowing the ship inside out. Which would rule out passengers. There were so many places off-limits to guests. Somebody unfamiliar with the ship would be taking a huge chance kidnapping someone without a clue of where he or she was going. That left the crew. And that could be anyone from a cabin boy to a store clerk. Though this was all true, something still nagged at me.

I turned back to Clive. "Did you see where they went?"

He blinked. "Won't do you any good."

"Why not?"

"Only I know where it is."

Chapter 14

I looked straight into Clive's eyes. "Then you'll take us."

Phyllis harrumphed. "Are you crazy? He can't even stand up."

This posed a problem. I looked around for inspiration. A pair of stilts the cruise director had used in a contest sat by a trunk of life preservers. No good. Skateboard? Another contest. Nope. In the corner of the deck, two wheelchairs sat folded into themselves. I asked the bartender if they were free to use.

"Be my guest," he said with a wave.

I left Clive with his head on the bar, then dodged for a wheelchair. I popped it open and wheeled it back over. "Okay, Clive, get in."

He rolled his head up, focusing a bloodshot eye on me. "In what?"

I jiggled the wheelchair. "This!"

He twisted around in his stool. "What for?"

"So you can take us to wherever it was you saw Sabrina take Tantig."

"*Hic.* Who's Sabrina?"

"Do you get the feeling you're going around in circles?" Phyllis twirled her index finger around her temple where a plastic apple was loosely hanging from her headpiece.

My life with Phyllis was a constant maze of circles. And *she* was pointing fingers.

"Rita Hayworth," I said to Clive. "You can show us where Rita took Tantig."

"Sure." He fell into the wheelchair. "Leth go."

We left the pool area, and Clive directed us to an elevator to the bottom floor, the last floor accessible to passengers. We traipsed off that elevator into a dark, foreboding area where we stopped in front of a service elevator marked *Off-limits*.

"I'm not getting in that." Phyllis folded her arms in front. "It says *Off-limits*."

I wasn't in any mood to coddle Phyllis. "Then stay here."

She looked around the shadowy area. "Unh-uh. I'm not staying here, either."

We piled into the elevator and rode down to the next level. After navigating further down several metal ramps, we finally came to a high-ceilinged, noisy engine room with overhead pipes, massive ductwork, and turbo generators. The air had a faint, damp smell, and there was endless wiring and machinery divided into smaller watertight compartments. Some compartments looked like they housed air-conditioning systems while others produced sounds like giant pistons hissing steam.

We huddled in the corner and looked down at half a dozen crew members busy at workstations. I glanced to the wall on my right. Hmm. A schedule for staff engineers, utility men, and other crew members. To the right of that was a sign stating unauthorized personnel would be fined if caught trespassing. Great. Another problem. We'd never get past this group of workers. Nothing but a dead end.

I took a defiant breath. This wasn't going to deter me. Maybe the captain thought Tantig was back in San Juan. But what if she wasn't, and I could locate her and set her free?

I thought about Holly's warning that there was a maniac loose and to watch my back. Then my gaze rolled to Clive, and I wondered if I should've reported the lanky little guy's theory. Right. He smelled like he was fermenting. Who'd believe him? I glanced from Clive to Phyllis and held back a groan. *Like it or not, Valentine, you're on your own.*

Turbulent waves rolled outside, and I could almost hear propellers whir under my feet. Clive leaned back and pointed above, trying to be heard over the pounding engines and whistling fans. "From here, you gotta take the ductwork."

I looked up at the 3' x 3' panel on the wall. "Take it where?"

He rotated his head in a big circle. "Down there. It's the only way you'll get past the workers, and it'll take you right to the secret room where the lady's being held hostage." He gazed up at me. "No matter what the schedule tells ya, there ain't no workers in that area."

I scrutinized Clive. He was barely coherent, and I was seriously believing every word he said. "And you climbed in the ductwork and made it down there."

He dropped his chin to his chest. "Yep." He pointed down at the bottom of the sixty-foot descent where the ductwork ended. There was a stack of huge crates beside what looked like unused old equipment. Behind all that was a barely visible gray door and a virtually unnoticed ceilinged-off room. "She's in there." He swung his head back at me.

I gaped down at the concealed room, another half level below the other workstations. I was still nervous about this idea. If I had any sense, I'd wheel Clive in the opposite direction and hightail it back to ocean level. Unfortunately, the only thing on my mind was finding Tantig.

I peered from Clive's scrawny body up to the panel on the wall. "How'd you get up there?"

He motored around in the wheelchair like it was second nature and opened a closet door. "Ladder." He gestured inside like he had more upstairs than I gave him credit for.

My heart grew more anxious by the minute. Nothing stopping me now.

I studied the screws on the ductwork, then turned back to Clive. "And opening the panel?"

He burped. "Swiss army knife." He patted his mostly naked body. "Never leave home without it."

I looked down at his black Speedo. If he had an army knife on him, I didn't want to know where it was.

It was spooky being deep in the cavity of the ship, but I studied where the ductwork ended above me, thankfully, out of sight from the action below. A heavy-duty nail file would undo the screws to allow me entrance into the ductwork. I looked over at the closet. Unless it had tools inside.

I wandered into the cubbyhole and scanned the area. A few buckets, mops, and other cleaning supplies. Nothing that would undo the plate. Nail file it was!

I shut the door and turned back to the others.

Phyllis was leaning against a control panel, her fruity hat askew on her head, her hand resting on a valve. She sighed. "My legs are sore."

"Phyllis," I said, not wanting to compound my fears, "could you step away from that valve?"

She straightened, looked at what she was leaning on, and backed away.

I combed through my bag, pulled out my nail file, and stepped toward the ductwork.

Clive reached for my arm. "You can't go now."

"Why not?"

"Becaush. She's not alone. Rita's there with her. And I'm tellin' ya, she won't like it when she sees you poking around."

"How do you know Sabrina's in there? You saw all this yesterday."

"I can smell her perfume."

"From here?" Maybe he had a point. I put my wrist to my nose. Despite the oily smells and dusty air from the fans, my perfume was distinct and lasted forever. I swept my arm in front of Clive. "Can you smell *my* perfume?"

He wiped his wet nose on my arm. "Heyyy, you're wearing the same one."

"You dolt," Phyllis said. "That *is* the perfume you're smelling."

"Okay," I said, trying to remain calm. "Assuming Sabrina's wearing the same perfume, is it possible she could be in there? When did you see her last, Phyllis?"

"Breakfast."

"And I saw her at lunch." When she kissed Football Guy and darted for the elevator. Maybe Clive was right. She could've left Football Guy and zipped straight to the secret room to keep an eye on Tantig. I fixed my stare back on the ductwork. I'd love to know how she made it down there. Surely, she didn't climb through the ductwork with Tantig. Which again had me thinking there had to be a connection to someone who knew the layout of the ship. "So, how am I going to get Tantig out?"

Clive shrugged. "But I wouldn't do it when the boyfriend's around. He looks big and mean."

"Boyfriend?"

"The guy with the shnake tattoo. He went storming into the room after Rita took Tantig in there."

I swallowed heavily. More puzzle pieces were being dumped on me, but I couldn't put them in place.

"This guy," I said, "with the snake tattoo. Did he look familiar?"

Clive hiccupped. "Never seen him before."

Of course. Clive couldn't remember meeting me five minutes ago. Why was I hoping he'd recognize the tattoo guy? If I'd been on the ball, I would've taken a picture of Football Guy in the bistro earlier. Another missed opportunity.

"Did he see you?" I asked.

"Are you kidding? He meant business. I hid in that compartment." He pointed to a metal box across from the hidden room with slanted vents on the two doors. Reminded me of my old high school locker, only shorter and wider. Not big enough for the Hulk, but comfortable for someone Clive's size. Or mine. "Wasn't nothing in it but bags of salt," he continued. "Rita came back out of the room with the boyfriend, and they did some talkin'. From what I gathered"—*burp*—"they're taking turns. I shaw Rita hang up the key after he left, then went back inshide."

"Did he leave through the ductwork?"

Clive shook his head. "Nope. He dishappeared around that corner of the room. Same way Rita came and went. I followed her this far, then I spotted her down on the lower level comin' around that corner. That's when I deshided to go down through the ductwork."

What scared me most was I was beginning to understand Clive's slurs and poor grammar, and worse, his thought process. "Where's the key she hung up?"

He pointed to a blue box near the door. "Over there, hanging on the other side of that box."

I glanced from the box to Clive. "Look, I can't leave Tantig down there another minute. I'm going down. You two can get help."

He clutched my arm. "You can't do that. If he comes back, he'll shoot you. And if *he* don't, she will."

"You aren't saying he has a gun." I shot him an apprehensive look. "Are you?"

"That's exactly what I'm saying."

I sniffed back a sob. Life wouldn't be the same without Tantig. "I don't care." Guilt and fear clawed at me, just thinking about abandoning her. "What kind of person would I be, leaving my great-aunt down there?"

"A smart person," Phyllis said.

Coming from her, I wasn't sure that was such a compliment.

"You're not thinking straight," Clive said. "And you're askin' for trouble. After I saw the hidey-hole earlier, I passed the boyfriend in the hall. I heard him say into his phone that if anyone tried to interfere with their plans, he'd kill the old girl." Clive shook his head. "He wasn't messing around. I wouldn't want Tantig's death on my plate."

I listened to his words, choking up inside at the thought of causing Tantig's death. The sensible thing to do would be to notify the captain. Let him handle it. But if he alerted the wrong people, and someone from the crew was involved, I'd potentially be putting Tantig in more danger.

"Lemme give you some advice." He straightened in his wheelchair and held his head up best he could. "Go back up to the shunny part of the ship and carry on as if nothing's happened. Then, come back down tonight when the big dinner is on."

"What big dinner?"

"The Western-themed dinner. Probably you'll see Rita and the boyfriend at the meal, and if they're there, you can come down here."

It made perfect sense. Of course, at the moment, I was willing to accept anything that sounded reasonable.

"All right," I said, thinking this through. "Since we're not sure if Tantig is alone, I'll come back later during dinner, use the key, and free her." It was possible later she wouldn't be alone either, but I was forcing myself to think positively. It was the only way I'd get through this.

"See?" Phyllis said. "Everything works out."

I shifted my stare to her, wondering how helpful she wanted to be. "Are you volunteering to come back later with me?"

Her eyes went wide. "Not on your life. I'm not climbing down no ductwork. My feet haven't circulated properly since my hike in the rainforest. And now I feel as if I've climbed down Mount Everest."

Clive's head dropped low like he was taking in Phyllis's feet. His matted beard brushed his knees, his lip curled up in disgust. "I need a drink." He closed one eye like a pirate and stared up at me. "How 'bout that promish you made."

I swallowed back another sob aching to surface but knew in my heart I had to act sensibly—not impulsively— where Tantig and her kidnappers were concerned.

We trekked back to the pool area, and I planted a fresh

espresso in front of Clive. Coffee vapors so strong curled my braided ends into knots.

"Hey!" Clive poked his head over the rim. "This isn't rum and coke."

"You're right. It's even better."

"You mean there's shum of that Irish liqueur in it?" He smiled eagerly.

I put on a smile I didn't feel. "There's *something* in it."

Twenty minutes later, Phyllis and I were back in our cabin. We left Clive at the pool bar, slurping espresso, waiting for the kick to kick in.

"I'm going to lie down," Phyllis said. "I gotta feel better by tonight."

"Why? It's just a Western-themed dinner."

"Then later they're showing *The Good, the Bad and the Ugly* under the stars. I want to get the best lounge chair, front and center. Don't you love that movie?"

"Never seen it." I worked with a staff every day that resembled the good, the bad, and the ugly. Who needed to watch it on the big screen?

"*What?* Who's never seen that Clint Eastwood movie? You should join me tonight. I'll save you a chair."

Like she forgot what I'd be doing later. "Thanks. I've got to go back for Tantig."

She threw her fruity hat onto the bunk, and the plastic apple toppled to the floor. "You're going through with this idiot scheme?"

"Yes, Phyllis, I am." I picked up the apple and tossed it on her bed.

"You don't even know if Clive's telling the truth. He's unreliable."

"*You're* the one who thought he had something to do with Tantig's disappearance." I had my hands on hips. "*You* were the one interrogating him like the Third Reich. Now, all of a sudden, he's unreliable."

She shrugged. "It's your life. Just don't cry to me when you need help. I'll be gazing at Clint Eastwood."

"When did I ever come to you for help?"

She tugged out of her sarong, and I was reminded of another idiot scheme. The one where Valentine Beaumont promised Grandma Maruska, on her deathbed, that she'd give her eighteenth cousin—fifty times removed—a job because said cousin was unskilled at everything else and was the sore on the family's butt. And because Valentine was a dope.

I dropped to the floor, tugged off my slip-ons, and gently removed the bandages from the backs of my heels. Blisters were down, redness subsiding. Nice to know something was going right.

"What are you wearing for this Western-themed dinner?" I asked.

"Something I made after my sewing course. I happened to bring it along. It's going to catch everyone's eye."

Phyllis was about the worst seamstress in the world, but she was right: her clothes did catch everyone's eye.

"What about a hat or cowboy boots?" Partying was the last thing I wanted to think about, but if the kidnappers saw me without a costume, they'd get suspicious.

"Hat's hanging in the bathroom." She bent under the bed. "And here are the boots. I picked them up in the costume shop this morning."

I slipped into Phyllis's extra-large boots and shuffled around the cabin like I was six years old, clopping around in my mother's high heels.

Phyllis snorted at me. Then the cabin phone rang.

She picked up. "It's Romero." She extended the phone to me.

My heart soared, then almost as fast, plummeted. "Tell him I'm not here." I clomped into the bathroom, plunked Phyllis's ten-gallon hat on my head, then dug myself out from under the brim.

Phyllis rolled her eyes and put the phone back to her ear. "She says she's not here."

Erg! I flipped my head forward and dropped the hat into the sink, praying Romero wouldn't be laughing.

Phyllis nodded into the phone, then held it out to me again. "He's got news on Lucy."

"I don't care. I don't want to speak to him."

Phyllis relayed this. "He said if you don't come to the phone, he's going to cuff your hands and feet when you get home and put your ass in a holding cell with a dozen other thugs until you *do* speak to him."

I balled my fists and stumbled out of the boots. How dare he! He couldn't do that. Could he? I plunked Phyllis's hat back on the hook and grabbed the phone. "What!" I shouted at Romero.

"Miss me that much?" I could almost see his full lips angling into that damned sexy smile. I shut my eyes tight, erasing his face from my mind. He was just a voice. A cop voice. Nothing more.

"I tried your cell," he said.

"It was off. No one I needed to speak to."

"I figured that." Silence. "Want to tell me why you're acting like I just drowned your cat?"

"You leave my cat out of this." I wasn't going to be all chummy with someone who was having a fling with Officer Belinda. And Lord knows who all else! Fine. I could talk business. I restrained myself and spoke professionally. "What's the news on Lucy?"

He cleared his throat and, I imagined, loosened his collar in frustration. "Got a copy of the autopsy report. Thought you might want to know Lucy's neck was broken."

I took a breath. "What? How?"

"Most likely from a fall. The angle of the break corresponds with the position of the head during probable force of impact. Even with the body freezing, time of death puts it at about eleven forty-five Saturday night, give or take an hour."

I thought about Chef Roy's words that Lucy had to be dead when she was stuffed in the ice machine. Then I recalled Kashi and the blue food coloring.

"Then she wasn't poisoned," I muttered to myself.

I heard him sigh. "You want to tell me what you're digging up?"

Awkward silence bridged the phone lines. No surprise, since I hadn't shared my earlier suspicions on Kashi.

"For whatever reason you're not making nice," he said, "I'm still going to confide in you."

"I'm listening."

"I want you to be careful. Along with a demented murderer on board, there may be a drug bust, and I don't want you in the middle of it."

"How do you know this?" Then it dawned on me. Jock. "Forget it. I already know."

"He's a good guy to have around. I just don't like the way he looks at you."

"What do you care how he looks at me? You've got"— I bit my tongue—"forget it."

I was glad I stopped myself. Romero would've only denied any relationship with Belinda, so what was the point? He was like all men. Untrustworthy and only interested in his own self-gain.

I wasn't sure how I felt about this new alliance between him and Jock. Part of me was relieved, but then there was a part of me that liked keeping my work separate from my private life. And up until recently, I thought Romero was becoming part of my private life.

"By the way," he said, "nothing on the Tic Tacs. To date, Tic Tacs haven't been sold on this cruise. Chances are somebody innocently dropped the pack outside your door, and you happened to pick the unlucky time to find them."

"What about the bag of Tic Tacs delivered to my door? Another unlucky discovery?"

"You lost me."

"You heard me. Last night, there was a whole bag left at my door."

The stillness told me he was considering this. "Okay. Probably not coincidental."

"Ya think? Especially when that woman they found in San Juan wasn't Tantig?"

He exhaled. "Sorry it wasn't her. They're still looking for your great-aunt. In the meantime, I think you better go everywhere in pairs."

"What am I, five years old?"

"Just a minute," he said.

And then I heard it. That damned silky voice. I should've taped it so Twix could hear the alluring tone, asking Romero if he was ready. Ready for what?

Heat soared from my toes to my eyeballs, almost blinding me with rage. How much more proof did I need that Romero was involved with his partner? This woman had shown up at his place. Talked to Twix like she was his lover. Even walked into his house. Now she was back in San Juan with him? Little holiday?

An ache stabbed my chest. I pressed the phone closer to my ear and thought I heard his low, sexy laugh. I knew that laugh and had thought he'd only intended it for me. Wrong again. *Loser.*

"Go ahead without me," Romero said to her. "I'll catch up to you later."

I'd been through this stage before. Cheating boyfriends. Spewed lies. After they walked all over me, they expected me to smile like I was a goodwill ambassador. Well, no more Mr. Nice Guy. I didn't need to be kind to a two-timing, cheating fink. Later, huh? He could later *this.* I slammed the phone down, picked it up again, and gave it another slam.

Phyllis stared at me, her mouth a foot from the floor. She swallowed and gave her head a slow shake. "Brother. No wonder you can't find a boyfriend."

While Phyllis napped, I did some packing, then called Mr. Brooks and enquired about Yitts.

"Boy, she's a good cat," he said. "Real happy to see me every morning. Sits patiently on my lap while I slide on her harness and leash. Even likes watching me work across the street."

My heart panged with a touch of longing to see Yitts again.

"Everything okay there?" he asked. "Sounds like there's an earthquake."

"Nothing serious." I frowned at Phyllis snoring. "Thanks again, Mr. Brooks, for taking care of Yitts. There's a bottle of rum in my luggage with your name on it."

He chuckled. "I look forward to it."

I hung up and stared at Phyllis's cowboy boots. With the way I was feeling, this Western affair would be another joyous event. I'd be better off stationed with Clive at the pool bar.

At least I had a plan. I'd put in an appearance in the dining room, then slip out, and head back to the bottom of the ship.

I took one last look at Phyllis sleeping, then tiptoed to the door, kicking something with my toe. I looked down at a scrap of white material, figuring it was something that had fallen off Phyllis's flimsy outfit. I picked it up, but it wasn't material at all. It was a piece of tissue paper, the kind for wrapping gifts, and scratched in blue ink across the front was *KEEP SEARCHING AND GRANDMA GETS A BULLET.*

I reread the note and gasped for air, huffing and puffing like I was drowning in peroxide. Phyllis stirred, and I inhaled and fanned my face, trying to get myself under control. *This wasn't happening.* But it *was* happening. Whoever had Tantig meant business. Clive was right. They'd kill her if they found me snooping.

Wait. All I had was Clive's word on any of this. What if he'd delivered the note? What if he was a deranged serial killer? Maybe the whole drunk act was a charade. Leading us to the bowels of the ship to find Tantig. Couldn't be. He smelled the part. But could I trust anything he said?

Was Football Guy really the big mean boyfriend? Had to be. I didn't tell Clive about the snake tattoo.

I crumpled the note in my palm and stepped out into the hall, looking both ways, hoping for clues as to who left it under our door. Up until now, I wasn't certain what to believe. But there was no mistaking it. Tantig had been kidnapped. And if I wanted to save her, I needed to be persistent and stay one step ahead of her captors. Perseverance I had. The rest I was hoping would fall into place.

I threw the note in my bag and closed the door behind me. Who even knew where our cabin was? Sabrina had never been here—that I knew. Molly and Polly...the Tic Tacs? Possibly. Kashi? Unlikely. *Think, Valentine, think.*

What about the cabin stewards? They were up and down the hall all the time, making beds, cleaning rooms. I'd never had any interaction with them, so I couldn't be sure I was heading in the right direction with this line of thinking. And apart from ordering room service for breakfast this morning, I hadn't had much to do with that staff either.

I walked by a cabin with a discarded tray out front, and suddenly I envisioned Devon, the guy from the dining room, wheeling his cart down the hall this morning, picking up dirty dishes.

I stared at the tray, pins of anxiety piercing my chest. Devon was well acquainted with the layout of the ship, wasn't he? He knew where my cabin was, ten thousand leagues under the sea. But he was an employee, like the housekeeping staff. I was a passenger. So what if he knew where my cabin was? Except I didn't like the fact that he knew. That bothered me. And what troubled me more was that I was bothered by this.

I told myself I was being ridiculous. It was his Fu Manchu mustache putting disturbing thoughts in my head. That didn't make him a suspect. And what had he done to look suspicious? There was no connection to Lucy or Sabrina that I knew. Still, I couldn't stop the unease plaguing me.

Let's say Devon was the kidnapper. Suppose he took Tantig. There had to be a reason. And what reason could there be other than her witnessing a crime or seeing something incriminating. The most obvious crime was Lucy's murder. Again, did Devon even know Lucy? Maybe he was the friend who came to the room Saturday night when Kashi was leaving. If so, he would've had a snake tattoo on his arm, and I'd only seen Devon in long sleeves.

What would Romero do to follow up this information? I rolled my eyes. I knew exactly what he'd do. He'd saunter up to Devon, flash his badge, and ask if he'd mind rolling up his sleeve. After gasping for air because of Romero's intimidating presence, Devon would roll over and play dead. End of problem. My trouble was, I couldn't swagger up to him like Iron Man and demand his cooperation. Ha! Wouldn't that be rich? Me, in high heels and a dress, scaring a guy like Devon.

I recalled Jock saying the captain suspected one of his staff was involved in a drug run. I figured he'd meant someone with power. A distinguished official. The first mate. A helmsman. But Devon? Was he at the bottom of this? Was he involved in Molly and Polly's dealings? Was that the drug run Jock was referring to?

What about the drug dealer's murder in New York? Was Devon involved in that, too? Was he the guy on the sidelines with the tattoo? Was it his arm in the ripped photo now missing from Lucy and Sabrina's cabin? I couldn't even research his background since all I had was a first name. Did I risk insulting Chef Roy by asking more questions about his staff?

I marched to the costume shop with purpose. I had no proof Devon was our man, but I had to get through the next few hours so I could free Tantig if she was where Clive had said she was.

The costume shop was along a galleria that housed other games and fun activity stores. The costumes displayed in the window ran from a knight in shining armor and pin-striped gangster suits to Wonder Woman and French maid getups. Maybe I'd find a saloon-girl dress and petticoat to wear, or something else frilly.

I wandered around aimlessly, gazing at beautiful costumes, my mind flip-flopping from Devon to Romero's news about Lucy. Suddenly, I was back to the night of her big win. If Devon was the guy who came to the door as Kashi left, what happened later in that cabin? Could Lucy have gotten into a fight with him? Or with Sabrina? Could one of them have broken her neck? She was three feet high. How could she have broken anything falling from a standing position? Unless she fell from a higher location.

The salesclerk watched me dig through outfits with a pick-something-already look on her face. I finally decided on a long tan duster, chaps, a holster, jeans, boots, toy rifle, red handkerchief, and a cowboy hat. It wasn't my first choice of getup, but the saloon-girl dresses were all taken.

I traipsed out of the shop with my outfit when Molly and Polly skipped over from the arcade. Great. I hadn't spoken to them since my episode in the steam room. And I wasn't too crazy about greeting them now.

"How are you, Valentine?" Polly peeked nosy-like in my bags.

Their cheery dispositions weren't fooling me. If Polly cared about my well-being, why'd she lock me in the steam room?

"Oh, you know." I gave a fake smile. "Going with the flow, so to speak."

"Going with the flow." Molly giggled. "You're funny, Valentine."

I did an internal eye roll.

"Got your costume for tonight?" she asked.

I lifted the bag in mock enthusiasm. "Yee-haw."

"We've been so busy we haven't had a chance to pick ours out."

Yeah. I grinded my teeth. Busy trying to kill me and flirting with Jock and the captain. I thought again about their illegal activities. Were they part of the drug scene that Romero had referred to when he said there may be a bust?

I certainly wasn't going to tip them off. "Get any more souvenirs yesterday?"

"Why do you ask that?" Molly stepped a foot closer, a shifty look on her face.

Prickles of perspiration dotted my forehead. "Because you said you were going back on land when you left the steam room."

"Oh yeah." She blushed. "We got a few."

"Come on, Molly," Polly said. "We better get on it. I don't want to be without a costume."

"Good luck," I said. "There's not much left to choose from."

I aimed toward the elevator when Polly grabbed my arm. "Did Sabrina find you yesterday?"

I gulped. "Sabrina?"

"Yes. When we left the steam room. We met her in the hallway. Said she was looking for you."

Chapter 15

It was after six by the time I arrived at the dining room. I walked under a large Western-style sparkly brown banner that read *Welcome to the Hoedown!* Stationing myself beside bales of hay, I listened to a country singer twang the latest country hit. Couples line danced on the chalk-dusted floor under festive lights, and Western cow folk moseyed into the mock saloon, barbershop, and general store.

Now that I was here, I had to play it cool. If the butterflies in my stomach settled, I'd grab a bite to eat, do some mingling, then dash off to find Tantig. I patted my jeans pocket, double-checking that the nail file was where I slid it when I'd dressed. I admitted I was ready for the challenge ahead of me. But first things first.

I attempted to look interested in the activity around me, gazing from the dance floor to the buffet table. My mouth watered at the sight of barbequed ribs, fried chicken, coleslaw, and corn on the cob. Guess I was hungry.

I stepped forward to check out the horseshoe-shaped table filled with assorted pies when a lasso flung past my head and snagged on a bale of hay next to me. Instinctively, I leaped away from whatever idiot was tossing a rope. I spun around and saw the idiot. *Phyllis*, in her ten-gallon hat, white blouse, and blue-jean skirt with enough dips and furls to cover Montana. Denim bunched at the seams, and frayed threads dangled to her boots. Phyllis couldn't sew a raft to save a sailor, but she did have tenacity.

She shook her lasso, trying to unsnag it from the bale of hay. "So, this is Western theme night. I could've told you it'd look like this. Being a seamstress, I've got a good sense of design."

Standing beside Phyllis, I looked like Woody from *Toy Story*. I gave her a half-hearted smile and tapped my three-pronged curling iron by my side. The cord was tucked inside my chaps, two prongs in the holster. Pretty slick since the costume shop had run out of revolvers. And if nobody looked closely, the third barrel was a dead ringer for a pistol. Just what I needed tonight.

I didn't see my parents and presumed they were missing out on account of Tantig. After tomorrow, we'd be heading back to Miami. Then what? A rush of familial guilt struck me. What was I doing here? Parading around like a cowboy when Tantig was in danger. *Stay calm. You'll get her.*

"Giddy-up," a voice sang behind me.

I turned around before getting galloped over by Max, slapping his leg in his cowboy suit, singing the theme song to some old Western show.

"When does the fun start?" He zoomed in on the mechanical bull.

"I don't know. I just got here." I poked the brim of my hat up with one finger and noticed him staring at me. "What!"

He shrugged. "You're not dressed how I expected."

I puffed out a sigh. "What did you expect?"

"Frills. Lace. Petticoat. Push-up bra."

I flattened my lips. "The Mae West costumes were all gone."

Max nodded toward a row of men waiting for shaves from Molly and Polly. "Looks like the Dallas Cowboys cheerleader costumes were taken, too."

I leaned on my rifle and watched the girls in their skimpy outfits lather up two clean-shaven men. "Not exactly Western clothes, are they?"

"I don't know," he said with a tilt of his head. "They're wearing cowboy boots."

I looked at their boots. "You're right. I didn't notice them."

"Neither did anyone else." He grinned, then looked pointedly at Phyllis, unraveling her lasso. "What's she doing?"

"Laying cable to Massachusetts."

Max rolled his eyes, and I focused on the staff, both of us trying not to watch Phyllis get more tangled in her cord. Max tugged out his gun, twirled it around his finger, then slid it back in the holster with a smack. "I can't stand it any longer. Oh Lord, why did You give me a conscience?" He helped Phyllis untangle her lasso, did some pointing to the mechanical bull, then sashayed to the buffet.

I wasn't sure what Max was up to, but before I joined him, I took note of the waiters, dressed in plaid shirts, jeans, and cowboy hats, serving trays of mini roasted wieners and gooey s'mores.

Devon was working his end, smile on his face, ponytail at his back. Fu Manchu goes country. He caught my eye, stopped what he was doing, and offered a friendly smile that sent shivers down to my boots. I pretended not to notice and quickly averted my eyes to the food line.

I spotted Sabrina selecting some ribs. She was dressed in a ruffled, high-collared blouse and a long skirt, and her hair was swept into a no-nonsense bun. She looked like the leader on a temperance committee from the Wild West. She didn't resemble a kidnapper.

I pursed my lips, recalling Molly and Polly's news that Sabrina had been looking for me after they'd left the steam room. A burning question hounded me. Did she lock me in that steaming room? It was easier to blame the bouncing duo, but the truth was they might be innocent. Sabrina might have wanted me to stop my search for Tantig, figuring heat exhaustion—or worse, death—would be the answer.

Was Sabrina holding Tantig captive? Was I getting too close to the truth about Lucy? I didn't know what to think. But instinct told me whoever was responsible for taking Tantig was the same person who killed Lucy. Tantig must've stumbled onto something she shouldn't have, and the killer wasn't taking chances.

I glanced from Sabrina to Devon, turning things over in my mind. If they were in this together, then nobody was with Tantig. I could make my exit now. But wait. Devon wasn't necessarily our man. Football Guy could be the boyfriend Clive had mentioned. I'd witnessed for myself Sabrina kissing him. They were involved. No question.

If Sabrina knew Devon, I had yet to see any communication between them. Wouldn't there be a twitch of recognition? A nod? A wink? I got nothing. No stares. No smiles. Nada. My mind went back to the dinner table the first night of the cruise. Lucy had teased Sabrina about snooping around the ship. That was what had been nagging me.

Sabrina might've looked carefree and relaxed, but she didn't seem like anyone's fool. I had a feeling she had a keen sense of what was going on around her at all times. But what if it was more than knowing her surroundings? What if she'd staked out the place because she was planning a murder? Or maybe she was an accomplice to murder. I narrowed my eyes on Devon. Why did I suspect he was the one involved in all this? Did I have an aversion to men who resembled Fu Manchu? To waitstaff?

If I was wrong and it was Football Guy, where was he now? I scanned the crowded dining room. The football posse was pigging out on corn on the cob, noisily toasting with beer mugs in the air. Candace, who'd snagged the Mae West costume, was in the middle of the gang.

Darn. I still hadn't asked what she'd seen, if anything, regarding tattoos and the sports jocks. I wasn't sure that even mattered anymore. Except, of course, for Football

Guy. And at the moment, the guys were all in long-sleeved Western shirts. One thing was certain. I didn't see Sabrina's main squeeze or know whether he was again with that group. If he was Tantig's abductor, he could be down in the depths, harming her.

A sick feeling roiled in my stomach. I had to get on with the night. I had to free Tantig.

Sabrina carried her food to our table where Max was sitting. I was anxious to break away from the crowd, but first I wanted to saddle up beside her and see if I'd learn anything about Tantig's disappearance.

I stepped forward and felt a hand slide under my duster and pinch my behind.

"Whoop!" I slapped my butt and spun around.

Jock. The devil. Good thing my gun wasn't loaded.

He stood there coolly, hands on his hips, dressed in black from his cowboy hat down to his boots. His hair spilled over his collar, and a bushy handlebar mustache covered his lips.

"I do reckon it's Calamity Jane," he said, not taking his eyes off the room.

I had a flashback of Jock naked in bed, large muscular thighs, hard rippling abdomen, larger *and* harder parts in between. *Hot. Air.* I grabbed a glass of lemonade from a nearby table, guzzled it back, then loosened the handkerchief around my neck.

He slid his hand on top of mine and stroked the rifle. "You're not planning on shooting anyone with that thing now, are you?"

I calmed my beating heart. "No, but the night's young." I snatched the rifle away from his wandering hands. "And I was going for Annie Oakley."

His face showed no sign of expression, but I could tell by the way his mustache twitched he was grinning underneath.

I tried not to be taken in by his extraordinary good looks or his suave gunslinger demeanor. He was an employee. Right?

I took a second to note all four of us were together in the same room. Just like at work. Yet we'd rarely been together all week on this huge city of a ship. And who knew where I'd be in another hour. I shuddered inside at the thought of trudging alone to the bottom of the vessel, rescuing Tantig. But I had no choice.

"Last time I saw you"—his eyes drifted to Molly and Polly—"you were scooping coffee beans off the plaza floor."

I gazed in the same direction. "You should've seen me an hour later."

"What?" He angled his head, the humor replaced with genuine interest. "Where were you?"

I squared my shoulders, attempting to show how brave I was. "In the pit of the ship."

I'd been hesitant at sharing anything with him because, for one thing, I didn't know if I could trust him. And secondly, there was his questionable association with Captain Madera—which, as it turned out, wasn't so questionable, but the fear rising up my spine prompted me to unload. If I searched for Tantig and never surfaced again, someone had to know where I'd gone.

I glanced over at Phyllis and swallowed the growing panic. Phyllis couldn't solve a multiplication problem. I wasn't going to trust that she'd help if I went missing.

"Is this another one of those stories where you used your tools to dig your way to China?"

I stuck out my bottom lip. "No. But contrary to popular belief, Tantig is not back in San Juan. I'm going on a reliable source that she's being held captive in a room off the engine room." I thought of Clive, my reliable source. I couldn't believe I was going through with this half-baked scheme because of a lead from a drunk who resembled a garden gnome. But there it was.

"And you're planning on rescuing her tonight."

"Yep."

"You think that's wise?" He crossed his arms, bringing my attention to his huge biceps tightening against the silky material of his black shirt.

"*Wise* has many definitions." I stared from his biceps into his eyes.

"I don't want you going down there alone," he said. "Not only that, you'll be entering a prohibited area. You need to involve security on this."

"No need. I have a plan." Yeah. Sneaking through a maze of ductwork and miraculously flying out of the metal contraption like a superhero. "And I won't be talked out of it. I'm going down, and I'm getting Tantig."

He sighed. "What if you get hurt?"

"Pff." I tapped my rifle. "Got it covered." My churning stomach didn't match my confident voice.

He peeked behind my shoulder. "Where's your beauty bag?"

"In the cabin."

"I thought you never left home without it."

I twirled around. "Wouldn't go with the outfit." Plus, I had what I needed.

My eyes slid over to Devon. "Tell me something. Do you know anything about that waiter with the Fu Manchu mustache?"

Jock gave Devon a discreet look. "I know I wouldn't go near him if I were you."

Exactly how I felt. "I received a warning earlier about searching for Tantig. I think he may have kidnapped her."

He grimaced. "Look, I can't let you go down there by yourself."

"You can't stop me."

He gave me a wicked grin.

"Jock, you are not stopping me. She's my great-aunt. I'll do anything to rescue her." I stuck out my chest. "Remember, I'm your boss." Like he gave two hoots about that.

"I know who you are. You're a reckless, determined, curious buttercup. And if I had any sense, I'd tie you to those saloon doors to keep your pretty ass safe."

I tried not to blush, but I knew I was unsuccessful.

"Now you sound like Romero. And if you don't mind, I'd rather not think about him at the moment."

He rolled his eyes, and his bushy mustache flattened. "I don't like this idea, and I can't help you because I'm going to be busy tonight." His eyes shifted once again to Molly and Polly. "If I wrap things up early, I'll join you."

I followed his gaze back to the blonds. *Gee, don't let me interrupt your night.* Why was everyone mesmerized by Molly and Polly? I watched them shave a couple of men, their breasts all but falling out of their teensy jackets. Okay, maybe I knew the answer to that question.

I was going to lay my life on the line, and Jock was likely planning a ménage à trois. *Ooh.* I wanted to trust him, but he wasn't making it easy. *Fine.* I wasn't going to waste time stewing about it. I didn't need him anyway. Good thing, too, because in a blink, he was gone.

I plodded to the buffet, feeling a pity party coming on. Jock was Mr. Worldly, and what did I have to show for my fabulous Caribbean cruise? I'd lost a contest, was in the middle of another murder investigation, I'd rescued Max from a Puerto Rican jail, had been embarrassed and injured in more ways than one, and the worst part was Tantig had been kidnapped. If this was a holiday, I'd have had a better time at home, inhaling second-hand smoke from Mrs. Calvino next door and watching Mr. Brooks crucify his yard with power tools.

I took some food from the buffet and joined Max, Phyllis, and Sabrina at my table. My heart was knocking in my chest, and my armpits were sweaty. *Breathe, Valentine, breathe. Act cool and composed.* I didn't want to tip off Sabrina that I was onto her. I just prayed Phyllis wouldn't drop the bomb either. Seemed I didn't need to worry. Phyllis was yakking Sabrina's ear off about her day in the rainforest. So Max took this opportunity to yak off mine.

"Guess what?" He buttered his corn on the cob.

I was biding my time until I could make my exit. "I'm all out of guesses. What?"

"I'm over my fear of water."

I gave him a dubious look. "How'd that come about?"

"It was due to Kashi." He leaned toward me, opened his vest, and stuck a colorful, hairy ornament under my nose. "Do you like it?"

I backed up in case it bit. "What is it?"

He looked offended. "It's one of Kashi's 'Get Out of Town' brooches."

"Why is it so colorful?"

"Because this is his rainbow version. Hairs of every color."

"Because you're so vibrant?"

"Exactly. Kashi calls it 'Get Out of Town Elton John.'"

Naturally. I looked around the dining room. "Where is Kashi? I haven't seen him all day."

Max wiped his hands on his napkin and lowered his voice. "After you left the pool, he came by. You know, lovey, he's not such a bad guy. Taught me Indian meditation exercises to calm myself when I'm agitated. It's helped. I don't feel anxious anymore near the ocean. We even tested it. I walked straight to the railing and viewed the rolling waves. Nothing. Not even a tummy flip. I'm cured."

I watched Phyllis nod at Sabrina, then lick butter off her plate like an animal.

"What else can he cure?" I muttered, shoveling coleslaw into my mouth.

"*What?*" Phyllis stopped short at something Sabrina said. "If that doesn't take the cake!" She swung her head so fast from Sabrina to me her ten-gallon hat almost toppled off her head. "Get a load of this." She nudged my arm. "When Sabrina got back from port yesterday, she found a bar of soap in her toilet. Boy, those cabin stewards don't deserve much of a tip."

I coughed and sputtered, trying to look innocent. Everyone gawked at me.

I pointed to my throat. "Cole...slaw...stuck."

Max gave me a hard wallop on my back that just about sent me into next week.

"Thanks." I cut him a gruff look, grabbed my water, and turned from the table, lapping it up. As water trickled down my throat, Football Guy sauntered into the dining room, dressed like Clint Eastwood in a spaghetti Western—maybe even *The Good, the Bad and the Ugly*. Poncho over his shoulders, flat-topped cowboy hat angled low over one eye, holster slung low on his hips. He caught sight of the team and within seconds his poncho was flipped back, and he was belly up to the bar, slugging beer with them. Hmm. Funny he didn't look for Sabrina. Maybe the romance was over.

This answered one question. Football Guy was one of the jocks, which also likely meant he wasn't part of the murder or kidnapping. After all, he was a passenger, and passengers didn't know the ship inside out. Right? Unless you were Sabrina—the cruise junkie. Of course, this didn't explain Clive being in the engine room. But wait. He was only following Sabrina. And if she was involved with Devon, Devon could've told her where to hide Tantig. Which also meant Tantig had most definitely witnessed something incriminating for them to have seized her.

Phyllis went on. "I told her strange things have been happening in our cabin as well."

I shook my head no. "Nothing so strange, Phyllis."

She gave me a flippant wave. "What do you mean, *nothing*! What about that bag of Tic Tacs that was delivered?"

I avoided Sabrina's gaze. If she looked into my eyes, she'd see the light bulb clicking on. It all made sense. Sabrina had planted those Tic Tacs on the doorknob. If she'd taken Tantig, the Tic Tacs were a warning. Maybe the lone container I'd stepped on earlier was Molly's missing Tic Tacs, an accident, a freak occurrence. But without a doubt, the bag on the doorknob was intentional. Who else would've put them there?

"And I don't know why," Phyllis continued, "but every time I walk into our cabin, it smells like nail polish remover." She glared at me. "Have you noticed that?"

I shook my head emphatically. "No. Must be your sinuses." I rubbed my forehead. "And speaking of sinuses, I feel a headache coming on. Probably the motion finally getting to me. I'm calling it a night."

"But lovey," Max said. "You're going to miss Phyllis showing us how to ride the bronco bull. Aren't you, Phyll?" he asked, hopeful, any compassion he'd held for her a few minutes ago swept away by a new desire to see her thrown off a mechanical bull.

"Welllll…" Phyllis puffed out her chest. "I know I'd be good at it."

"You can tell me all about it in the morning."

"What about *The Good, the Bad and the Ugly*?" Phyllis asked. "You need to watch the movie."

What was this? Normally, no one cared where I went. Now, all of a sudden, everyone needed me here. "Look, I'm going to rest. My duster weighs ten pounds, this hat's rubbing on my ears, and I didn't sleep well last night."

"Don't look at me," Phyllis said. "I can't help it if you didn't sleep."

"I hope you're feeling better in the morning," Sabrina said.

Her words were soothing, so why did I have this feeling a knife was about to be stuck in my back?

Chapter 16

I made it halfway through the dining room when Candace bustled up to me in her Mae West costume, a large-brimmed red feathery hat on top of her head, a tight red gown pushing up her boobs. "Where are you sneaking off to?" She backed me into a corner.

I squeezed my toy rifle, half wishing it was loaded. *Calm breath.* I still wanted answers from Candace about the jocks and their tattoos. Retaliating with sarcastic remarks would only make things ugly. "Nowhere. Just heading to the bathroom."

She pulled back a long plume, dangling in her face. "*I'm* not going *anywhere.*" She glanced over her shoulder. "Those boys are what a girl needs." She smiled wickedly. "*This* girl, anyway."

"I'm glad you're having a good time." I was all out of niceness and decided to simply come out with it, hating that I had to ask Candace anything. "Speaking of the boys, have you noticed if any of them have a snake tattoo on their arm?"

"*Snake tattoo.*" She gave me an odd look. "What's this all about, Valentine? You changing your hobby from assaulting men's genitals to breaking arms with tattoos?"

I gave a fake laugh. "Something like that."

She curled up her lip, pulling back her feather again.

"I've only seen one guy with a snake tattoo on this cruise, and it belongs to that little drunk who looks like Papa Smurf."

I blinked, wide-eyed. "Clive?"

"That his name? I don't pay much attention to men unless they're tall, dark, and handsome."

Don't forget loaded. "Then how do you know he has a snake tattoo?"

She blew out air through her collagen-enhanced lips. "I saw him at the bar the other day and asked what was underneath the bandage."

"And you're sure he said it was a snake tattoo. I mean, he slurs a lot. Maybe he said he had a mole removed. Snake tattoo. Mole removed. Almost rhymes."

Her eyes bugged out at me. "What do you take me for? Some kind of idiot?" She huffed. "He said *snake tattoo*. I even saw a bit of it poking out from under the gauze. End of story." She glanced over her shoulder. "Now, if you'll excuse me, I've got a posse to round up." She shoved up her boobs, thrust back her shoulders, and pranced back to the gang. Mae West reincarnated.

I stood there, stumped. Was Candace playing with me? If not, and Clive had a snake tattoo, why would he be wearing a bandage over it? Was it new and he was told to keep it covered? Was it really a snake? If so, why didn't he mention this coincidence when he told Phyllis and me about the boyfriend's snake tattoo? This was too absurd to be anything but a fluke.

I was still thinking about this when I turned on my way out of the dining room and plowed into Kashi. He was dressed in white. White cowboy hat. White T-shirt. White jeans. White boots. He looked like an Indian version of Mr. Clean, with a touch of yee-haw. And he was in a hurry to get past me.

"Whoa, Nellie," I said.

"Who is Nellie?" He panted, pushing his glasses up his nose. "And more importantly, am I late?"

"*Whoa, Nellie* means slow down. And late for what?"

"The bronco riding contest." He breathed past my shoulder. "I, Kashi, am an expert bronco rider. When I was a child, still living in India, I sometimes rode cows bareback. They like to wander the streets, you do know."

"Yes. I've heard that."

He dipped his head. "As an expert bronco rider, I will show their scrawny butts how it is done."

I moved aside. "Don't let me stop you."

Ten minutes later, I'd commandeered a wheelchair from the pool area. I didn't see Clive anywhere and didn't know if I should be thankful or worried, especially after learning about his tattoo. Logic told me he was simply a passenger who liked his booze. No need to be troubled by a rosy-cheeked guy like that, right? He could've moved from the pool bar to one of the lounges. Then again, he could've passed out on his way from the pool bar to one of the lounges. But I couldn't concern myself with Clive or his whereabouts now. I had Tantig to think about.

I didn't know what condition she'd be in when I found her, and I wanted to be prepared. How I'd hoist her back up through the ductwork was another issue. But one problem at a time. I steered the wheelchair down to the last level where the service elevator let me off. So far, so good. Everything was as I remembered.

Psyching myself up, I trekked down the metal ramps that led me to the noisy engine room. I stopped at the spot Clive had shown Phyllis and me earlier. From my corner I saw crew members, like before, busy at workstations below.

Part of me thought again about going for help since the last thing I needed was to be stopped and reproached by the crew. But I didn't know who to trust. What if there were others involved in Lucy's murder or Tantig's kidnapping? I couldn't take a chance. If I handled this right, I wouldn't run into anyone. I'd find Tantig, free her, and no one would see us.

My heart hammered a thousand beats a minute, hiking up my anxiety level. All guilty parties—that I knew—were above sea level, playing cowboy. I swallowed, determined to ignore my reservations, and center on what I had to do.

I backed the wheelchair into the corner by the closet, hung my cowboy hat on the handle, threw my duster on the back, and leaned my rifle against the side. I dragged the ladder out of the closet, pulled out my nail file, and pushed up my sleeves. I could almost hear the *Mission Impossible* music while I undid the panel that would provide me access into the ductwork.

Once the last screw was loose, I popped open the metal plate, set it on the ground, and gaped into the passage. *Gulp*. No one said it was going to be this narrow. Not good when you were mildly claustrophobic.

I pushed back a quiver and thought about what Tantig had been through. What if she'd been beaten? Starved? Humiliated? There was a lot more at stake here than my fear of suffocation. I'd waited long enough to come back down. I couldn't chicken out now.

I rammed the nail file back in my pocket. I had no choice. I had to go in that tunnel.

I went to grab my bag. Right. Didn't have it with me. I cuffed my forehead with the heel of my hand. *Dummy*. There was barely enough room for me in that passage. How did I suppose I was going to lug my beauty bag? Maybe, while I was at it, I could shove in the wheelchair.

Okay, Valentine. You're overanxious.

Darn right I was overanxious. How could I have thought I was up for this challenge? It was a lunatic, pea-brained plan. That's what it was.

I took several deep breaths to calm myself and said a short prayer. Then I wiped a wayward tear off my cheek and climbed to the top of the ladder. I crawled headfirst into the ductwork. I got three feet in when I scrambled back out and almost fell down the rungs.

My heart was racing, and I couldn't catch my breath. I paced the corner, blinking madly, shaking the nervousness from my hands and shoulders. "Come on, Valentine. You can do this."

No, you can't, a voice said inside my head.

"I have to!" I drew in air through my nose and out through my mouth, repeating this until I wasn't shaking fiercely. I needed something that would relax me. I closed my eyes, pretending I was on a warm beach, listening to soft waves rolling onto the shore. That usually worked. The tenseness eased out of my shoulders, slid down my arms, and fled from my fingertips. Okay. Now I was ready.

I shoved myself back into the passage and edged forward on my hands and knees, my mind bouncing back and forth between saving Tantig to the calm, sandy beach. Pinging, humming, and whirring noises above and below were muffled by the steel shaft. I considered this a good thing. I just hoped the sounds of me inching along would be muffled as well.

What seemed like three days later, I reached the bottom panel, undid the plate, and hammered it open. I dropped to the ground, inhaled fresh air big time, and did an all-over shake at being free. Then I looked over my shoulder to make sure there wasn't anyone around. *Whew*. Clive was right. A few pumps and fans for scenery and oodles of crates and old equipment. But the area was secure.

Not wasting any time, I grabbed the key, crept past the crates and paraphernalia, and found the secret room Clive had said Tantig was in. My heart pounded so violently at what I might see, I did more deep breathing to prepare myself. Then I undid the lock and safety latch, slid the key in my pocket, and slowly opened the door.

A table and chair were the first things that greeted me. Sitting on top of the table were a box of crackers, a dirty mug, papers, a pencil, and small cans of brown paint and glitter. Plastic bins of old theme-dinner and cruise props were scattered across the room. Silk flowers, napkin holders, soiled tablecloths, and party supplies poked out of the bins.

A toilet and a roll of toilet paper sat in the far-right

corner of the room. The unpleasant smell in the air told me there was a plumbing problem and clearly no ventilation. I put my wrist to my nose and sniffed hard on my Musk's floral scent. Whoever kept house never would've passed my mother's inspection. Despite that, I didn't intend on staying long in this...this forgotten storage room.

My gaze drifted from the toilet to the other side of the room, and the sight there made my heart swell. Facing the left wall in a recliner in the upright position was Tantig watching one of her soaps on a TV. She didn't seem to hear me enter. Either that, or she didn't care. She certainly didn't look agitated or afraid or like she'd been hurt. She was in a paisley-patterned dress with support hose on her legs and Velcro running shoes on her feet.

"Tantig!" I rushed over, stumbling past the table and chair, momentarily forgetting about the stagnant smell.

She gave me a vacant look, unconcerned that I was dressed like a woman of the Wild West, rescuing her from the bowels of the ship.

"Are you okay?" I bent in front of her, checking for bruises or marks of any kind.

She tipped her head past me, focusing on the TV. "You're in the way."

I was so filled with relief, tears pooled in my eyes. "We were worried about you." I hugged her and smoothed back her mussed hair off her forehead. "Have you eaten?" I looked at the crackers on the table. "Are you hungry?"

"I ate a sug-air-free chocolate bar the other day," she said without emotion. "My blood sug-air went *sky* high."

She'd said this exact line two weeks ago, which left me as confused then as it did now. Uncertain if she'd had a chocolate bar since she'd been abducted, I grabbed some crackers from the box, gave them a sniff, and put them on her armrest. They weren't fresh or top-of-the-line, but I didn't think they'd kill her.

She gave them a glance, then went back to watching the TV.

"Who brought you here?" I asked.

She blinked straight ahead. "The lady with the long red hair. She's nice. She watches channel four news back home."

"How did you get down here? She didn't force you, did she?"

"No. We took an elevat-air." Her gaze didn't leave the TV. "I met her when I was walk-ink our first morning here. Then I saw her again Sunday morning. I told her I'd rather be watching my soaps than obeying Stuck-air. And the next day she said if I came with her I could watch my shows all day."

"Sabrina promised you that?"

She nodded. "Last time I went to Stuck-air, I made him paklava. He did not return my Tupp-air-ware."

Following Tantig's thought process was useless. "I'm sure he just forgot."

She clicked her tongue on the roof of her mouth.

"And nobody's harmed you?"

She blinked and raised her chin, along with another *tsk*. The silent *no*.

"Tantig, did Sabrina ask you about Lucy's murder?"

She looked up at me. "Who-hk?"

"The little person who was killed. Remember? You were at the Captain's Gala when she was wheeled into the dining room, frozen in an ice statue."

She rolled her eyes, like *who-hk cares?* and fixed her gaze back on the TV. "I saw a suitcase."

"A suitcase." I was trying to unravel this mystery, and Tantig was talking luggage.

"It was around two-thirty in the morning. The same night I had my hair done in that contest." She closed her eyes and tilted her head back like she was remembering that catastrophic event. Then she pressed her lips together and reopened her eyes. "I couldn't sleep. I went for a walk. Then I saw the nice lady with a man. They were dragging a suitcase behind them. It had a fing-air sticking out."

I sucked in, Lucy's murder becoming more real. "A finger! Are you sure?"

She nodded at the TV.

"Did they see you?"

"I talked to them."

"What did you say?"

"I asked if they were leaving. They said no. Just rearranging luggage."

I suddenly remembered Tantig's confusion the morning we arrived in Nassau. She'd seen the cruise director wheel out her bag of tricks and had thought everyone was leaving because she'd seen other people dragging luggage around. More specifically, she'd seen Sabrina and most likely Devon wheeling around a suitcase in the wee hours of the morning. They were probably in such a hurry to dispose of Lucy they decided to deal with a confused elderly woman later. And how easy that turned out to be. All they had to do was promise she could watch her soaps on TV.

Now it made sense why Sabrina's room seemed empty when I searched it. Her clothes were piled neatly in drawers, but her luggage was gone.

"What color was the suitcase, Tantig?"

"White snakeskin."

Exactly what I'd seen Sabrina wheel into the ship the day we boarded. Where was it now? In Devon's cabin? I glanced at the closed door. Outside this room in one of those crates?

I paced back and forth, putting this all together. I stopped at the table and noticed glittery brown smudges on top of the worn laminate. Where had I seen brown smudges like this before? I jogged my memory. It was somewhere earlier today. The bistro? The pool? Then it hit me. Devon had shiny brown grease on his sleeve when he picked up my tray this morning. But it wasn't grease. It was paint. And the shine was glitter. The same paint and glitter used on the sign for the hoedown. I stared down at the cans. The same paint and glitter sitting on the table.

I gaped at the small quarters surrounding me. Was this Devon's hideaway? His lair? I'd read that cruise-ship crew shared tight cabin space with up to six people. Was this a spot where he could have secret privacy and downtime? Where he could plan drug smuggling? Murder?

I dragged my thoughts back to the luggage. Devon and Sabrina must've killed Lucy, stuffed her in the suitcase, and rolled her to the kitchen to be frozen. Less suspicious than hauling a dead body around by its feet. I shivered at that. "Come on." I rushed over to Tantig. "Mom will want to see you're okay."

I helped her out of her seat, opened the door, and spied the backs of Molly and Polly, twenty feet away, working on opening the metal box where Clive had hidden. I took a giant step back. *Jeepers.* Did everyone know about this area? Thank heavens for the constant hum of the engines. Molly and Polly didn't seem to hear me. I left the door open a crack so I could watch what they were doing.

They pulled a large bag labeled *FLOWER PRESERV- ATIVE* from the locker and dipped their fingers inside. Then they put their fingers to their noses. Huh? Why were they snorting preservative? Holy crap! That wasn't preservative. That was cocaine. Hold on. Clive had said salt was in the bags. Then again, when he was inside the locker it was dark, and Clive's vision wasn't all that great. Probably the first thing that came to mind.

Shoot.

I closed and locked the door.

"What is it?" Tantig asked.

"We can't leave yet. Go sit down. I'll let you know when it's time."

She hobbled back to the recliner, and I did a more thorough survey of the room. I inspected a grimy calendar taped to the wall, marked with notes on when to switch flower containers, set up displays, and check supplies. There was a slash across Sunday and Monday of this week, and *Deal* was written on both days.

Were those the days drug deals were made in Nassau and San Juan? I thought about Molly and Polly out in the engine room and remembered the duffel bag Max had seen them holding in San Juan. Was it full of money? If the florist shop was a front for this smuggling operation, were they all in this together?

I recalled interaction I'd seen between Molly and Polly and Sabrina and Lucy. Judging from the first night at dinner, it seemed like the beach babes had just met Sabrina and Lucy. But that didn't mean they didn't all have a role in running drugs. Was it possible this job was so huge that these twosomes sailed on the same ship but didn't know of the other's participation?

Maybe Molly and Polly weren't in charge of transporting drugs on board. Maybe they just paid for them once Devon confirmed the drugs were safely on the ship. But how did the drugs get on the ship? Who else was involved?

My heartbeat quickened with each new question. With trembling hands, I rifled through stray papers on the table. Nothing but work notes and doodles.

Suddenly, the door handle wiggled. I jumped back, then patted my pocket where I'd stuffed the key. *Whew!* The tugging on the handle stopped. Then a second later, Sabrina flew in, looking like a pissed-off school marm, hair sprouting out of her bun, eyes blazing. *Damn.* How many keys were there to this place?

"Headache, huh?" She banged the door shut and whipped a knife out of her boot. "I knew you'd be here. I could smell your perfume miles away."

Darn lasting fragrance. Sweat bubbled on my lip, and my shoulders tensed at the angry glare in her eyes. "I came to get Tantig," I said.

She gave a short huff out her nose. "You can forget that. She's not going anywhere. And neither are you."

My insides were like jelly, and I was back to being eight years old with Holly telling me I couldn't eat cake in the living room. Like she was the boss over me. Well, I wasn't eight anymore, and I wasn't too fond of being told what I could or could not do. I wiped the sweat off my lip and raised my chin.

"What is it with your family anyway?" Sabrina asked. "First, your great-aunt follows Dev and me halfway to the kitchen. Now you show up here. Don't you people have anything better to do with your time than meddle?"

I rolled my fingers into a tight ball. "I guess it's in the blood."

"When Dev sees you here, the blood's going to flow."

My pulse throbbed between my ears. But my first consideration was Tantig. "Let her go. She hasn't harmed anyone."

"She's done plenty of harm." She wielded her knife in front of me. "If she hadn't seen Dev and me carting Lucy away, she wouldn't be here right now. At first, we weren't going to kidnap her. Then I heard her remark to someone about a finger and rolling suitcases. I thought, who'd believe a senile old lady? But then you and your meddling background became a concern, and we knew it'd only be a matter of time until you stuck your nose in. See? We had to keep her locked up and out of the way until the coke is off the ship in Miami. We couldn't trust she wouldn't blab about any of this to the wrong person."

"Who could she possibly blab to? She says very little to anyone."

She tapped the blade of the knife under her jaw. "Hmm. Let's see. Jock was your date at the Gala, was he not? And considering he's chummy with the captain and has been asking questions about drugs and trafficking— even before Lucy died—I'd say he's at the top of the list."

I tried to think of something to say to dissuade this line of thinking, but she plowed on.

"Then there's Detective Romero who arrived after Lucy died and who'd caused problems for her in the past." She sneered. "More interesting, good old Uncle Sam told me Romero was your boyfriend."

"Mr. Jaworski?" The nosy gossip. What did he know?

I gave a defiant head shake. "Romero's no boyfriend of mine."

She shrugged. "Be that as it may, *you've* solved murders

before. What was stopping your great-aunt from blabbing to *you*?"

I had no answer. I cracked my knuckles and glanced over my shoulder at Tantig—eyes glued to the TV. I gave a silent moan. I was trying to save her life, and she was watching soaps.

I turned back to Sabrina, afraid to ask what they intended to do with us. Tantig had seen her captors. She could describe them. That wouldn't change once the cruise was over. What might have seemed like a crazy story about a suitcase and a finger would become much more credible after she'd been missing for several days.

I couldn't stop trembling inside. I had to get Sabrina to soften. Maybe if she talked this out, she'd at least set Tantig free. It was worth a shot.

I rolled back in my mind to the newspaper article about the drug dealer who was found dead at Lucy's salon. "Just tell me," I said. "Was this all connected to the murder at Shortcuts?"

"You heard about that, did you?"

I gave a pompous look. "I read the papers." Much.

"You could say it was connected." She shrugged again, and I could tell that's all she was going to say on the matter. "Lucy was always hard up for cash, and she knew the cops were watching her like a hawk—especially since the homicide. She was trying to lay low, but she got greedy."

"So you killed her."

She shook her head. "It wasn't intentional. But you probably wouldn't believe that."

"Maybe I would." She was holding a knife under my nose. I could be open-minded.

"It wouldn't have happened if she hadn't lunged for Dev. He was making arrangements for Lucy and me to bring the coke back to New York, freeing up the bikers who usually deliver the shipments."

Aha. Lucy's comment about Jock—and recognizing a biker a mile away—instantly came to mind. So smuggling drugs from Miami to New York wasn't a first.

"This time," Sabrina continued, "we decided to take the beauty cruise and rent a car to drive back. But Lucy started bitching about her share, how it was her business on the line, and she just freaked. Dove headfirst off the top bunk, aiming for Dev. He scrambled out of the way, and a second later she was lying on the floor with her head snapped." She shook all over as if to erase the horrible memory.

"Then you hauled her to the kitchen and dumped her in the mold."

Her eyebrows went up. "We had to get her off our hands. Seemed like the simplest thing to do."

"You could've thrown her overboard."

"True. But where's the creativity in that?" She grinned. "Actually, the ice sculpture was a warning to the guy loading the stash into the hull. He was getting cold feet"— she chuckled to herself—"about smuggling the last shipment on board in San Juan, but there was no choice. There are others we have to answer to. We had to see this thing through."

I considered the size of the operation. "What about Molly and Polly?"

"What about them?"

"You didn't see…" My gaze wandered to the door.

"See what?" She waved her knife back and forth like she was cutting through fog.

Something told me to shut up. Obviously, Sabrina hadn't run into them a moment ago outside of this room. "Uh, see them at the Western theme night, shaving men."

She rolled her eyes. "Yes, I saw them. They're not very good at what they do. Those men were walking away with bandages on their throats."

I doubted they cared.

"But they *are* funny." She smirked. "During the contest, when Lucy clouted that little drunk with a hairbrush and all hell broke loose, Molly whispered that she wondered how long it'd be before Lucy got what was coming to her." She gave a thin laugh. "I told her it wouldn't be long."

"I guess you were right." I frowned, my thoughts circling back to this whole drug business. "What happens to the drugs once they're loaded onto the ship?"

She gave a heavy sigh. "Dev locates the boxes marked from the florists, then removes the bags from inside and stashes them in the locker."

"The bags of 'preservative.'"

"Yes. That stuff's a perfect double for coke. Some of the other floral boxes loaded into the hull contain fresh flowers, floral foam, and real preservative. And since Dev personally handles picking the best flowers for Chef Roy's dining room, he manages incoming loads. The coke goes in the locker, the preservative and bouquets go in the vases, and everybody's happy. Genius, don't you think?"

"Clever. And helpful of him to do all the grunt work for the displays."

"It's worth it. Getting the coke off the ship is more challenging." Her gaze veered to Tantig, then settled back on me. "After the large flower arrangements have been discarded, Dev hollows out the floral foam at the bottom of the jars. Then he hides the drugs sealed in small plastic bags inside the foam and sets the foam in the bottom of the vases. The used vases are sent to the florist on land where eventually fresh flowers are inserted and brought onto the ship for the start of the next cruise."

"After the drugs have been removed from the vases," I confirmed, "involving another florist in Miami."

She made a check mark in the air with her knife. "You're a quick one, Valentine."

I ignored the jab and thought about our first stop in Nassau Sunday. "Is this where you were the night of the captain's dinner? Checking to see if your first delivery had arrived while Lucy was wheeled into the dining room?"

She gave a smug smile. "Yes. Dev had to work. Everything was running like clockwork." Her smile gave way to a frown. "Of course, having a death and kidnapping on our hands didn't exactly add into the equation."

"Why don't you explain Lucy's death was accidental?

As for Tantig, she won't remember any of this tomorrow."
That was a fifty-fifty chance.

"You think?"

"I've known her all my life. Some days she still asks
who I am."

She looked as if she was considering, then she straightened her shoulders. "No. Dev would kill me if I let her go."

I narrowed my eyes on her. "What is your relationship
with Dev?"

She bobbed her head slightly. "He's my boyfriend."

Huh? "But I saw you with Football Guy."

"Who?"

"The football jock who's here with his buddies." I
spread my arms high and wide. "Built like an offensive
lineman."

"Oh. Him. He was just a one-nighter." She grinned.
"Okay, two-nighter. Ends up we were raised in the same
town outside Boston. And I know what you're thinking.
How could I? Right?"

I was head-over-heels crazy for Romero, and yesterday
I woke up in Jock's bed. Who was I to judge? "I wasn't
thinking anything."

"Dev and I have been together forever. With
everything that's happened on this cruise, Football Guy, as
you called him, was a diversion."

I pictured Football Guy's tattoo and suddenly recalled
the photograph of Lucy, Sabrina, and a third person who
was cut off. "Then who was in the photo with you and
Lucy in your cabin?"

She pushed back stray hairs from her face. "Dev,
except his body was folded behind the frame."

Which meant Dev was the guy with the snake tattoo
Kashi saw the night of the celebration.

"Lucy insisted we take the picture and cart it with us
for luck, but we all agreed nobody could know of any
relationship between us and Dev."

"What happened to the picture?"

She looked at me strangely. "What makes you think it went anywhere?"

My nose twitched. "Guessing?" Would she suspect I'd been snooping in her cabin? I hoped my perfume wasn't *that* lasting that she'd sensed it.

"You guessed right. I destroyed it after Lucy died. That's all I needed. A picture with the three of us together."

I let out a breath. "What about the bag of Tic Tacs?"

She shook her head. "Your aunt offered me one that first day on the deck and one the next time I saw her." She looked beyond my shoulder again at Tantig. "The woman evidently has a thing for Tic Tacs." She did an eye roll. "And with you showing her picture around, I thought a bag delivered to your door would give you something to think about."

"But I got them when we thought Tantig was safely on land."

"I know. Kind of fun psyching you out."

She wagged the knife at me. "Before you ask, yes, it was me who locked you in the steam room. I saw you and Molly and Polly heading there, and I followed you. After they left, I broke and jammed the door handle, hoping it'd trap you inside."

"You went to a lot of trouble to keep me silent."

"Dev saw you go into the galley and talk to Chef Roy. You were a threat. We couldn't take any chances you'd learn the truth." She angled the knife sideways, studying the gleaming blade. "There's a lot of money at stake here. But when Dev's done with you, we won't need to worry about that."

Chapter 17

I tried swallowing, but my throat seized up.

"Don't get comfortable," Sabrina said. "Dev won't be long."

She was serious. Devon was going to come down and make sushi out of Tantig and me.

I'd avoided seasickness the whole cruise, but now nausea was hitting me. Or maybe it was the fact I was facing imminent death. I felt light-headed, and I was certain the color had drained from my face. Sabrina didn't seem to notice. She turned on her heels and slammed out of the room, locking the door and loudly securing the safety latch behind her.

I reached for the chair, my knuckles white, nausea rising in my throat. I gagged, afraid I was going to throw up. *Keep it down, Valentine.* This room wasn't equipped for sickness. No sink. No bags. No first-aid kit. I gave a fleeting look at the smelly toilet and gagged again. Wonderful. I'd be dead within hours. What did it matter where I barfed?

I peered over at Tantig—oblivious and content. The only sound other than my gurgling stomach was the TV emitting kissing sounds and soothing words of love. Outside the room, loud whirring and humming noises continued.

A terrified voice inside my head kept repeating, *you're both going to die*. What if this was it? What if I never saw Tantig again? All her funny sayings and gestures swam around in my mind. Tears welled in my eyes. I wasn't ready to lose her. Nor could I bear the thought of causing her death.

I took deep breaths, thinking they might be my last, when a strange emotion surfaced. If I was going to die, I wasn't going down without a fight. I had to save myself. And I had to save Tantig.

I swiped my eyes, swallowed soberly, and staggered to the door. I jiggled the handle. Yep. Locked. And there was no way to unlock the latch from inside. I pounded on the door and screamed for help. Maybe Molly and Polly were still out there. I waited a beat. Nothing. The noise outside the room was horrendous. No one would hear me. And Molly and Polly were probably under the stars by now, watching *The Good, the Bad and the Ugly*. I clenched my fists, doing my best to remain calm and focused.

Hold on. There were dozens of machines beyond that door, machines that needed tools for repairs. Surely there had to be a hammer or wrench or screwdriver in here to ward off Devon.

I darted around the room, tearing things apart, spotting a long cardboard roll of tissue paper among other useless things. I hustled over and grabbed the roll, whacking it on my palm. Maybe not the best line of defense, but I could still bonk Devon on the head with this.

I took a closer look at my weapon. A corner of the tissue had been ripped off, and something had been imprinted on the layers underneath. A code? A private message?

I snatched the pencil off the table, held it on an angle, and swept it back and forth across the engraved portion. The area darkened, and the lettering underneath appeared in white and read *KEEP SEARCHING AND GRANDMA GETS A BULLET*.

I pressed my lips together, anger surging inside. This wasn't a code. This was where Devon wrote the threatening note. I tossed the roll against the wall. Who was I kidding? Like that was going to have any impact. Silk flowers and napkin holders weren't going to cut it either. Good grief! There had to be something!

Without warning, I gagged again. This time it wouldn't stay down. I dashed for the toilet, choked at the smelly sight inside, and retched into the filthy bowl.

Sweat broke out across my forehead, my nose dripped, and my eyes teared. Not one of my prettier moments. My curling iron hanging in my holster knocked against the porcelain toilet. I unleashed it and tossed it on the ground while I finished my business. Ugh. I gave a shaky moan, stood up, and cleaned myself with a wad of toilet paper.

Tantig mumbled something about her show, undisturbed I'd just puked behind her.

I'm fine. I dabbed my forehead, turning slightly toward her. *Thanks for asking.*

I shivered and tossed the toilet paper in the bowl. Then my curling iron caught my eye, and an idea struck me. I peered over to my great-aunt. "Tantig, let me curl your hair."

She blinked back at me. "What are you talk-ink about?"

"Your hair looks untidy." This was an understatement. Tantig's hairdo looked like she'd been through a typhoon. A good brushing probably would've done the trick, but I didn't need a brush for what I was planning. I swiped my palms on my pants, plugged in the curling iron, then combed my fingers through her hair.

While time ticked away, I fussed and curled and probably created a world's record for number of ways to use a three-pronged curling iron on short, fine hair. I was telling myself everything was going to be okay when Devon stomped into the room, his Fu Manchu mustache wilting from the corners of his mouth. He had a gun with a silencer in hand, boots on his feet, and a cowboy hat hanging by strings down his back. All he needed was a kid's stick horse between his legs to complete the Western getup. Unfortunately, he'd still look sinister and creepy.

He shut the door behind him, blocking out the drone of machinery. Meanwhile, I continued curling Tantig's hair like my life depended on it.

Tantig moved her head slightly toward Devon. "Who-hk are you?"

"John Wayne." He smirked. "Giddy-up."

Tantig rolled her eyes and went back to watching soaps.

I wore a stiff upper lip and tried to keep my hands firm on the curling iron. I'd already vomited once. I couldn't promise I wouldn't do it again.

Devon nodded at me. "Like my hideout, do you?" He didn't wait for an answer. "Stumbled upon it a while ago when Chef Roy sent me down for extra tins in the kitchen storage rooms."

"Nice."

He scrunched up his nose. "That all you can say? It's more than *nice*. It's private. And it's going to stay that way. So let's go, partner. I'm running two jobs at the moment. I haven't got time to piss around while you play hairdresser with your aunt."

"Great-aunt." I tightened my grip on the curling iron, not liking one bit the way he was speaking in front of Tantig.

"Who cares? In a few minutes, she'll be a dead aunt." He chuckled and waved his gun in the direction of the door. "Bad enough I had to endure a bronco contest between that Indian and ten-gallon-hat broad. If I'd had my gun on me, I swear I'd have blown a hole right through that bull just to end the suffering."

I pictured Kashi and Phyllis taking turns on the bronco bull. "Who won the contest?"

"You kidding? The Indian, hands down. That sourpuss broad got thrown a second after starting. What a sucker for punishment. Kept getting back on. Thrown each time right after pressing the button."

Sounded like Phyllis.

"Boy. Dumb or what." He stepped a foot toward the door. "Come on. I haven't got all day."

I yanked the curling-iron cord from the wall. "Where are we going?"

"Gee, I don't know. You have a preference where you're killed?"

"I guess not. But how do you know nobody will interfere with your plan?"

He guffawed and glimpsed at his gun. "You're outta luck. Nobody's interfering with nothin'. You make one peep, and you get a bullet through the skull."

He moved a foot closer to me and curled up his lip. "*Eeeyew*. What's that smell?" He shoved past me and ogled the toilet bowl. "That's disgusting."

While he examined things, I asked God for strength. Then I sucked in air, poised my curling iron at him, and jumped on his back. Caught off guard, he lost his balance, and his cowboy hat went flying. I hung on with everything I had inside and branded his neck with the scorching metal barrels.

"*Aaaaah!*" He fell to his knees. "Stop that! You insane?"

I yanked hard on his hair and poked him again and again. He staggered to his feet, and we went around in circles. He tried to grab the curling iron and throw me off his back, but I hung on tight like lice on hair.

"You're dead meat!" he shrieked. "Hear me? *Dead meat!*"

Adrenaline flowed through me, and all I could think was I refused to die in the belly of this ship. At that, I whacked the hot iron on the side of his face.

"*Aaaaah!*" He shook his head, and the smell of freshly burned skin wafted through the air.

I gasped at my great-aunt. "Run, Tantig! Run!"

For once, Tantig showed speed. She shuffled to the door while I clung on hard to Devon. He jerked me off his back, and the gun flew into the toilet. We both stared at it, sinking to the bottom of the gross stew. I let out a cough, and he rolled up his sleeve and plunged for the gun.

I saw the snake tattoo on his arm, and a fresh surge of anger surfaced. Like a madwoman, I shoved his head down into the bowl, hammering his neck with the curling iron.

"*Ouch! Stop it!*" He whipped his head out of the toilet, and brown slime ran down his temples. Red-eyed, with burn marks on his cheeks, he aimed the gun at the door. Then he fired a shot. I swiveled my head and saw blood sprout on the side of Tantig's dress. She slouched and disappeared around the corner.

I went ballistic.

I screamed at Devon, gulping for air. With all my might, I wound my curling-iron arm around like a Red Sox pitcher and clocked him upside the head. He staggered sideways, crashed into the table and some boxes, and landed on the ground. I ran out of the room, slammed the door behind me, and flung open the locker. I was barely thinking straight, but I figured if I took a bag of cocaine, guaranteed Devon would come after me and not Tantig.

I peeked around pistons and fans, doing my best not to follow the spots of blood on the concrete floor. Suddenly, hollow gunshots sounded, then ping, ping, ping. Bullets fired in every direction, ricocheting off ductwork and overhead pipes.

I looked behind me and saw Devon aiming his gun at me. Blood stained his face from where I'd clouted him, and a putrid smell followed him from the room.

He kept firing, and I dove for cover. But he was too quick. He dropped his gun at his feet and was on top of me in seconds, struggling to wrestle the cocaine and curling iron out of my arms. He had me by about sixty pounds, but I kicked and hammered and screamed for all I was worth.

I stabbed the searing barrels into the bag. The heat melted the plastic, sending white powder everywhere. Devon yelped and finally ripped the curling iron out of my grasp.

We rolled on the ground, smacking and scratching each other, his weight suffocating me. I was spent and ready to quit, but I spied Tantig's shoes from under the machinery, twenty feet away, and a jolt of superhuman power came over me. I thrashed around, looking for his gun or any type of weapon. The only thing surrounding me was cocaine. Gathering my wits, I scraped together a handful and flung it in his face.

He coughed and sputtered and tried to roll me over. I wrestled back, but something jabbed me in the hip.

My nail file!

Without hesitation, I dug it out of my pocket and knifed him in the ribs. He screeched and swatted the file from me, gawking in disbelief from my face to the blood seeping through his shirt. Panicking, he backhanded me hard across the mouth, then lunged for the bag and swept cocaine back inside.

I lay there, my mouth burning in pain, blood on my tongue. Urging myself on, I leaned on my elbow and reached for the gun. Only, he got to it first. Then we heard a loud voice.

"Drop the gun and put your hands in the air!"

Everything went still. We gaped to an upper metal ramp where Jock stood with several security officers—one with a megaphone. Molly, Polly, and Sabrina cowered next to Jock with their hands behind their backs.

Devon blindly fired shots. I scrambled away. Everyone else ducked.

Devon caught me and yanked me to my feet. He wrapped his grimy arm around my neck, his tattoo directly under my nose. He pressed the gun to my temple. By now, the engineers and engine crew had joined Jock and the others. Everyone froze. I wasn't sure I was even breathing.

The officer with the megaphone spoke. "Put the gun down, Devon, and walk away."

"Not on your life!" he shouted back, jabbing the gun harder into my head.

Tears were streaming down my face, and blood trickled from my mouth. Past the corner of my eye, I saw Tantig slumped in a chair, head down. Out of desperation to live, or for Tantig's sake, I bit down on Devon's arm. The gun discharged and hit something that gave off a disturbing, rumbling sound.

Please, Lord. Tell me that wasn't the wall of the ship.

There was a moment when everyone held their breath. Then, vast amounts of water sprayed inside the engine room. Within seconds, boisterous alarms honked with angry determination, and everyone sprang into action. Security officers cleared the area, taking the girls with them.

Devon threw me away like yesterday's scraps and made a run for it. He got about two feet when he slipped on a mass of tiny white ball bearings. His arms went wide, the gun sailed through the air, and his feet flew up like they'd been snagged out from under him. He hit his head hard on the ground and went out like a light.

I crawled over to Tantig, turning a blind eye to Devon's beat-up face and blood soaking through his shirt. Trying to gain control, I wrapped my arms around my great-aunt. I wanted to see her open her eyes, even if it was only to give me her blasé look. But she remained unresponsive.

I rocked her in my arms, praying she'd be okay. Just then, she opened one eye and grinned up at me. Shocked, I looked from her, back to the tiny ball bearings, wondering what the grin was about. Then realization dawned. Those weren't ball bearings. They were Tic Tacs. Tantig's Tic Tacs. She must've had a container on her. And Sabrina said she was a senile old lady! I hugged the stuffing out of Tantig, choking back tears of joy.

"You're going to brrreak my neck," she said.

"Are you hurt?" I eased up on squeezing her. "I saw Devon shoot you."

She reached into her pocket and pulled out a candy bar with a clean hole through it.

"That's what he shot?"

She nodded.

I sighed. The lighting down here wasn't the best, and I'd mistaken the chocolate drops on the ground for blood. At least this proved Devon and Sabrina had fed her something.

Two officers charged toward Devon. Another aided Tantig.

The sounds of hissing pipes and deafening sirens continued, and a dense fog had developed. The magnitude of the devastation was overwhelming. I was blurry-eyed and drained, but I inhaled a triumphant, shaky breath and told myself it was all over. The killers had been caught, and Tantig and I were going to be fine.

I turned away from the blood and cocaine and room filling with water and trailed behind the others to safety. I had my head down, counting my blessings, when out of the fog, wading toward me through several inches of water, was Jock.

He pulled me close and looked from my bloody, swollen lip into my eyes. Wordlessly, he cupped my face and placed a gentle kiss on the tip of my nose. "You're my hero."

Not expecting that, a fresh tear sprang to my eye.

He wiped away the tear, scooped me up into his arms, and held me tight against his chest. Then, without another word, he carried me out of the wet dungeon.

Chapter 18

The island sun shone on my belly, and clear turquoise water swayed along the shoreline, gently nipping my toes. My skin glistened with coconut oil, my Babajaan hat covered my head, and I was tanning to the right shade of bronze in my white bikini.

I'd found a remote spot on the beach and was sitting on a lounge chair at the ocean's edge, sipping from a refreshing bottle of water. The only sound, other than peaceful waves, came from exotic birds trilling in the distance.

The ship had reached port last night after disaster struck. Everyone had disembarked with most of their things. Thousands of passengers were put up in ocean resorts while others slumbered along the beach in cabanas provided by the resorts. Others still stood with bated breath at the dock, waiting to see if their rum and cigars would go down with the ship. My parents were among those guests.

Phyllis got over being dragged away from *The Good, the Bad and the Ugly*. She and Max acted like a married couple and shared a room at the nearest resort. I had a cabana all to myself on a stretch of white sand, and I slept like a baby.

I knew Jock hadn't slept. Once he'd set me on dry land and made sure I was okay, he'd jogged back to the pier to assist others in disembarking. I was just glad Devon and Sabrina had been taken away and that Tantig was uninjured.

I learned Jock had been keeping tabs on Molly and Polly, faking interest in them to see how much they'd divulge about their drug involvement. He'd also been tracking Sabrina and Devon's whereabouts, disclosing he'd been looking for Sabrina when he'd muffled me outside my cabin door.

I relished the quiet time on the beach and reflected on my emotions regarding Jock. He was a hero and knight in shining armor. He'd assisted in seizing the crooks and had worked tirelessly to rescue passengers. Whenever I wanted to doubt him, he proved he was an honorable man, a lord among men. I trusted Jock at work, but deep down I knew I could trust him with my life.

All things considered, I should've been falling for the man. And maybe part of me was. But there was another part that needed to keep him at a distance.

Lord knew my heart beat nervously when I was near him, and I could only dream about the life he'd led, and what it'd be like with me in it. But more than that, I liked seeing this Hercules every day, working alongside him, laughing, and okay, flirting. I didn't want that to disappear. If our relationship turned into something more, and then it ended—like they always ended—it'd be goodbye Jock. I wasn't ready to let that happen. I didn't know if I'd ever be ready.

I took a break from sunbathing and ran into Clive sipping margaritas at the resort's beach bar. It was past noon, and he was already rosy-cheeked. He offered me a drink, but after Lucy's death and my big night with ouzo, I was staying clear of anything that remotely smelled of alcohol.

We toasted with my virgin margarita, and Clive repositioned his skinny butt on the barstool.

"All's well that ends well!" He held up his glass with his bandaged arm in a limp salute.

I sipped my drink. "Tell me, Clive." I gestured to his arm. "What's the story on your snake tattoo?"

He sloshed his drink, holding his arm up in front of his eyes. "It's not a shnake tattoo. Whoever told ya that?"

I did a mental head slap, taking Candace's word that Clive had a snake tattoo on his arm.

"Nobody important. She must've been mixed up." Or trying to lead me astray. The witch.

Clive gave his head a shake, then set his drink down, and unwound the gauze. "I mighta said it *looks* like a shnake *now*. But it once was a bee-u-ti-ful mermaid with a long, glorioush tail. Ole ball and chain made me remove it."

I stared at the faint image of a mermaid, the squiggly tail now red and partially scarred. I cut Candace some slack. In the right lighting, it could've been mistaken for a snake.

Clive frowned. "The little missus said it looked too wrinkled on my skin. Gosh," he slurred. "Ith it any wonder I came on a cruise? Can't drink. Can't have a tattoo. Wha-the world coming to?"

I smoothed my hand over his arm. "You're one in a million, Clive. I'm sure your wife will be glad when you return home."

He sipped on his drink. "Ya think?"

I pictured my own parents, not happy unless they were arguing. "I'm sure of it."

He gave a dopey nod and saluted me again. "By the way, my name's not Clive. Ith Henry."

I shook my head, confused. "How'd Phyllis get Clive from Henry."

"Beaths me." He gazed up at me. "That sourpuss works for you?"

I refrained from rolling my eyes. "Yes."

He held up his glass. "And I'm the one drinking?"

I kissed the top of his head and said goodbye, then

moseyed back down to the beach, thinking about home and how my goal of donating money to the hospital went awry. I went on the cruise to win a contest. With Lucy's murder and Tantig's kidnapping, I'd lost sight of that. Okay. I failed miserably at making goals. There had to be a way I could help.

I pulled my chair back from the shoreline, put my feet up, and reopened my water bottle, pondering how to come up with some money. Fast. I enjoyed playing the piano. Still had it in me. But did I want to spend my nights in a bar? The answer to that was always no.

My gaze fell to my sandals, half-covered in the sand, and my thoughts turned to my shoe that fell in the lifeboat. Then I was hearing Mr. Jaworski's shoe tirades. I shrugged. Maybe he had a point. It wouldn't kill me to part with some fancy heels and make a few dollars at the same time. Probably a good idea to scale down anyway, right? Ridiculous owning so many shoes. And in the grand scheme of things, what did a few girly possessions mean? Heels and jewelry could be replaced. Children couldn't.

I was plotting my purge on eBay when a pair of feet striding along the shoreline entered my line of vision. I raised my chin under my wide-brimmed hat to get a better look. Hmm. A tanned pair of muscular legs, too. I tilted my chin up another notch and checked out the long white swim trunks printed with huge orange flowers. Then I saw a bare, hard-muscled chest covered with dark hair.

I chugged water so I could take a friendly look without seeming interested. My hat tipped back, and I had a perfect view of the wavy hair curling over his ears and dark stubble on his jaw.

Romero!

I sprayed water onto my belly, my heart skipping a beat. What was *he* doing here? Looking all virile in nothing but a pair of swim trunks.

I tugged my hat back in place and gave my stomach an angry swipe. Like I should be happy to see him. *Ha!* What about Twix's discovery and the new woman who was moving in? If I could've trusted he cared about me, if he wasn't a two-timing jerk, I would've run into his arms. But I resisted. And my beautiful serene moment had just ended.

I swiveled myself in the opposite direction and sprang off the chair. I checked my bikini was in place and huffed down the beach. Not an easy feat with my bare heels sinking in the sand. Well, who cared what I looked like? I had nothing to say to Detective Romero.

On second thought, I spun around and stomped toward him. "What are you doing on my beach?"

We were standing six feet apart, and he used that space to his advantage, taking his sweet time appraising me from my head, down the curves of my bikini, to my toes.

Standing this close on an almost secluded beach, under the hot sun...*holy moly*. Sexual tension escalated inside from his penetrating stare, and my breath caught in my throat as a familiar ache swamped me. I'd gone two days without seeing him, and instantly I was back to being drawn in by his raw masculinity and charm.

He winked and that almost undid me. "When I heard a cruise ship was on the brink of sinking in the Bahamas, I told the staff sergeant I needed to come out here." He paused, trying hard to keep from smiling. "And I didn't know it was your beach."

"Well, it is. And you're trespassing."

"Like how you trespassed into an unauthorized area on the ship a mere day ago? Instead of telling security and leaving it to the professionals to save Tantig?" He cocked an eyebrow. "Good thing charges aren't being brought."

I was relieved about that, too, but I crossed my arms in front, acting all indignant.

"And I just ran into your father. He told me you were over here."

I fumed. "What makes you think the man was my father?"

"He was dressed like a buccaneer. I figured he was related."

I rolled my eyes. "He's going through a phase. And just so you know, I had nothing to do with that hole in the ship…directly. Anyway, they patched things up."

He took a step closer, his voice deep and sexy. "They patched things up."

My knees went weak from the way he repeated those words, and I avoided looking up into his eyes. "Yep."

Amused, he took his thumb and gently brushed my lower lip. "Swollen mouth you've got there." He said this as if he wanted to do something about it, and not in a medicinal way.

I wasn't sure if it was the scorching sun, or his enticing Arctic Spruce scent drifting in my direction, or his touch that blazed into me like fire on ice, but my insides quivered like I was being licked with hot flames. In a moment, I was going to melt into the sand.

I angled back so I could regain some perspective. "It looks worse than it is, and if that's all you came to say, I guess you'll be leaving now."

He didn't budge. "I have a few more things to say."

"Such as?" I put my hands on my hips. I was at a disadvantage being half-naked. But I put on a bold face, refusing to feel intimidated by his powerful presence.

"You were pretty brave, putting your life on the line to save your great-aunt."

Why did he have to go and say something so sweet? I swiped away a bead of sweat rolling down the center of my stomach, finding it difficult to look tough when I was getting turned on.

"And I thought you might like to know the case I was working on in California was tangled up in this mess."

My eyes went wide. "It was?"

He nodded. "Molly and Polly were working for a drug lord who divides his time between California and his homes in Boston and New York. Guy goes by the name Toro. Has quite the harem. Likes women with big…hair." He grinned. "Sends them on drug runs so he can stay home and operate his racketeering business. Actually believes he's doing someone a favor offering protection."

I thought this through. "So Molly and Polly weren't hairstylists."

"What?"

"They took part in the makeover contest. I thought they were hairstylists." I recalled the Western hoedown and guys lining up to be shaved by the girls. No wonder men were walking away with nicks on their faces and throats. Molly and Polly couldn't shave a balloon to save their lives.

"They were nothing but coke addicts," Romero said, "willing to do anything for a high."

They did always seem extra happy. Maybe they'd shared some of that happiness with the guy loading boxes into the hull in hopes of discovering where the cocaine was hidden.

Romero grimaced, and tiny lines of frustration creased the corners of his mouth. "Toro's tentacles stretch from Boston and New York to California, the Caribbean, and Miami. We almost brought him down several years ago when one of his New York dealers was found dead in Rueland. But his lawyers are savvy, and he got off. Then a year ago, another member of his New York posse was caught trafficking. The guy didn't like the idea of wearing an orange jumpsuit for the next ten years, so he decided to turn state's evidence against Toro. A week before the trial, the stoolie was found trick-or-treating as a corpse."

"The body on Lucy's salon awning."

"The very same. Lucy's shop basement was a depot. Drugs were running in and out of there like Grand Central Station. A couple of her employees quit, not wanting to be involved in any illegal activity. Sabrina stayed on." He shook his head. "Devon had a perfect setup on the cruise ship. As long as someone smuggled drugs on board, Devon moved them into Miami via flower vases and floral foam. Another crook distributed from there."

I wasn't sure I understood all this. "Why didn't the parties know about each other's involvement?"

"That's how Toro operates. Drop-off points. Pickup

times. Everyone's allocated a duty. No overlaps into another's territory."

I wiggled my toes in the sand, thinking how coincidental it was that Molly and Polly were assigned the same table on the cruise as Sabrina and Lucy. Was this intentional on Toro's part? Stretching his tentacles even onto the ship to keep his eye on his operation?

"Then what was Devon doing in New York?" I asked. "I saw his picture in the *New York Post* from last year."

"Seven years ago, he started working in New York City at Chef Roy's restaurant—one of Toro's favorites. Probably when he'd met Lucy and Sabrina. Then a year ago, he got recruited to work on the cruise ship with Chef Roy. Jumped at the chance. Being employed at the restaurant, he overheard and learned a lot about Toro's dealings. Maybe Devon approached Toro, seeing this as the perfect opportunity to make some big scores smuggling. He'd already been laundering drug money, so Toro likely asked him to prove himself by becoming the assassin, and Devon agreed."

He shifted his weight and wiped the sweat off his brow. "Devon probably hung around the crime scene for kicks when the media showed up. He'd just started with the cruise line, and after the murder he conveniently disappeared. Nobody fingered him, and we didn't know the connection to Sabrina until Jock tied the pieces together."

"But what were you doing in California?"

"Putting heat on Toro. We knew he was there, and it was a matter of days before making an arrest, this time, one that would stick. When I worked in New York, he was the boil on the backside of vice. Seeing him walk after the Rueland murder was like cutting off my right arm. I wasn't going to let him go free again."

Romero had lived through a drug case about five years ago that hit close to home. I knew how important it was for him to see justice prevail.

The sun beat down on him, outlining his broad

shoulders and lean hips. He caught the appreciation in my eyes but stayed focused. "With murder, racketeering, trafficking, possession for the purpose of trafficking, importing and exporting, carrying a concealed weapon without a permit, and a few other charges, Toro will be backing into the corner of the prison shower for a long time."

He rubbed his chin, his powerful gaze on me. "I have a question for you."

I gave my lip a gentle bite. "Yes?"

"I just came from interviewing Devon. Why does his face look like a George Foreman grill?"

I tried to look innocent, but I could see by the know-it-all grin on Romero's face I'd have a better chance at being swallowed by a shark than getting one by him. "It's this three-pronged curling iron I have."

He put up his palms. "I've already heard enough."

"Then why'd you ask?"

He gave me a stern look, then pulled something that resembled a black tarantula out of his back pocket.

I screamed and jumped back, falling ass to the sand. "What is it?"

"Don't worry. It's not alive." Sand covered his feet as he bent down and helped me up.

Once I was standing again, we studied the furry object in his hand. Black hair strands laced around black gems, and there was a tiny sparkly boat glued on top.

"A little Indian guy at the pier pressed it into my palm. Told me to give it to you." He dropped it in my hand. "Said he'd do it himself, but he didn't trust your impulsive nature."

I pressed my lips tight at that remark. I took my finger and pushed it around in my palm just in case it sprang at me. In a weird way, it was kind of beautiful even though my inner instinct was to squash it with my foot.

"He called it a 'Get Out of Town' brooch. What the hell is a 'Get Out of Town' brooch?"

"Kashi, the little Indian guy, makes them." I twirled it

in my hand, amazed at the intricate detail. "Did he have a specific name for it? He names all his brooches."

Romero gave a thoughtful nod. "He did. Said this was his 'Get Out of Town Titanic.' He made it especially for you because you're scary"—he pointed to the spidery limbs—"and everywhere you go, disaster follows." He tapped the miniature ship and chuckled.

I swept away his menacing fingers. "Yes, I got that. Thank you."

"Before I forget," he said. "The cruise line is awarding you two thousand dollars for helping in uncovering a smuggling ring."

I straightened. "What?"

"I told them you couldn't accept since you're partly responsible for the *patch* on the ship."

I smacked his arm. "You did not!"

I couldn't believe it. It wasn't the full amount I wanted to donate to the new wing at Rueland Memorial, but it was a hefty start.

He gave me another sexy wink. "The check will be waiting for you when you get home."

"Great."

None of this explained the new love in his life and who was playing house back in Rueland. Well, I wasn't going to stand around, pretending everything was okay. "Now that you've explained things, goodbye."

He sighed big time, looking down at me. "I'd bend you over my knee and tan your pretty hide if I thought I'd get away with it. But Nancy Drew might exact revenge by setting fire to my house."

"You needn't worry about *Twix*." I huffed. "She's got more interesting things to do than try to understand why you'd drop me for Belinda."

He creased his brows. "Am I missing something here?"

I was glad it was out. "Yes. Your partner."

"That's what this is all about? Belinda?"

"Gee, I don't know. Every time we talked on the phone, she seemed to be in stroking distance." A breeze swept by, and I yanked my hat down to keep it from blowing off. "Sounded like she was practically attached at the hip in San Juan."

He massaged his forehead in exasperation. Who could blame him? I was acting like a child. But I couldn't help it. I wanted the truth. I needed to hear with my own ears he was moving on.

"For your information," he said, "Belinda is no longer assigned to me."

My eyebrows went up. "Why not?"

"Because I requested she be transferred to another precinct."

I narrowed my eyes. "Why?"

"Because I didn't like her work habits or attitude." He gave me a grim look. "And before you ask *why* again, let's just say she was insubordinate. I already have one female in my life who drives me crazy. I couldn't handle another."

I crossed my arms, choosing to ignore that. "Even if she looked like a Victoria's Secret model?"

He gave a short burst of laughter. "Where'd you get that impression?"

"Nowhere." Damn Holly. Putting ideas in my head. "Then what was she doing in San Juan?"

"She wasn't." He frowned, clearly not understanding. Then he gave a slow nod. "Ohhh, the phone call yesterday." Like he just realized what I was talking about. "The woman you heard in the background was one of the officers in San Juan. Some of the cops were having drinks after their shift. They were trying to make me feel welcome."

He stared at me long and hard, then blew out air. "As for Twix, tell her the next time she wants to snoop at my place, I'll leave the back door open. The neighbors won't get the wrong idea that way."

"She was just being a good friend."

"And Cynthia was being a good sister."

"Cynthia? It *was* her?"

He nodded, folding his arms in front of his toned chest.

"Sounded like she wanted Twix to believe she was something more."

He gave a wicked smile. "I told you before she could be a pain in the ass. She was just having some fun."

"It wasn't funny to me."

"Because you thought I wanted Belinda."

I glared at the water. "Maybe? And because you seemed unconcerned when you saw Jock and me together in my cabin." Out of the corner of my eye I saw him shake his head.

"You want to know the truth?" He rested his hands on his hips. "You drive me insane, and sometimes I want to throttle you."

"Is that supposed to make me feel better, 'cause so far you're failing miserably."

He widened his stance. "During an investigation, I have to keep a level head. That means staying disciplined and tough. Knowing you work with Mr. Universe every day is a little hard on the ego. And seeing you with him on the cruise was worse than I'd imagined. But I put up with it when I thought he'd protect you when I couldn't. The truth is, I'm crazy about you. Crazy about the silly things you say. Crazy about your smile. Crazy about your impulsiveness. Felons don't make me crazy the way you do."

I stuck out my bottom lip at that.

"Now…" He dug his heels in the sand. "I've got two days off. I can either go back to Rueland and fix that damn lock on your laundry room door, or…"

I avoided his stare at the subtle reminder of how he'd found Jock and me locked in the laundry room at work. "Or?"

"Or I could stay here with you, spend some time together, and escort you back home."

I let my gaze wander back up into his penetrating blue eyes, the devotion I saw there undeniable. The truth was I was at my most vulnerable when I was with Romero. I wanted to reach out to touch him, to trust him, to bury the old me, but I was terrified to let myself go.

Yet I realized in some ways, I'd found peace. I'd learned to believe in myself more, and I'd gleaned a smidgen of self-confidence. I was a work in progress. And works in progress, like any good hair color, took time to develop.

I gave a one-shoulder shrug. "I guess you could stay here."

He took his finger and tipped up my chin. "Not the answer I was looking for." He placed a firm hand behind my neck, flung my straw hat on the ground, and pulled me into him with an authoritative tug. My hair spilled down my back. Sand trickled between my toes, every nerve ending suddenly alive.

Once my body was molded into his, he took my mouth with raw hunger. Shivers coursed down my spine, and heat surged between my thighs. The taste of his lips on mine, the feel of his hands on my skin, the urgency, the need, the no-holds-barred. Desire and longing that had escalated over the past months came to a forceful head.

Romero lived by a code of self-control and cool emotions, but there was no amount of composure that would rein in the intensity and passion he evidently felt at this moment.

He broke away from kissing my lips and worked his way down my neck, sucking, nipping, driving me crazy with his touch. He slipped his hand down my back, inside my bikini line, his caress deft and proficient. My legs all but gave out, and when I thought I couldn't take any more, he recaptured my mouth.

I pulled him in closer yet, yearning and warmth flowing through my veins. His strength cradled me, his length pressed into me. He kissed me long and hard and finally dragged himself away to catch his breath. "I've wanted to kiss you like that since the first time I laid eyes on you."

I breathed in his intoxicating scent, cupping his rugged jaw with both hands. "What stopped you?"

His eyes took in my entire face, his hands stroked my bare hips. "Not everyone is as impulsive as Valentine Beaumont."

Okay, he had me there. But I was too giddy inside to feel anything but joy. He felt so right, and the bliss that overcame me when I was in his arms gave me hope for what was ahead. Maybe Grandma Maruska was right. It *was* the future that counted.

He rubbed my swollen bottom lip again and gave the bruised flesh short, sweet kisses. "I know this may be an odd request"—kiss—"but do you think we could maintain a somewhat normal relationship when we get home?"

I peered up at him through my lashes, amazed I was still standing. "A somewhat normal relationship?"

"Yeah. You know. No more perm rods in unsavory places, keep the curling irons strictly for hair. That sort of thing."

I shrugged with an air of innocence. "I'll give it some thought."

He leaned in for another kiss. "With you, that's all I can ask."

Other Books in
The Valentine Beaumont Mysteries

BOOK 1

MURDER, CURLERS, AND CREAM

Valentine Beaumont is a beautician with a problem. Not only has she got a meddling mother, a wacky staff, and a dying business, but now she's got a dead client who was strangled while awaiting her facial.

With business the way it is, combing through this mystery may be the only way to save her salon. Until a second murder, an explosion, a kidnapping, death threats, and the hard-nosed Detective Romero complicate things. But Valentine will do anything to untangle the crime. That's if she can keep her tools of the trade in her bag, keep herself alive, and avoid falling for the tough detective.

In the end, how hard can that be?

BOOK 2

MURDER, CURLERS, AND CANES

Valentine Beaumont is back in her second hair-raising mystery, this time, trying to find out who had it in for an elderly nun. Only trouble is there are others standing in her way: hot but tough Detective Romero, sexy new stylist Jock de Marco, and some zany locals who all have a theory on the nun's death.

Making things worse: the dead nun's secret that haunts Valentine, another murder, car chases, death threats, mysterious clues, an interfering mother, and a crazy staff.

Between brushing off Jock's advances and splitting hairs with handsome Detective Romero, Valentine struggles to comb through the crime, utilizing her tools of the trade in some outrageous situations. Question is, will she succeed?

Book Club Discussion Questions

Share these questions with your book club. Enjoy the banter!

1. What suspects were on your radar throughout the story?

2. Twix spies on Romero as a favor to Valentine. What lengths have you gone to for a friend?

3. Max has a fear of open water. What is your biggest fear?

4. Tattoos play an important role in the story, providing Valentine with different leads and suspects. Do you have a tattoo? If not, would you ever get one? If so, of what?

5. Tantig is known for carrying Tic Tacs everywhere. Is there a certain candy or mint you (or someone you know) always have on hand?

6. Phyllis has a rough time on her hike through the rainforest, ending up sunburned and sore. What is the worst experience you've had with nature?

7. Kashi makes special "Get Out of Town" brooches and bestows them on people. If he were to make a brooch for you, what do you think it would be?

8. Valentine's mother is a relentless matchmaker. Is there anyone in your life who plays this role?

9. As the series continues, which hero do you want to see Valentine with?

10. What was your favorite scene? Favorite character?

Note to Readers

Thank you for taking the time to read MURDER, CURLERS, AND CRUISES. If you enjoyed Valentine's story, please consider telling your friends or posting a short review. Word of mouth is an author's best friend and much appreciated. Thank you!

Social Media Links

Website: www.arlenemcfarlane.com

Newsletter Sign-up:
www.arlenemcfarlane.com/signup/signup5.html

Facebook: facebook.com/ArleneMcFarlaneAuthor/

Facebook Readers' Group:
www.facebook.com/groups/1253793228097364/

Twitter: @mcfa_arlene

Pinterest: pinterest.com/amcfarlane0990

Arlene McFarlane is the author of the *Murder, Curlers* series. Previously an aesthetician, hairstylist, and owner of a full-service salon, Arlene now writes full time. When she's not making up stories or being a wife, mother, daughter, sister, friend, cat-mom, or makeover artist, you'll find her making music on the piano.

Arlene is a member of Romance Writers of America, Sisters in Crime, Toronto Romance Writers, SOWG, and the Golden Network. She's won and placed in over 30 contests, including twice in the Golden Heart and twice in the Daphne du Maurier.

Arlene lives with her family in Canada.

www.arlenemcfarlane.com